THE SEASONWIFE

A NOVEL

THE SEASONWIFE

A NOVEL

Saige England

BATEMAN
BOOKS

Published in 2023 by David Bateman Ltd,
Unit 2/5 Workspace Drive, Hobsonville,
Auckland 0618, New Zealand
www.batemanbooks.co.nz

ISBN: 978-1-77689-083-5

A catalogue record for this book is available from the National Library of New Zealand.

Cover design: Keely O'Shannessy
Internal design: Katrina Duncan

Printed in China by Toppan Leefung Printing Ltd

*To those who have gone before. To those who grace
this side of life — for whom I thank my lucky stars —
mo anam cara, John, and my precious sons, Kelynge,
Benjamin and Marco, children of the Pacific.*

Historical note

At the time this novel is set, the early 1830s, the North and South Islands of New Zealand were known to Europeans as the North and the Middle Island, and were governed from New South Wales. Likewise, Māori were referred to as New Zealanders.

Note on glossaries

For the definition of key words and phrases in te reo Māori, the language of the indigenous people of these islands, as well as Irish Gaelic and colloquial cant and whaler slang, please refer to the glossaries that begin on p. 275 of this book.

CAST OF CHARACTERS

Tangata whenua*

Manaia	A young woman born to a mother of low status
Rima	Manaia's mother
Manutaki	Manaia's uncle (her mother's brother)
Te Rākaunui	Tohunga of tā moko, a renowned tattoo artist, and expert in related spiritual matters
Te Iho o Ranginui	The community's highest leader in spiritual matters
Kauri	A young man of high birth, Manaia's lover
Rāwhiti	A young man in the village
Kāhu Kōrako	Highest rangatira of Manaia's community
Keteiwi	A village woman
Manawa	A village woman
Te Mārire	A village man

The immigrants**

Bridie Murphy	A young Irish woman
Róisín Murphy	Bridie's mother
Tom Murphy	Bridie's brother
Robbie Fitch	A whaler and trader. Also known by Manaia as Ropi
Quentin Cuthbert	A disgraced missionary
Mallet	Quartermaster on Robbie's ship
Jake	The master's mate
Old Bill	The cooper on Robbie's ship
Young Bill	The cooper's son
Ivory	A crewman on Robbie's ship
Gibson	A crewman on Robbie's ship
Nob	The cook and a whaler on Robbie's ship
Musgrove	Sailmaker on Robbie's ship
Cox	Sailmaker's mate
Caddock	The butcher
Jenny	A barmaid
The Abbess	Mistress at The Shipwright's Compass
Judge Wells	A Sydney-based judge
Jimmy	Róisín's lover

---

*   The people of the land, known to the immigrants as New Zealanders
**   Known to the tangata whenua as the tauiwi

PROLOGUE

The hunters who come for him are brash, not brave. Heaving boots, snapping branches, hoisting guns. Crunch of leaves, crack of a bough. The boy inhales the tart and pungent reek, warm skin of trees, soil-baking light. Presses his hands against his ribs to stay his breath, for breath might betray him as he stands stock still in the blue shade. Trees in this forest have spaces between, are not close enough to keep him safe; stood apart, they are as distant from each other as a family after a quarrel.

Earlier that afternoon he had left Sydney to escape the myriad sounds of nature being smashed and broken. Stones bashed and baked into bricks, trees felled for logs to build boats, houses, mills. Sydney offered opportunity but no solace, no space to hear the voices of the ancestors. Solitariness is different to loneliness. No matter how far he travelled from New Zealand, swapping ships, pulling in, pulling out, all the different ports, never was he far from his tīpuna.

He had drifted through the forest until he felt nourished. Slowed to rest in the dry nest of a trunk, cradled in dreams, warmed under blue heat-drugged trees. Until the forest warned him, and now, into the ragged rim of his sight the hunters manifest from a chorus of thrashing and shouts.

Fear was a trickle finding shape, is now a taniwha. Writhes, scours his skin, arches to bite the back of his throat. Five hunters. Four wearing round hats, one whose hat is higher, whose beard is longer, whose watch chain is gold not silver, who wears the garb of a gentleman; but the boy has learned from experience that few gentlemen are gentle.

A different stink meets the airborne fumes of gum-smoked leaves, the earthbound perfume of sun-peeled bark. From the pits under his arms to the fur between his buttocks comes the stench of a man planning a kill.

'Fine tattoos you have there, boy.'

A hunter steps forward, touches his face. A trespass this, for the head is tapu. The man draws a finger down, around the left nostril, around the curl of the koru. This man would not understand the koru, the power in the leaf before it unfurls.

'Fix your glaziers on this, Fitch. Fine tattoos, delicate as fern fronds.'

The boy knows the way this will end, has seen this look before in the eyes of men calculating the price of oil as they watch a whale rise and spume. Sweat drips and runs in rivulets between the blue-black ridges that are his river, his mountain, the beauty of his skin adorned by the tohunga. And this man, this hunter, is traversing his skin.

A rush of feathers, the great wind of them. A chance given, the boy turns and runs. Darts through trees, weaves around trunks, wades through strips of pink bark. Slows breath, lengthens stride, silently thanks the tohunga who had taught him since boyhood how to make wings of his feet. A sound of falling. His fine London hat has toppled, is rolling over the ragged brown edge of the cliff.

He pauses as the hat whirls into the haze of blue-green mist. The most expensive hat he ever owned. Purchased in the season before this, on the day he met the girl. Girl turning woman. Her look held him as she crossed George Street, unafraid of her own legs. Steps unlike the narrow steps of settlers who put on their character like they put on their clothes. More like a cornstalk planted in the colony, feet seeking roots, arms swaying, face turned to bask in the sun's warmth.

Her finger had danced but not touched the long green stone dangling from his ear. Pounamu, he had said, when she touched the hard warmth. Roimata, he had said as she gazed at the black specks in the river of the stone.

'In the English language it means tears. See how the stone cries.'

Laughed at her attempt to mimic the words in his language. Her finger hovering — not touching — the coils on his face. My map, he told her. A map of myself. Her eyes glanced light, drifted calm. Under the fresh splash is the mysterious depth. He is about to plunge when someone calls.

Startles them out of their reverie, the call. A lilting voice from a shadowed arch, tongue of the Irish, tone motherly. Slower her steps then, the girl who had skipped towards him, dragged against departure.

The canopy lifts, wild wings scrape the sky. The forest warning that the hunting party is nearly upon him. He climbs up a mound, presses against a tree the way a man presses into a woman, seeking protection, seeking entry, seeking escape from death.

Surely these men are playing, may strip him, mock him, would not kill him? Would it hurt to die? His chest heaves, his heart pleads. Give me more, more of life. How will the last beat measure out? Will he reel and scream, fly with the strange white birds, try to return to his own land? No, he will rise to haunt these men who hunt him, who want him for a token to put on a shelf.

Voices whisper around him. Beloved by his whānau, protected by the tīpuna, rousing the spark, stirring the flame to challenge this end. He breathes out slowly and then takes the deepest breath — a breath huge and full. Legs stretched, muscles taut, he leaps. Leaps high and wide.

The last sound he hears is the Englishman barking orders.

'Take your mark with care, Fitch. Fire at the heart, not the head.'

CHAPTER I

Sydney, 1832

There must be a tool to keep a mother in life. Bridie scours for it now, searches every sand-piled corner for a net to trap and restore the soul to her mother's bereft and sagging body. For on the bed she lies, Róisín. Green eyes roving, mouth a cavernous wound. Straining for voice, words, song. Stretches and cracks the corners of her lips. Drags breath like a fire gulping air so it can flutter life. Bridie seizes the dry-skin folded wings of the bellows beside the hearth.

Hollers at her brother to lay one hand beneath their mother's head, and with his other hand stretch wide the mouth. Wider still. Róisín simmers and writhes, struggles as though they mean her harm. Frantic, flummoxed, failing to find words of reassurance, Bridie forces the point of the bellows into her mother's mouth. Pumps. Gasp, gasp, gasp. Róisín heaves herself high, bursting from the damp mattress like a fish jumping from the ocean. One large last force of self, a shudder and she is sunk. The girl turns the empty bellows over in her hands, feels the emptiness, the flat, sad skin of it.

'We must try again.'

———

Outside, on the rocky shelves that shelve houses, day is burying night. Shivering haloes of light thread through dusking shadows. Shawls hooded over heads, crossed over chests, wound around waists, lanterns held high, mourning women coming to wake Róisín Murphy.

Bridie peers down as the lanterns meet puddles and splashes of light from the lamps above the Saracen's Head. As usual Saracen's is spilling fighters and braggards. She prays to Brighid that the party of women will pause and be thwarted by booze into idle forgetting, abandon their mournful mission to this small abode on The Rocks.

But still they come and their coming confirms her dread. There is sickness in her belly. Sadness scrapes tears from her eyes. Teetering against the scowling wind and snarl of waves, she opens her mouth like a cave open to the ocean, screams into the void. Would, if she could, shift shape. Wing-borne or sea-borne, fly far from her mother's cloying sickness and her young brother's foolery.

Blind the sky now, void of stars. Only the churn and curdle of white froth and spume. Directly below, on the cusp of the curve of the beach are dark lumps — rocks where they sat only a week past. Ma and herself, hair flying as they leaned against each other. Briny stink of oysters scraped from the rocks, shucked and sucked fresh, slapped on pillows of bread.

The procession of light is closer. Please, Brighid, make the wind scoop the lot of them over the cliff. Hears her mother admonishing her. Apologises to the dark whirl of night as she rushes to protect her ma from visitors who will prod the dying into death.

Curses the door for its reluctance to close so she can slide the black bolt. Heavy, the bolt. Prays for Brighid to give her strength. At last the door shuts, the bolt slides. Rushes across the sandy floor and out the back. Fetches a shirt that flaps like a rebel under the iron roof of the scullery. Must have escaped from her arms the shirt, blown and hung itself on the line where hang charred pots. She had gathered the washing earlier on cause of rain that threatened to fall — a wasted effort for the rain failed to fall, failed to fill the most-often-dry well.

Slides the bolt on this door, slams out the din of bluebottle flies circling the shit hole at the end of the path and the festering stink of the dunnekin. Stronger stink even than the stink of seaweed on the salt wind. Inside, hands batting moths, boots scudding sand. If she tidies the house Ma must wake to set eyes on the tidiness. Pushes the broom on the hardwood floor, stirring sand hidden in cracks between planks to rise and settle. Each breezing brings more sand, soft as flour through the unglazed window. The sand does not want to leave. Piles of it — sand, leaves, twigs in every corner. The more she tries to push nature out the more it howls, begs, pleads, insists on its presence.

Sobs coming out of her loud, she pulls the patched-rags curtain around the bed. Ma is surely only taking rest, cannot be dead. Ignores the sagging skin, its pallor. Certain, she is, that soon these lungs will rasp for life, Ma's tongue will search again for speech or water or Bridie knows not what. She pulls it shut, the curtain, to stay Tom from the stench of sickness and sweat rising from the drenched nightgown and damp mattress ticking. Hollers at him now, her brother, to help in rolling puncheons and kegs against the doors.

'Pack a force against them, we will.'

'What force, for why?'

Sweet in looks and stupid inside the head is Tom. Regrets this thought the instant she hears it. Her mother would wish her to be, if not kind to her little brother, not mean.

'Against the mnàthan-tuirim. She won't find the will to rouse herself if they come for the caoineadh.'

Blanker still, the look on him. She, Bridie, had turned too, to the language of the sterling settlers, the way to be distinguished from convict stock is talk like the toffs, speak English. Guilt stabs her — guilt for arguing with her mother, for shunning the Gaelic.

'Irish women, the mourners, come to keen.'

She says the word flat now, like the English say it. Keen. Without the lilt. True cornstalk, Tom, sprouted here rather than

Éire. Taking the hammer she bangs nails in the oat-smelling sack that serves as a curtain against the unglazed window. Bites each nail between her teeth and bangs, banishes with each bang of that hammer thoughts bothersome and regretful. Bangs until the coverlet is taut, leaving no gap for these intruders. Snuffs out the stubs of the candle. Pitches into darkness the centrepiece. Beside the candle, the porcelain figurine cherished by her mother. Cast aside by an English merchant's wife on cause of a tiny chip, but her ma loved it so, flaw and all. Can hear her voice.

'Don't trust something that isn't a little bit broken. Finest-looking skin can't cover rottenist deeds.'

Tom is bobbing up beside Bridie, bringing her back to the ache of the now, this too awful, sad time. She hisses, curses in Gaelic, pulls him to herself to crouch in the darkness. Slaps her hand over his gabbing mouth, wrestles his body still.

———

The stench of dead seal oil seeps through the cracks and hinges. The light casts shadows against the unglazed window, seal ghosts gallop against the sacking. The seal-oil-lantern-carrying women whimper and sob outside like beggars begging to maw and mourn.

Bridie prays to Brighid to give Ma the strength to rouse and strike the women for not coming earlier, for not coming to save her. Feels her lip tremble, feels astonished at what is coming out of her, a sound from deep inside and outside of herself, mouth gagging, sobbing. The song of herself, a harsh agony finding rhythm with the great bash of waves stirred by wind and ocean.

On the other side of the door, silence. Perhaps now the women will leave, but the wind outside stirs, rises, snatches and claws at chatter. Skips a sentence off the cliff, leaves another to dangle.

'—has in her pocket scissors or a knife?'

A pause in the rumble of voices. She knows the way of them, the plan, that on the other side of the door fingers are sliding through seams of skirts and aprons, fishing inside drawstring pockets that hide innermost collections from protectors, thieves and drunken men. Sifting through coin, shells, thimbles, announcing the find of half an apple, a dried chunk of bread. Screeches of success. Sounds like one of the Reilly women, the loudest shriek.

Sewing scissors and knives snap at the coarse coverlet, hands tear and loosen nails which fall and roll. The coverlet falls from the window. The cold wind comes first, then one after the other, two of the younger women clamber through the unglazed window. One holds a tin lantern, another pulls the latch on the door. The bolt slides treacherously, the door opens easily, not with so much as a creak or a groan. Bridie makes one last effort to stave them off.

'Ma might rise yet. Might not be properly dead.'

———

Pale and light, the lightest white loaves folded in linen, they tell her. Laying the bread on the table beside the slightly broken figurine. For she was deserving of the lighter, the whiter, the higher in price — Róisín of Éireann, for she was so loved. An earthen jug swishes milk under wrinkled skin, like the skim yellow colour of her mother in sickness. Sugar crumbs broken from sugar blocks ferried from a far-off country. Oysters scraped off rocks. Beef in a tub of blood. Eels smoked and peeled from their black skins. These are the gifts carried by heavy arms, under faces flushed, eyes scalding, foreheads knuckled.

They tug aside the curtain of patched scraps that shields the bed. Gasp and sigh. So, she is gone indeed and oh so quick, poor dear Róisín Murphy who endured so much in her short time on this earth. Released now she is, gone to God, gone to Jesus, gone to Mary, gone to Patrick, gone to Brighid.

As they move forward, crossing themselves, Bridie paws at her mother. Pats the belly, the hands, her face. As though her mother is not cold in death, is waking into the world instead of waking out.

'Please rise, Ma,' her voice breaks. 'I will speak the Irish like you want, only the Gaelic if you want. I won't argue no more.'

Tom is blubbering into his hands.

They touch Bridie and croon, lift Tom and sing a thread of tune like a shuttle running across the loom. Daughters, sisters, mothers, neighbours all sing to wring relief from the saddest spell.

Like cows lowing lovingly to a field, the women closest in friendship wash the palms and soles of hands and feet, each finger and toe stretched and washed and all the folds of skin between. Bridie catches a thought that floats not from herself, from somewhere above and around. Grateful am I that my tired-out body should be so gently tended by these dear friends. It is not herself who thinks this for Bridie is not grateful, nor does she consider the women to be dear.

The song folds into talk and the talk is of times gone. Of babes born dead, of a boy drowned in his own mother's well, of a girl drowned in Tank Stream, of the evil sodding government men, of the Tank Stream stewing muck — haven't they all seen a soldier using it as a chamber pot? Talk of Russian troops pulling out of Poland but no one is sure about that. The Romanovs are quite a family. So far off, though; France is close enough. Boney — Bonaparte was secretly transported. Escaped he did, hides in the Australian bush now, to steal the young. Boys and girls are pork to him. A warehouse down by the wharves is selling chamber pots with his face painted on the bottom, mouth open to swallow — well, you know what. Rustle of laughter, ripple of giggles.

After wiping every corner of her mother's body they brush knots from strands, form a wide fan of hair. Under the murky oil light the women braid it, sparks of gold, sparks of red. Ah, the women say and oh, such a beauty she was, Róisín Murphy, fierce of temper at times — oh the stories they could tell — but such fine hair.

Bridie kneels before her mother's sea-rusted chest, its clasp broken, straps free. Trawls through garments — black cotton and brown worsted stockings, coarse shawls down to the most precious thing — unbinds the linen and the ribbon from her mother's fine silk shawl, sheen of it green. Green of the land out of which she was torn, caged, carted as livestock over the ocean to here. To be wedged into a thing called freedom, ocean on one side, untamed hinterland on the other, to have her daughter taken from her, to only keep children if she had a protector.

Someone offers Bridie fig-candy, she shakes her head. The hand passes to Tom's half-parted mouth. As they lift her mother from the bed onto the table, Bridie sweeps out of the way the stub of the candle and the figurine her mother had cherished. Lays the figurine at the head of the table to look over her now.

Occupied the faces, all intent on folding the sallow, sunken flesh in the sea of the fine green shawl. Cross the arms, clasp hands over the green mound.

One woman sways, plucks an invisible thread from the air and pulls it down, wraps a song around all those who wear grief, for grief is ever present in those who have left home. Woven in this thread are sadness and suffering; for Róisín, so brave, so young, so fine; for Róisín, so Irish, has flown home. The sound of the song becomes the sea bashing rocks like the English bashing the Irish and the verses about the English grow wild and hard.

———

Quentin Cuthbert comes in quietly, removes his stovepipe hat and lays down on the table, beside the dead woman, his damp, rained-upon Bible. Bridie pulls herself up high, fixes her eyes on him. Stomps a heel on the hardwood floor. Another woman stomps, and another. A verse flies from Bridie:

'Latch the doors to stay the storm, kindle branches on the hearth, heat the iron on the stove, but when you set the table —'

She pauses in her lament, seeing Cuthbert's gestures, his nodding as though she is to cease her grief to serve him. Ignoring him, she resumes:

'— do not spare a place for death.'

An older woman pulls on the thread of anguish, bringing the voice of the women who birthed these women, waking the women who woke them into life, and the women before, all the way back to Brighid. They clutch hands, holding one another up, swaying, their voices echoing and hovering and ringing as the missionary flaps his hands to stop their gaping mouths, frantic in his effort to banish the sound. The singing only grows louder as he shuffles into his coat, seizes a loaf and, clutching his topper, rushes into the night, muttering about Satan being present among them.

Bridie follows him, wanting him gone but struggling with guilt and resentment as she watches his lantern dip down the path. Needing to be alone, she tightens her shawl and takes the path to the back. A cold breeze flicks sparks from a crack in the oven out the open scullery and into the yard. She takes a breath of darkness so deep it shuts out the light of stars.

Senses a movement beyond the scullery and the vegetable patch, near the dunnekin. Bulk of that shadow causes her to gasp in fear.

Robbie Fitch, holding up his lantern in one hand, shifting his baubles into his pants with the other, is coming down the path from the dunnekin. Curses the buttons he has buttoned uneven. Breath on him strong. Croons as though she is all child and not halfway to being a woman:

He nothing said,
but by the fire laid down the bread.
When lo, as when a blossom blows —
To a vast loaf the manchet rose . . .

The lamplight shows a change since she last set eyes on him. A lock of grey over his eyes, black tainted grey the curls of his beard. Finest beaver from America, he tells her as he doffs his hat. She's seen an etching of beavers in a periodical, clever creatures building a dam. Robbie winks as he strokes the topper now, watches her. Humming theatrical, breaking into song, pretends he is stroking some other thing. In the dim solace of shocking grief she finds the line that follows, the line she must throw out to shift herself away from him.

'In angry wonder, standing by,' shivering in the colding air, her voice, 'the girl sent forth a wild, rude cry, and, feathering fast into a fowl, flew to the woods a wailing owl.'

Seeing into her, he is, as she sees into him. In his high-legged boots, best of the imports from India, no doubt. Black greatcoat cut from finest cloth. Neck chokered by a cravat. Cloth of it wrought from the best Spitalfields silk, handed down from the best of the Huguenot weavers. The finest of everything has Robbie Fitch.

His eyes on her now, as though he is trying to lift her out of the dream of herself standing here wondering what he is like at sea, captaining the ship that sails the ocean, fetching seals, whales and flax from the New Zealand islands. Does the brute flirt and flap on his ship? If only her mother were here to accost him with her tongue, if only she herself and Tom were safe, safe from the government, safe from the likes of him. If only death had not locked life in a dream.

She turns towards the light and huddle of women inside, but he thrusts a hard arm around her waist. Propels her past the vegetable patch, past the hot stink of the dunnekin, up and around layers of rock to the crust at the top.

Night is a black silk gown; cameo moon drags clouds of lace. That which is gone will never come again. Her mother's quick sickness and quicker death. Smell of whale off Robbie Fitch as he stands behind, hands on her shoulders, grasp of him hard as he marches her to the edge of the cliff.

'Remember when you were little and I held you like this, kept you from falling?'

'No.'

Since forever it seems, he has played the part of the friendly uncle, but whatever he was to her ma was not kind nor brotherly.

'Should you wish to die . . .'

Splintering herself, the pain would shatter the beach.

'Tom has need of me.'

His guffaw is her flush of humiliation. Scooping his beaver hat before the wind prises it off, he laughs. No merriment in the laugh, more a volley of gunfire.

'Should you wish to die poor you can spend your life in the service of the gentry.' Shouting now he is, above the din of the sea. 'If you wish to acquire wealth you must . . .'

Was there more to the sentence? Were the words lost to the wind? Silence is the angry sea. The wind whipping up a cry from a ravine. A gull cawing to a mate. Sadness is in the rocks. Striving to find a way out.

'It'd be a cruel fate to lay those luscious locks in the clod.'

Strangely quiet now the sea, slumbering. His words heard clear, slide to lock in her mind. She summons up the harsh caw of a creature of fifteen years, a girl in the before world, a woman in the after world. Raining curses, she runs from the baccy and booze smell of the devil riding high on the salt wind.

———

Inside, the mourning women are prayerful, heads bowed, backs pressed to the walls. A man stands at the table, his back to Bridie, his apron strings, his bare bald head. Caddock, the butcher, raising a knife. Across his left hand lies Róisín's mane of hair, twisted into a rope. Pulled taut, sliced.

Bridie leaps at the butcher. He holds the rope of hair away from her. He turns towards Robbie who has grabbed the girl.

'I don't want no trouble.'

'The girl will come around.'

Robbie is taking her right hand in his, prising open her clenched fist. Crosses her palm with a handful of Henshall's coin.

'Sharp on the morrow your Uncle Robbie will take you out to buy some pretties to wear to the funeral.'

'I want a pretty with red hair,' says Tom.

She snaps at this foolishness, even as the women around him smirk. Scatters the coin on the hardwood floor, gulps bile as the women swoop to scoop this prize.

'We don't need anything from you, you evil fartleberry.'

Tom giggles. 'Poop poop a fartleberry.'

Laughter from the mourners. Fixing a look on the lot of them, Bridie scolds Tom.

'Shut your mouth, simplewit. Think on our ma.'

'Swiped Ma's figurine as well, he did,' says Tom, helpful now.

'Bad luck that will bring, angling at a wake.'

That from a mourner. Bridie eyes them all but their eyes shift; whoever spoke has hastily sealed her lips. Draws her breath as Robbie, leaving with Caddock, pauses at the unglazed window. He leans through, ducks his head, his hat crouches between two women.

'Until the morrow.'

As he tips his beaver topper, she hopes the spirit of the animal will rise, will haunt his way home, cause him to trip and roll, wake him in the small hours with a tooth-bared growl.

Turning up lamps that stain walls with the yellow tannin of seal oil, the mourners resume their talk. Bridie gauges that talk of the stolen hair and the stolen figurine will grow on the walk home, spread in days that follow, cause outrage that will die when the women need meat from the butcher. Feels a longing for her mother to latch her voice to theirs. Turns to clutch her brother and finds him at the table, slurping milk from a bowl; glazed with blood and urine, the bowl.

Flops herself beside Tom. Cradles her tired head in her tired arms. The pair of them beside Róisín, her hair sold, to be worn most likely by ladies, cursed English scum. May Ma's spirit rise from the wig to haunt the wearer, may she spark sickness into the heart of the bearer.

The wind is lamenting. Her job done, the bean sídhe gallops over the sea, flies above the rocks. Sound drags up from the guts of Bridie's belly. Puddle she is, drenched in tears, dredging grief. Dreading the dawn that will return him, her mother's first protector in the colony, the protector who comes and goes from Australia to the Middle Island of New Zealand. The man who did nothing to stop the government men, probably encouraged them, landing her in the Parramatta orphanage, a man she distrusts with all the muscle and might inside herself. Robbie Fitch.

CHAPTER 2

Full to the brim he is, full to bursting and overflowing with disgust. First the wretched mourners screeching like wounded seagulls, then the next abode he had been required to visit. Man and wife. She, the queen bee of bickering, had refused to give her husband his rights, had allowed another to claim her. Cuthbert thought the case clear: she needed to plead forgiveness — from God and husband — but the wife was unrepentant. Angry, even. Shouting at him that she had given herself to a young sailor who had more manhood in his little finger than her husband had in the whole of his body. Two quiet Bible readings he attempted, but the woman threatened to bash both his good self and her husband with a brick. Said she would sooner appear before the bench than beg forgiveness from any man. Daily, nightly, almost hourly, Cuthbert prays for good, God-fearing women, but where are they — the moral and the pure?

His hungry belly makes a sound like a barrow being hauled over cobbles. As he shifts his arms to chew a piece of bread the wind snatches from his head his hat. Spins his hat over the cliffs and drops it into the hungry sea. Dammit. The curse is inward; he begs forgiveness. That the Lord is testing him is only natural. Testing his wit, his patience, his pocket.

His topper will be among those that bob ashore to be fetched up by boys who sell goods back to bereft owners. No point in pointing out to them the sin of making a market from misfortune, for this is

Sydney and Sydney is no different to London. On the wash table in his stuffy Sydney lodging room he keeps a caddy of currency for this very purpose. Henshall's Spanish counter stamped, Dutch guilders and ducats, Indian rupees and Portuguese johannas to purchase stolen goods from saucy sun-flecked urchins.

Later he will drag wretched urchins from their abodes. Children need discipline, duty, service. It is the mothers who pose the problem. The noise they make when he comes to collect a child. Beg, pray, curse, knead his chest, pound him with bruises, kick his shins, stamp on his boots, wilfully failing to see that it is a mercy he is performing as he gathers their children for the Parramatta orphanage. Upriver even the wildest child cannot escape over the rough road or over water. Let mothers curse him to Hell and home. He is secure in the knowledge he is saving young souls.

Now his thoughts are disrupted by a figure on the narrow road ahead. Stumbling forward, he is annoyed at the misfortune of being caught bareheaded. The man cuts quite a figure, back to the wind, topper miraculously firm on his head, greatcoat swirling in the brew of this storm. Few men conjure such a manly figure of adventure. Here, before him, is Robbie Fitch, the man he most seeks to avoid.

As Robbie turns toward him — has he been waiting? — above the sound of the sea gnashing on rocks comes another sound — whistling. Such carelessness when the sky itself is wearing the scowling face of Satan! Clutching at his wayward hair, he prepares to greet the villain and be on his way. But Fitch moves fast, swamps him with feigned friendliness.

'Hey-ho.'

Pressed into a pit of felted underarm sweat and the blubbery stench of whale — shifted into stranglehold when he tries to shift away — Cuthbert is shunted against his will. The whistle gone, marched he is, to the tune of Fitch's garbled gossip, along McLeary Lane, past Muttonchop Ruth's and fist-fighting Caroline's. Shoved under the sign of the Saracen's Head, where he stumbles into tallowed light and falls against a whitewashed stone-stubbled wall.

Inside is disorderly merriment, a storm of entertainment. A comely woman bumps into him, breasts bumping him first, sails a smile at him, as though the encounter could go further, as though he could tickle her fancy. How easy it would be to succumb. The folk before him play with each other but all too soon they will play to the court and the newspapers will flourish their squabbles and trials.

Above his head a thatch of black iron sprouting candles reminds him of winter in London, snow on the gnarly branches of the Bethnal Green mulberries. The room shakes, the branch shudders. Rough boots stomp, flick dust. Broom ends knock, pan handles bang. Fingers click. Lifting their skirts, raising their arms, women sing and trail circles with ribbons tugged to loosen their hair.

A fire spits flames and smoke from the far side of the room. Towards the black hearth Fitch leads him now. To a recessed alcove where tough men lean over a bench making deals, stirring the darkness out and out. The men nod, shift and stagger to the bar, giving up the alcove for Robbie who roars for a jug and gestures for Cuthbert's coat. Cuthbert resists, presses his back and his coat against the wall. Robbie's coat has layers of flowing capes, his own has one. With the lack of a hat and his less than great coat, he feels unmanned. Undefended. His inferior coat is evidence of low rank.

Staring at the smoke rising from the hearth, he searches for the wings of angels, reassurance that all is not lost, that he is not. Lost. Oh, the head of the Christian Mission Society, Samuel Marsden, can hire convicts to tend his home and farm while the working missionary — he, Cuthbert — is paid a stipend on which he can barely survive.

Moreover, those who do the real work are blamed when it all goes horribly wrong. No one — not Marsden, not anyone — had warned him that the wasteland was not at all a wasted land. No one had informed him that when he arrived in New Zealand he would find enterprising farmers and fishermen who sold fish and potatoes and fresh water and flax to whalers. He was under instruction to teach heathens about agriculture and God when — truth be known — the native New Zealanders had sheltered him, fed him, nourished him, right up until that disaster on the beach.

'You seem vexed, Mr Sky Pilot.'

Makes a great show of pulling off his gloves, Robbie. Finger by finger, a flamboyant battle with the finest red leather.

'Sorry business about Róisín Murphy,' he continues, waving a naked finger. 'A temptress with a temper, kept strong men at bay, that one.'

Crosses Cuthbert's mind, it does, that Robbie is speaking from experience.

'True enough, more tigress than lady.'

A gust of wind shrieks down the chimney into the hearth, gives him a start.

'Tigress coming to make you mind yourself, Mr Sky Pilot. Best refrain from speaking ill of the dead lest they come bothering us.'

Nudged by the gust, a burning log rolls, rests precariously across the brass firedog, spraying sparks and ash over the missionary's boots. Fitch grabs the poker, pokes the cindered crust, pushes the log back. Returning to the table, he waggles his forefinger at the missionary. Thick gold band on this finger, sparkling green. Other fingers wear different gems.

A woman arrives with a scarred wooden tray; laden atop are a pitted earthen jug, pewter tankards dinged and dented, a platter of stinking cheese, a stale hunk of bread. As the woman bends forward, Cuthbert tries to quell a desire to tug the lace kerchief stuffed between the bulge of her breasts. His cock — how apt that word — stirs in its nest like a plucky rooster seeking a mate.

Fitch, quick, grips the woman's waist.

'Ah Jenny, gimme a kiss.'

In answer Jenny plucks Fitch's hand, turns it over, palm down. Bends and skims with her lips the dry skin of his knuckles. Then she turns to lift Cuthbert's hand. He hesitates. Rude to snatch it away. Burdened by the lingering heat of her eyes, the hellish fire, his great-coat that is less great than Robbie's. The heat of so many layers he wishes he could shed.

———

Sometime in the night, between the candles on the table turning into stubs and the light of those candles melting away, something shifts the image Cuthbert has of himself.

'There you were handing out guns—'

The audacity of the man, bringing it up now as though it amuses him.

'What choice had I, with you and your crew arming the other tribes? My people were ducks in the shooting season.'

'Oh yes, it was a mercy you did them, providing them with guns for — what was it you got out of it?'

'Potatoes and water.'

'Wasn't a wife part of the bargain?'

Cuthbert feels the smoke rising in his throat, choking him. Coughs.

'A woman helped me comprehend the ways of her people and I imparted to her people the way of God.'

'I heard she was adept at giving you her tongue.'

The missionary rubs his face. Feels himself trapped.

'Oh don't take me wrong,' says Fitch. 'I never quite got a handle on the lingo myself but I heard you grew quite fluent in the gibberish.'

Cuthbert takes a slug of ale. Feels himself overwhelmed by the memory of her, the prospect of leaving, of staying. Of all he tries to erase. Robbie on the wharf, boasting about his cargo. The New Zealanders blaming all Europeans. The quick escape, all on account of the whalers and their unsavoury cargo.

'Funny when you think on it now — and no doubt you are — how I dropped that sack and they spilled out, plop, plop.'

Day, night, he strives to forget. Her people. The grandfather, the uncles, the aunts. The tears that could fill a river.

'Hilarious, how you just stood there while they ran down the beach waving their sticks, firing their guns. Lucky for you that I took you with us, gathered you up. Saddens me it does now to see all your fine skills going to the mission. Taking children and raising them in an orphanage so they can be served up to be fucked by the fucking gentry.'

'They thought I had tricked them. That I had colluded with you.'

Robbie takes a swill from his tankard, dark eyes focused on Cuthbert.

'Once you've had a woman who's happy to touch your lap you want nothing less. You want your offspring to say their prayers in your wooden church. A pretty vicarage with three chimneys, rolling meadows and a flock of lazy sheep. The mission won't hand you nothing like that. You need land aplenty to grow a grand view.'

Robbie bangs his mug of ale.

'Would you care for a long spoon?'

'For why? If you're offering a meal, some broth would soothe the tongue.'

And settle the tiger that is clawing up his belly. He regrets now that he did not stay to break bread with the mourners at Róisín Murphy's.

'To sup with the devil.'

Across from him, in the midst of smoke, Robbie is grinning. Reaches his big paw over and clasps Cuthbert's.

'I jest; this devil doesn't sup with a spoon, Mr Sky Pilot. He pitches a fork.'

Clarity comes later in patches, light bursting through dirty cloud. Robert Fitch and other men with ravaged faces hollering about an isolated place in the Middle Island where the native tattooist is an artisan. A memory of himself rolling onto the floor like a fallen log, mumbling about the fire being like a woman dancing. Trying to speak, slipping into the old Gaelic. Later he wonders whether it was a dream or memory — black stockings and white thighs, lingering essence of toilet water, lavender flowers drowned in alcohol. He will ask himself whether it was lust that led him to agree to accompany Robbie Fitch to New Zealand and serve as his translator. Or was it that he was simply, completely, utterly, as he heard Fitch say, three sheets to the wind?

CHAPTER 3

Dawn brings a daze that carries the children like fallen prey. The sun is out of place and all the world has changed. Knowledge is a cruel trick Bridie longs to swallow, but there is the cold, sunken mound, the spikes of shorn hair poking out of the green shawl.

Outside, the halo of the sun expands over waves that sigh, fall and whisper a lullaby. The absence of human arms to shelter this girl and her brother is sensed by the sun, by the sea and the rocks. Banging at their senses, nature insists that death is a veil, not a wall.

Bridie, so little in the dream of this new tide of life, feels the pull of the sun's shine all the way from the line of the horizon to herself. But something is coming besides, like the chill wind over a bad tide. In the haze of this strange light they come, Robbie and two of his mob. Traversing the top rocks and stomping down through scrub, crunching through the vegetable patch.

Robbie greets her now as though she never kicked a keg at the butcher. The men behind him stand rigid, one thin, one burly. Have in common the shift and dart of their eyes. The burly one meets her eyes for an awkward moment, and away. A man surely afraid the target will see the intent.

Bridie's voice is a shock to herself, seems to come from above her, not inside.

'She's to be buried in Brickfields Cemetery, buried proper into a properly dug grave.'

'Conveyed this to you, did she?' Robbie has scooped the beaver from its crouching position on his head. Bridie cannot see the creature as a hat, sees instead the terror of eyes facing the barrel of a gun. Sees the ghost taunt the man.

'Do otherwise and she will return as a furious spirit to haunt you all your days.'

Her voice wavering now, she clasps her hands to her chest to still the shake in herself.

'Róisín was a fury unto herself, but you'll not catch me speaking ill of the dead,' says Robbie. 'Mallet and Jake will keep her safe while I take you on a little outing. You'd like that, wouldn't you, young Tom?'

Infuriatingly eager is Tom, only too eager to leave behind their poor, dead, robbed-of-hair mother.

Bridie bides time by excusing herself. Seizes a log from the scullery and lugs it down the path, pushes it against the door of the draughty dunnekin. Tugs down her skirt, tucks up her blouse. Presses her hands flat on the wooden bench, tries to hold herself up, must not let her buttocks touch the mucky rim. Prays in this private place to Brighid, her protector.

Wending her way back to Robbie and his men, she snaps a bough from the wind-battered tree that leans over the vegetable patch, catches the whiff of stale cat piss. Inside, she lays the green and yellow bough on the chest of her cold, shrouded mother. Backs to her they have: Robbie, the fake protector, and Tom. She looks to where they look, out to the great blue carpet as it rolls up and lies down. She draws a salty breath and feels a stab of guilt for Ma who has breathed her last.

———

In the hackney coach — which Robbie calls a rumbler, driven by a man he calls a flunkey — they face each other on narrow wooden seats. Tom opposite, Robbie beside. As the flunkey ferries them around Sydney township Robbie barks commands. Keeping her face angled towards her brother, Bridie surveys Robbie's beard, black with coils of grey, his skin above scrunched by salt wind and savage light. Voice a bellowing contrast to red-gloved fingers which fly and flutter to describe the difference between this side of Sydney, The Rocks, and the other where live the toffs. Takes it on himself to teach them a thing or two, he says. Here on this side nothing is settled. All is clutter and chatter. Jigs and ditties, dirt-rinsed gossip, tears over broken china.

'Here we are, my chav, my chavi,' he says as the trap swings into the soft green of Hyde Park. Seen the original himself he has, London's Hyde, walked that green in his youth.

'Here we have the great buttock of the bay, the barracks, great bleeding arse — excuse my parley, little lady, little gent. Regard the law.'

Flaps his red-gloved hands at the wide stone building.

'Fraud starts with the toffs fiddling deals under the sticky shadow of the law. But we can learn from them, my dears. To beat the masters, you must master their games.

'Across from the barracks we have yet another grand design, yes lady and gent, here's where the deal flies, a hospital built by three crooked merchants and what did they get?'

He cups his ear towards Tom.

'Coin you say, boy? Wrong. A deal to bring in all the liquor to the colony. You might call that a rum deal.'

Laughs. Slaps his knees. A puff of dust.

'Known as Macquarie's when Macquarrelsome was around, the hospital is nought but a murder house.'

Almost captivated by this flank of Sydney with its bold stone houses, the likes of which she has never seen in The Rocks, Bridie sees that the windows are dark eyes sneering at her, passing judgments.

'Remember, young gent,' Robbie is saying, 'if you don't rise up you fall down.'

Learn the trickery of the toffs, Robbie instructs Tom, for Bridie notices it is Tom he fixes on, whose hand he eagerly grasps to snatch at air. Listening to him she wonders, is he right? Is there no respectable way to step across the slippery carpet and up the ladder to the land of the gentry?

'Outwit them so the dark arrow never lands on us again. We'll settle on the Middle Isle,' he is saying.

'Middle of where?' says Tom.

'The Middle Island of New Zealand, part of New South Wales.'

'But there's a sea between here and there,' says Tom.

'And the great colony of New South Wales stretches all that way. The Northern Island has a grand little town,' says Robbie. 'Kororāreka. Gomorrah of the Pacific.'

He laughs at a memory Bridie can ill imagine.

'Top of the Middle Isle is still ripe for plucking, ideal for all deals — there we could build a port for trade, a town for amusements and entertainments. We will dupe the New Zealanders, become gentry. I'll be King, you'll be Queen.'

His dream falters, for the flunkey is slowing. Bridie follows his gaze to a group of red coats.

'Tra-la-la, count them caterpillars, Master Tom.'

The flunkey draws the rumbler over to make room for a cart hauled by three soldiers, and a sergeant striding behind. Bridie takes in the shine of buttons and buckles, red coats, white breeches, black boots.

In the cart are the bodies of a native man and woman, the man on his back, the woman thrown across him. Naked the woman, naked the man. Every part of their bodies exposed — breasts and hair, curl of a cock. Wounds that look rude, gashes, bruises. Evidence of how they were killed in marks from the coil of a rope. The man's eyes are closed but the woman's eyes are open. Terrible the terror in those eyes. Bridie shudders, feels in that shudder something from the woman passing to herself; what it is she does not know, cannot yet know.

Beside her, Robbie sounds like a man strangling a cough. As the sergeant marches past, Robbie leans over, spits at the black gleam of boots. The sergeant barks and raises his cane. Robbie swings out over the step. Left hand scoops the beaver hat over the dust rising from wheels and hooves. Scoops the hat to salute his forehead.

'Beg pardon, sir, I will mark my aim with more care next time.'

The sergeant hesitates. Taps the cane once, considering. Strides away. Robbie slaps Bridie's leg.

'Give me a pistol and I'll mark my aim all right.'

Bridie moans.

'It's all right,' he says, patting her in a way that makes her hate his hand.

'Poor things.'

'Blackies,' he snarls.

'You're crying for our ma, aren't you, Bridie?' says Tom.

'Shut up, boy,' says Robbie.

She wonders whether Robbie knows she has been working at the new native mission, teaching children their new Christian names, along with English words and manners. She is supposed to whip the children if they insist on keeping their old names, feels something inside her curdle when she is told to obey this rule.

'They're not doing anyone any harm so why kill them?' she asks Robbie now.

'The only way to stop their interferences is to get rid of them.'

'Interfering how?'

'Helping themselves to crops, stealing fish.'

'The women we know share their catch with the folk of The Rocks, don't they, Tom?'

'They all deserve hanging,' says Robbie.

There is a pause into which neither of them ventures until Tom pesters Bridie again to explain why she is upset.

'Shut your gabber or I'll cut your tongue,' says Robbie.

'Will they be buried at Brickfields like Ma?' she dares ask.

'Buried?' He has adopted a toff's tone now, mocking her. 'They'll be off to the Shipwright's Compass where a physician will — let us say — attend to them.'

He laughs.

'Off with their heads, as the King would say, to be pickled in barrels.'

Unbidden, the moan comes from so deep inside her, the sound seems older than herself.

'Disgust is something the likes of us can ill afford.'

Robbie thumps Tom's leg, makes the boy jump.

'But it's the heads of New Zealanders that fetch the highest price, my boy. Finest tattoos in the world. All those pretty whorls and coils.'

'Hasn't it been outlawed?' says Bridie.

He ignores her, speaks to Tom.

'The market was flooded, drove the price down. Now that it's against the law, the price for heads is back up.'

'What market? Where?' asks Tom.

'England. Fine ladies, fine gents want heads to decorate their curiosity cabinets. Talking point in the withdrawing room.'

Up in the rumbler now, up so high she can see the way the world slides. Tilts back her head. A cloud above is a child's thumbprint pressed in flour, stamped on a wide bolt of blue silk.

Here comes Robbie stomping over her thoughts.

'You've too much spark in you to make a good domestic.'

Her gaze travels down from the sky to the man himself. To the gap of tanned flesh between the cuff of his grey sleeve and the rim of his red dust-coated glove. Imagines biting hard through the cloth to the flesh, tearing it with her teeth to draw blood. Lets her thoughts tie him in chains, weigh the man down. As though her thoughts reach him, he spreads his arm over her and squeezes her shoulders until she feels herself become a tiny shrunken thing.

'Take the melancholy out of yourself. You don't want to wind up on a slab like your broganeer mother, mourning herself to death for that urinal of the planets. No man wants to dunk himself in a well of misery.'

She is about to tell him that she isn't a well for dunking when Tom pipes up.

'What were Ma a beginner of?'

'Broganeer, not beginner, Master Foolery,' she sighs. 'Mr Fitch is saying that our ma grieved for Éire. Mr Fitch thinks it a nonsense to mourn fields and hills stolen from under the people. Ma would tell him that the thing he calls melancholy is sadness turned to fury and it be the fury that lives in the Irish who want to claim back their country.'

Robbie sneezes like a man sneezing out snuff.

'Try a rebellion and you'll wind up like all the other rebels. Washcloths swinging in the wind.'

'I don't want to be a washcloth,' says Tom.

'No fear of that, boy, if you ignore your sister and follow me.'

Harks on his words, Tom, and sinks back reassured. She shifts her hand under her brother, pincers her fingers, pinches. Passes her pain to him.

'Bet it's that sky pilot who's been twisting your mind about natives,' says Robbie. 'Bet he forgot to tell you about the fun he had banging his gingabobs against the gates of sin.'

'Sky pilot?'

'Clergymen. Bad luck they be, but Cuthbert has his uses.'

On the far, shaded side of the street stands a group of six New Zealanders, two in feathered cloaks and top hats, the other four wearing sailor hats and greatcoats, sea blue in colour. She waves and they wave back. Absent from the group is the young New Zealander she met some short time ago.

Bored by Ma trying on yet another bonnet she had no means to purchase, Bridie had skipped across George Street to the storehouse opposite. Stepped up to the New Zealander. When he turned and smiled, she had feigned interest in the stone attached to his ear, attracted, rather, to the tattooed face, the ridges swirling up and down and around. She had been startled when he spoke. His voice seemed to come from a place of strength. He touched her hand, moved her fingers to touch the stone. She longed to touch his face but the stone was second to best.

She gave him her name. He repeated it, tasted the trill, tried to say it, pronounced it wrong. She had laughed as he tried again. Starts with B not P, she had told him. His eyes had measured hers and she fell. Brown dappled light in a pool. She saw the deep of him. Drowned, she did, in those depths for a time so brief, until Ma's voice tugged her to cross back again.

He seems to have disappeared. She seeks him out now from the height of this wooden perch. Surveys these other New Zealanders: too old, too large, too thin. Perhaps he has taken up work in Parramatta, wandered to the hinterland to clear trees, or left the country on a ship.

———

The horse blows knowingly as the rumbler draws to a clattering halt outside a rumbling ken. Robbie tips his hat at a crudely carved figure above the door. Bridie follows his gaze over poached-egg nipples, rolls of stomach and tail scooping a ship.

'A mermaid,' says Tom.

'Murúch, she be,' snaps Bridie. 'Use your Irish like Ma taught you. Men fear them and on good cause.'

'A clever man can tempt a merrow to shed her caulk and live with him forever.' Robbie's voice is Irish mimicry. 'Here we are, our port of call,' switched back now, the voice of him.

'The Shipwright's Compass, Miss Lady, Master Gent. At this fine establishment we lay our arses to anchor. Now bail out.'

He leaps down, gestures for them to wait by the door. Strides to the corner, peers around the back, seems to check something, reappears, heaves a large sack from the rumbler, lugs it around the corner.

'What you got there, Mr Fitch?' asks Tom. 'Herrings? Guns?'

'Mind your business and your tongue.'

But the boy is after Robbie, skittering behind the building. Bridie hesitates. Should she follow, should she wait? She runs her fingers down one of the runnels between blocks of stone marked by hammers. Peers into the white haze of a yard. Rope. Flap of a ripped shirt. Astounded eyes, twisted gape, stretched necks. The haunting is surely a trick of light?

Every corner of every yard in The Rocks, every line of washing can shift, so easily become nine Irish rebels slung up like beasts. For all her not less than fifteen years she has been fed stories about the men, one version from the orphanage, another from Ma. In Ma's version the rebels did not twist and turn on the gibbet, they seized a ship and sailed to claim Éire from the English.

Back now, Tom. Face pale, skittle shaken out of him.

'What he took out the back, the stash. It's heads.'

'Pig heads or fish?'

'Something worse. Awful. He swore me not to tell.'

She feels the bile rise inside, a sourness in her mouth. Where can they run? Out bush where men as bad as the worst whalers hide themselves. Upriver lies Parramatta, the orphanage, the mission, where the whip is used against all the stolen children. At every turn and all around there is danger. Fear is a rock inside her now. Settled cold, settled hard.

Streets, crowded when they arrived, are empty. A stray toddler stumbling towards her is hurriedly scooped away and inside by its mother. Lucky child to have a ma. She hears the door bang shut, crack of the bolt sliding home, leaving her to face this danger alone.

CHAPTER 4

Seated at a scarred wooden bench inside the Shipwright's Compass, Bridie twists her forefinger over her middle finger, then her middle finger over the fore. Makes of her fingers tiny legs that flirt-a-jig over the bubbled stream to the candlestick, flirt-a-jig to the flame. The flame shudders like a girl straining for life.

'Here blows the Abbess,' says Robbie.

'Like the abbess in a convent?' says Tom.

'This one's married to more than three men,' says Robbie, laughing at the Abbess as she approaches their bench. 'You wouldn't stick to God the father, Jesus and the Holy Ghost, would you, my darling?'

'Watch your tongue.'

A slosh stain on the woman's gown. Breasts that meet the rolls under her chin. As the Abbess casts her eyes towards her, Bridie feels her worth assessed like a shank of meat.

'How old's the mot?'

A hot blush comes over Bridie's face as she tries to scowl; how dare her skin flush in betrayal?

'Fine fresh colour in them cheeks. What age would you be? Fifteen, sixteen?'

'She's five times ten,' says Tom.

'Five *and* ten.' Bridie rolls her eyes at her brother, warns him quiet.

Her tongue is so dry and rough she can only nod as the Abbess proffers an earthen jug. Longs to grab the whole jug and glug. Cupping bowls for dear life, they both slurp the brew, another, and a third.

A cordwainer appears, proffering his wares — soft slippers and boots. Such fine, soft leather and hard of heel. Refers to Robbie as the King of the Crimpers. Robbie strokes the leather, grins at Bridie and raises a brow.

'Men prefer young skin to old.'

The Abbess lays a gown on the bench. Green the colour of it, emerald with tucks and trails and a golden sheen, the dress of a woman who would live in a six-chimneyed house.

Another bowl sloshes on the table. Dimly, Bridie hears Tom bleat. Robbie's voice is muffled, his speech a merry dance, and she can hardly stand. She touches the table. Smells the wet of her own armpits like the damp stain of the stone brick walls, the smell of the place, of herself, all the way down to underneath.

Robbie heaves the gown over Bridie's head, passing it back to the Abbess.

'Take this flumadiddle. Check the parts. Fancy her up.'

———

Fingers of light grope into a room that is part storeroom, part boudoir. The Abbess shoves Bridie down onto a hard, cold bench. A damp pillow, stink of straw and urine. The wall above the bench has been scratched with initials. How many girls have lain here scraping their names? The candle glowers. Against the wall, shadows leap, try so hard to escape.

She struggles as her blouse is pulled over her head, her skirt tugged down, tries to cover herself but her hands only flap and the woman keeps tugging. Tries to muster a scream but gags instead, against the woman's hand. Somewhere in the struggle she stops. Her nod promises silence. She scours the woman's face, sees lines of anger and something else — laughter? Kindness?

'Please don't do this. Perhaps you knew my ma, she—'

The woman twists Bridie's wrist.

'Take what comes easy. Should it turn nasty, you'll suffer worse. We'll all suffer then.'

Her legs are pulled up and out. It hurts to be split apart. Feels herself a cold, dead bird, prodded, examined. Does the soul of a bird rise? Does it see itself roasted, gazed upon, served up as people laugh in merriment? Cold, white and goose-bumped her skin, her hands clenched in helpless fear. A sob turns to a lump of ice in her throat. She is trapped, unable to flee as the Abbess surveys every part of her.

Bridie's sadness weighs heavier as merrily, cheerily, the woman sings about boiling an egg and straining it through a ladder.

'The tongue of an urchin, the sting of an adder. Boiled in a blanket in a shower of rain. With seven notes of music to make her the gladder, and it will replace her maidenhead again.'

The Abbess washes her hands in a dirty pail, dries them on a bloodstained rag.

'All over and done. There will be no need of fakery with you, my dear.'

'May I go and bury Ma now?'

The woman laughs. 'You are about to be seduced.'

Thick white paste on her face dries to a mask. The Abbess pulls and brushes her hair, piles it high. Makes her pull on stockings whiter than legs. Finally, the gown, loathsome now. Dressed at last, Bridie is, but not as herself.

'Proper little lady,' says the Abbess.

When the Abbess holds up the looking glass Bridie sees a monster.

Her skin itches, her body aches. She longs to scrape off the thick raw pastry that is now her skin.

———

She blinks when she sees Tom. What must he think? She strains to pass a smile; it pains her for it is weak not strong, false not real.

Robbie's brows raise a question to the Abbess. The woman nods.

'She's not been spoiled.'

He grins.

'Not yet.'

He seizes Bridie's hand, prises open her clenched fingers, puts inside her palm something hard and cold. The curse comes from outside her, like a wind, whistles out of her mouth, spits at his face.

'Go ndeine an diabhal dréimire de cnámh.'

Knows, she does, that he, with all his secret language, will loathe her use of words he cannot understand. She uncurls her fingers. Lying in her palm is a comb made from something hard, flecked like amber in water. She hears a voice, a woman — Ma? — telling her that not all gifts are a blessing; some are a curse that keep you forever from the life you were meant to live. She wants nothing from him — not garments, not boots, not this comb. Poises her hand to hurl it from herself.

'Give it to me,' calls a woman.

'Me-e-e-e,' chorus the other women.

Only the Abbess is silent.

'Ungrateful little bitch.'

Robbie grabs her hand, pulls her fingers back, seizes the amber-flecked comb. All performance, he turns and bows to the gallery of women and men, speaks loud for her. To them.

'Trade is one thing turned to another, my dimber. Take this comb here — what was it first? A shell? Not any shell. Not a shell lying on the beach being nothing-else-first shell. This comb here was a shell that sheltered a turtle.'

He waves the comb in the air.

'Pooping eggs on a beach on a South Sea island till I happened upon her.'

His words carry hot breath, cause her spine to tingle.

'Pulled her neck I did — reached in and stretched it out.'

He grabs Bridie by the hair, pulls her back and drives the cold teeth of the comb into the back of her head.

'Drove the knife under her shell. Sliced right around, ripped that shell off her back. Easy as ripping out a fingernail. The shell, like bone, attached to the flesh.'

Bridie's head is pulled so far back she fears her neck will break. The teeth of the comb are digging into her hair and piercing her scalp.

'Still alive she was, but oh dearie me, not for long.'

He pulls out his knife, holds the cold end of it to the nape of her neck. She winces under the tip of the blade, feels the pressure on each notch of her spine as he traces it down her back. It is as though her curse on Robbie has turned on her — her own backbone has become the devil's backbone and soon she might be plucking apples from the garden of Hell. Prod. Prod.

'The flesh under her shell was so tender,' Robbie goes on. 'Sweet turtle soup we supped that night.'

He thrusts Bridie forward, towards the large looking-glass above the bar. Pushes her to face the strange girl, powdered and pained. What Bridie sees is not a comb jammed into her hair but a shell, and in the shell a creature with a face, eyes closing. A turtle mourning an island. Its presence sears into her. How could a creature leave forever the vessel that carried it?

Robbie flourishes a bow, the show of him for the crowd. The Abbess laughs, the women laugh. Tom is where? Robbie scoops Bridie into him; his whiskers scratch her lips, his tongue slides rudely between her teeth. The bile of disgust rises in her throat. She cannot scream, she cannot weep.

He takes her shoulders. Pinions her arms. Her breath comes hard, a dog panting before death. He drags her all the way to the end of the room, stopping outside a door that is black and arched like the door in a church.

'Heed this, my dimber. Every man's face is an anchor. Brows, nose, mouth. Some look hard and hold nothing of substance. Others look soft that deceive.'

'You can stop this now, Robbie. Let us go home, me and Tom, let us go to Brickfields and bury Ma.'

He rolls his eyes and mocks her with an exaggerated sigh. She sees that there is no escape from what is to come.

'The man inside this room wants your youth and your purity. He won't brook no nonsense — don't be fooled by his soft skin. The gentry are all hard. Cross them, there'll be a cross above you.'

He twists the black loop handle, pulls the heavy door. They leave behind the filthy haze of the dark-burning oil and enter a room shining with whale-oil brightness. In any other world she might gasp at the ceiling with its midnight sky and crescent moon. The walls drip flowers and burgundy grapes; silken rugs depict skipping horses and squint-eyed huntsmen. Furnishings focus on a ruby red settee. The only perfume is her own unbottled fear.

On a large desk sits a decanter of light, shards of gold. Behind the desk sits a man of middling age. Skin so pale and transparent she can see the blue veins beneath. Pink cushion cheeks sprout a beard that tries and fails to be full. His how-do greeting gives her a glint of hope that slides away. In his hands he holds a red apple and a knife. Slowly he peels long thin slices from the fruit.

'A man who is skilled with a gun should be skilled with a knife, no?'

His voice is the crisp crackle of autumn leaves underfoot. He wipes his weak grey beard with a serviette. Scrutinises her.

'I assure you, this one's whole,' says Robbie.

'You'd better be sure, because the last was a disappointment I was forced to expel.'

Robbie throws an arm across Bridie's neck, yanks her head back, lifts her gown.

'I assure you, no man's entered her cunny. Not as yet.'

'Return in an hour.'

'Right then. And those quality items you ordered have been delivered out back. Spectacular pieces, true merit.'

Bridie's eyes follow Robbie's to the cabinet with its rows of carvings, pipe heads and artefacts, shells. A row of human heads. She gasps. One stirs a memory of a man she met some short time ago. She stares at the dark hair falling over squeezed-shut eyes, the deep round-and-round tattoos like ferns over his cheeks, over his nose. Familiar the tattooed map on his face, but no sign of the green stone in his ear. Is it him, is it not? Deep, the ache that rises from her stomach to her throat, causes her to bend and vomit a gush of milky rum.

Something comes now, comes from the cage that is the cabinet, the raging range of spirits whose remains have become an Englishman's ornament. A thousand breezes, wisps and whispers, feathers stirring the air above her, the winds of anger flying together to form a cloud — a cloak.

Robbie and the gentleman should see it but they do not. Do not know it has been given to her. On and on they talk. Negotiating a deal — but what deal is this?

'How many are you after from our next run?'

'A dozen? Thirty? As many as you can procure. You deliver and I will settle.'

As Robbie turns to leave, the gent steps forward, takes his arm.

'The demand is for quality. You hear me?'

'Aye, only the best for you, Mr Judge, my lord, sir.'

'I trust you're not mocking me, Robert.'

'No fear. I was respecting you, Mr Judge. The great, good and fine judge of Sydney, quite rightly. Deferential I'm being. Absolument. Deferential.'

'I'm no fool. You'll not be paid if you try plying me with heads done after they're dead. I know how quickly they sag into something crumpled and mort. My buyers are superior sterling after quality ornaments — the fine, the deep and the fancy.'

'You're right there, Sir Judge. Don't ask me how the faces tattooed in life retain their liveliness, but they do. Like this fine lad we tracked.' He points. 'Come all the way from New Zealand to Sydney and now he's sitting pretty on your shelf. What is he about to say, do you think?'

Fury rises from Bridie. Through her burning throat it pitches.

'I'll speak on his behalf,' she says. 'He'd say, "Up the arse and down the mouth, fuck you both to Hell".'

Hurls her whole self now, a fighting ball of hair and claws unfurling at the men. She feels her anger turning her into the bean sídhe, spewing blood and orange sparks of fury.

Snatches her comb, stabs at waistcoats, arms and heads.

An earthen bottle blocks the light; the sound is of herself splintering.

'You fool, Fitch. You struck her too hard. You must learn to hook a girl like a fish. Ever so slowly. The joy lies in the struggle.'

A dark hour later she drifts from the aches in her body to find her arms have been racked, her legs wrenched. Drifts in half sleep to shadows, to the stink of cheap oil and spilt rum. The stink underneath is the stink of something dead, something escaped, something that can never come back. The stink of blood trickling from herself, from her own cunt as she is swung between two men. One man has her arms, the other her legs. Swaying her between them, they walk behind the counter. The Abbess hovers over her.

'— all be over soon.'

What comes out of her mouth this time is not a scream but spittle and froth followed by muck that, coming out, tastes worse than the murky liquid she drank. She struggles as they pull a sack over her body. Glimpses something being lifted from the floor behind the counter, a trapdoor. A fall, a slide down a shaft. Suffocating darkness until she hits the hard floor. Grind of cold stone on flesh-covered bone.

In the dusty light from the trapdoor above she sees two rolling figures crawling out of sacks on the floor. Tom, dear Tom, and another — but surely not — the familiar sloped shoulders of the missionary, Cuthbert. Darkness as the trapdoor slams shut.

She sinks into the small death of sleep.

CHAPTER 5

Piripiri Bay, Te Waipounamu

A trickle. A gush. Water hauls itself down the mountain, splashes over boulders, hurls itself over the cliff. Under the fall, lapping light, edges shadowed by trees, it pools before resuming its journey through the forest, around the swamp and out. Out and out, to be embraced and engulfed by the sea.

In the pool beneath the fall, Manaia plays with ngā kakerangi. Her laughter sparkles like all the raining droplets from the fresh fall of water as she plays with seals, babies. This lake is full of the life of them. Reluctantly, she rises from the pool, turning her back on their come-and-play eyes. Shakes the water from her hair, stamps the cold from her body, stomps on damp moss. She steps aside to avoid a baby clambering upstream.

'E noho rā.'

They stay but she must go. Springing from a boulder to reach the bank, she clambers up and into the archway of leaves that form the entrance to the forest above the stream. All around is singing. The stream sings in its race to reach the mouth of the sea. Birds sing of water falling from leaves. Manaia sings with them, joins the voice of the forest and birds and stream. Sings all the way to the clearing high above the wet valley of harakeke, sings to the valley that tumbles to the bay.

The path takes her down and then back up, deep into the black heart of the forest where the path merges with long shadows from the tōtara, across tangled roots and vines. She hears a whisper as she brushes the wide feathery fan of a ponga. Here is the sound of things decaying and new life stirring.

At last she casts her gaze down the plateau of gardens, the bridges across trenches, the platforms and drying racks. Tall gates. Rows of fences. Thatched roofs. All are signs of protection. Such a feeling she has that it overcomes her, makes her eyes fill with water. Love she feels, love and longing. When she looks at the warm smoke she wonders at the gossip, stories and laughter she has missed. She touches her hair. Dry. Dried by the wind. At least no one will realise she has been bathing.

Boys are already running to report her arrival, girls are already making up stories about where she has been and what she has been doing, none of it true. She moves aside for two women carrying kete of fernroot. Steps into a man swinging a rolled mat onto his shoulder. Boys with fishing spears, girls with baskets laden with harakeke.

A passing cloud casts a shadow. She looks up. Not a cloud, a bird. As she stands transfixed, people part and swirl around her, oblivious to the invisible line between herself and the bird above, a kāhu. The hawk has been her guardian since she was a little fish of a girl. Something is wrong. As the kāhu wheels and cries, every sense in Manaia springs awake.

Worried, she hastens through the throng to the whare where her lover, Kauri, is receiving the final stage of his tā moko from Te Rākaunui. The tohunga is so renowned that people from other hapū choose to be tattooed by him. So many preparations have led to this day — preparations made even before Kauri was born, the traditions handed down from the tīpuna.

Te Rākaunui is guided by Papatūānuku and Ranginui in all things; he respects the worlds of the sky, the land and the sea and all the life within. He has sought the blessings of all the atua and listens beyond this realm to the great power that resides in Te Kore, the womb where all life is stirred. Yet still Manaia worries, for even with these powers to draw on, with all his great knowledge, when this tohunga carves the face, the body, it is not unheard of for the spirit of a boy or man receiving the tā moko to grow weak. If this happens to Kauri it will cause him to bleed too much for too long, and suffer greatly. He might even die.

Two small boys are standing in front of the whare of the tohunga. She cannot tell whether they are being nosy or have been recruited as guards. She commands them to step aside. One runs off but the other remains.

'Kāore,' he says, barring her entry.

Annoyed, she picks him up and plants him on the path, telling him to be off before she does worse. At the whare she finds a gap where the binding between the ponga logs has unravelled. She peers into this gap.

Under a lamp of burning pigeon fat, Kauri is sprawled on his back, head laid into the hollow of a river-washed boulder. His eyes roll under eyelids squeezed closed as Te Rākaunui taps the uhi to slice small cuts in the skin. The smell of him is damp earth and dry fear. His fists are clenched as he fights the pain.

Somehow she must help him maintain the strength to receive his moko. She turns back, looking towards the colourless sky where the kāhu flies in smaller circles. Shutting her eyes, in the deep darkness she still sees the bird. She inhales, hā ki roto. Counts. Tahi, rua, toru. Toru. Toru. Toru. Exhales through the crack between the black logs, hā ki waho. Sends the strength of this wind towards Kauri.

She sends him strength until she senses a change, like the change in the wind when it turns from cold to warm. Kauri is breathing easily now, is even chattering. The hand holding the uhi is poised as Te Rākaunui looks down at Kauri in surprise. Fearful that the tohunga will hear her, Manaia holds herself still. She does not dare breathe again until he resumes his mahi.

As she walks away, she smiles and holds her head high. Her healing ability is a secret that will not earn her a reputation or praise, but she is satisfied. In relieving Kauri's suffering, she has made it easier for the tattoo artist to perform his best work.

———

Groaning loudly, complaining as she lifts a heavy pole of eels, she sees Kauri. Healed, handsome, and striding his long stride. Keen to show him her strength she lifts the eels higher, swings the pole onto her shoulders, catches his gaze which shifts to her breasts and away. His face is more beautiful than ever, expertly adorned. As he saunters towards her, her eyes explore the intricate tā moko and more of him, all of him. Slowly her gaze traverses the muscles on his abdomen, down and down to his tight, strong thighs. She raises her head, closes her eyes in preparation for the hongi when her breath and his will mingle, when she will feel the rise of the energy, the life force that is his beautiful wairua.

Around her, the mothers tease. Wouldn't she like to bathe him, soothe his skin, feel the new ridges of his freshly tattooed flesh? Āe, āe. They nudge and prod one another, squeal with laughter.

She opens her eyes, raises a hand to silence them, but they laugh more, spill about like eels, slipping and sliding. So near he is now, he will hear them, hear them humiliating her; they will distract him from his intention — for surely it is his intention — to suggest that they meet later, in one of their many places. Instead, his gaze is beyond. What could be so interesting? She looks over her shoulder, past the eel fishers bringing up the nets, to a girl standing with her legs apart, hands on hips. Surely not that scrawny creature? Āe, he is striding towards her, one of the young women who do less work than those who are not born so high. A woman whose eyes are smiling, whose breasts are pushing in his direction, who is right now touching his nose with hers, sharing her breath with him. Manaia wants to vomit. Watches them walk away together so quickly the sand around the river stones stirs beneath their feet.

She whirls, causing the pole of eels across her shoulders to slip, the eels to slap at her back. Hears her mother's voice rising above the others, weaving the way of the talk while the other women chatter in a stream of advice for Manaia. Some of the best treasures her mother has given her are words of wisdom, the whakatauki she can carry through her life. Her mother is uttering one now.

'The new cloak might look attractive, but the familiar cloak knows the shape of the man.'

———

There is only one path to take in the late afternoon — the path to clean and scrape and cook for the rangatira — but Manaia does not follow this path. Arms wrapped around her legs, she crouches under the bough of a ngaio and listens to the wind sing to the trees and the trees sing to the birds. A few days ago she would have composed a waiata aroha for Kauri, but now it would be a waiata tangi. Her song would sob. Perhaps she should talk to the namu, send a mob of the tiny soundless winged creatures to strike his new lover in the night. Better to send one of the naenae, instruct it to weave that thin piercing whine, wake her out of dreams, stab her skin, suck her blood, leave a mark. A tamaiti taps her arm, as irritating as a namu. Pestering, jabbing at her skin.

'Get off me,' she says.

Irritatingly gleeful, the boy tells her everyone is fed up with her.

The boy drags her to the whāea, who are prising open steaming cockles, piling kūmara into wooden bowls, preparing the kai for the rangatira. It hits her hard. How could she have been so selfish as to forsake this work to dream of a man? It is Rima, the mother who birthed her, who inflicts the deepest wound as she stares with water-filled eyes, an expression of shame. Ashamed of a daughter who lets others do her work.

No one speaks as the kai is served with great care to the ranga-tira, no one speaks as the scraps are cleared and the wooden bowls are cleaned. No one speaks as the workers eat. Only afterwards do the women release their irritation with her. In the whare moenga, legs crossed, hands clasped, head bowed before her mother, her other mothers, before Manutaki, her mother's dearest brother, and the other men who are her fathers, her uncles, her guardians who protect her, who raise her up after casting her down. She shifts restlessly, is told to sit still. She will never again ask, as she did once, whether the old scratchy mat beneath her should be thrown out and replaced. A kuia had rebuked and shamed her.

'Will you throw out your own mother when she is all worn? No? Then keep your clever notions to yourself.'

Exhausted, the mothers and fathers and children slump into sleep, their heads resting on the long black ponga log that stretches the length of the whare moenga.

For Manaia, though, this day is not over. It is the worst she has known, for she has lost her lover, her Kauri, to another. Angrily she plugs her eyes. Do not cry. But sadness is an overflowing thing, like water tumbling over a cliff.

A shuffle, a rustle. It is not a rat but Manutaki. Her mother's older brother habitually gets up in the night to make sure that the scouts younger and less experienced than himself are awake and alert. He has done this for as long as she can remember and for as long as that she has crawled after him to wait. Only twice has she followed him but he was quick to hear her footsteps and send her back.

In the doorway she huddles, watching as the flame of his torch disappears into the deep darkness. In her mind, she sees him make his way down the path, past the plantations. On the way back he will stand on the cliffs. He would check the moon but there is no moon this night. He will gauge the movement of the clouds, the stars and the waves.

She is roused from dreams by a blast of light that smells of pigeon fat. After planting the torch he squats beside her and sighs. The weight of his sigh makes her feel sad and yet she is hopeful. Surely he can advise her how to win back Kauri.

'A woman should look for a man who has hard hands, for that man is a worker.'

'And a man, what should he look for?'

'A woman must have a special skill. Should not be too lazy to use that skill.'

She waits in the dark, moonless silence for him to tell her that her skill is scrubbing kūmara or carrying eels, or perhaps if she is lucky serving the rangatira.

'You hear the tīpuna. You know things that are yet to come.'

He has never spoken to her like this.

'You need to work on this.'

'So I can win Kauri back? It's not hopeless?'

His laugh is sad; somehow she has disappointed him.

'I thought you were ready,' he says.

She wants to tell him she is, but he is already crawling back into the whare.

———

In darkness the space between mothers and fathers disappears. Even the sky and the earth seem inseparable. As she lays herself down, her head next to her mother's head, her foot knocks against her mother, whose foot kicks at her mother's brother who is, of course, Manutaki. She wonders if he has forgotten to make his pronouncement on the weather.

'Mutu-whenua,' he says loudly, causing as always the sleepers to turn and stir. 'Tomorrow will be a bad day for fishing.'

CHAPTER 6

*Somewhere on the ocean, the highway
between Australia and New Zealand*

At night, sounds on the ship subside. A few songs, wistful, rise. Curses dwindle and fade. Cold drafts whistle through the planks to underneath, to the bed where Bridie lies, for the deck forms the roof of this cabin she shares with Robbie. Wonders, she does, if the ship likes the night, relishes the freedom of being less manned. But she herself detests the nights. The cabin confines, the bed-box rocks endlessly on its gimbals.

Robbie's big body smells of the gut of the ocean. How she loathes the sea-broth stink of him, the whiskers that scrub her skin and burn her mouth. Dreads the way his delight rises as she struggles against him. Meat she is, meat to this man, a slab of salt beef, to be gnawed and devoured. As the mattress swings, as the ship sways, as her stomach heaves, his sour wheezing breath hastens. He fumbles, grabs her hand to slide back and forth, to push and tug. Music of his murmured flash twists her gut. Chiv lis adré. Put it in.

Bridie recoils. Hates his manhood — would hack it off if she could. Get him drunken, tie his arms to the gimbals, stuff his mouth with the stockings he bought her, knock him out with — with something, she will think of something. With a rusty blade back and forth she would hacksaw across the shrunken — for they would shrink — pebbles of his balls. Slice the sausage cock, let it fall, dribble blood. She would slip down the steps to the hold. Skirts would drag in the dark stink water; she would hold her breath so as not to breathe the stink. Flick of tinder, light meeting the gleam of eyes from the raised cages: six chickens, three goats, two grovelling pigs. She would if she could — dreams she would — poke through the bars of the pig cage the little sausage, the two shrivelled tomatoes of his chopped-off manhood; hear the snuffle of snouts shovelling up the stew. Would he imagine such an end for his tools? He would not.

When he takes her flesh, she reaches deep within the darkness, far within the walls of herself. Hauls for light as women have for centuries hauled light from these depths. Hauls deep inside for the self that is spirit, this small shining self that is light, that from this place, this time, will take her in flight.

———

Nights are terrible, days scarcely bearable. Now it is morning again and she is on the wooden stage, surrounded by low bowed walls of wood, creaking curtains that strain against the wind. A beast in a marketplace, tied to one of the ship's three masts. Roped for her own safety until she gets her sea legs, Robbie has said. She walks gingerly so as not to slide her thin-soled boots on the wet boards of the deck. She is not stupid as he surely supposes, for she senses the pleasure he takes in displaying his prize, feels herself humiliated, for the men surely entertain themselves by imagining what he does to her by night.

The high sleeves of her gown have become sad little bags sagging from her shoulders. Every hour or so she bunches and squeezes the fabric of this gown — the very same green gown the Abbess dressed her in — and the water in it pours out, as on a washday. The waves that spew over the runnels of the ship soak her. The rope rubs wrists already seared by ropes.

What is it — five days since she was abducted? Time seems to have lost its way. Five days since she was hauled through the tunnel from the cool cellar of the Shipwright's to the jagged hole in the cliff and the thin crumbling path down to the shore. Even then she wondered on it, as she does now — the wonder of how nature produces theatre, for that night was full of sinister scenic beauty. Surely the sky and earth conspire at such times, create a theatre set to please an audience. Or perhaps the beauty of that stage is a creation to stir comfort in the victims of misfortune. It gave no comfort to her. Full of fear she was when the waves patched with lantern light sloshed around a boat rowed by straight-backed men under the last quarter of a dying moon. Heave-ho. Singing and grunting. Rowed them to the ship that now carries the sad carcass that is herself.

She has heard names applied to the flint-faced, firm-jawed men who stomp the deck, hauling, pulling, straining, swinging, hammering, polishing. Ivory, Mallet and Jake, whose eyes slide sideways with complaints they dare not voice. A cooper called Bill and his son, Bill the younger, a ship's boy like Tom. Besides all the big, hard men there are others who nervously work in the shadows of the ropes, ghostly boys and men, ghouls, made human only by the stink of fear in their sweat. Speeding their spirits to work are songs. Leery songs about prigging and boozing.

She changes the words around as she walks back and forth and around and out. When a man nears her she changes the words back, sings the manly words. But when no man draws close she sings of the sea, of Éire, of her mother, of loss and of a longing to slit the throat of a brutal man.

———

Cuthbert the missionary has been lying low since their journey out of the tunnel from the Shipwright's Compass to the ship. Silent his eyes that night, shifting quickly from hers whenever the lantern swept its glow. Once on board she caught no sign of his presence, knows not whether he has been hiding from shame or suffering from sickness, but of a sudden he seems to have returned to himself. His familiar voice sweeps between shrieks of wind, spatter of spray.

Here he is, pointing at her roped to the mast, at little Tom slipping on the sea-soaked deck. Then Robbie's voice slams against the masthead, over the fresh, cold surge of salt water washing into her hair, her mouth. Oblivious to her soaked state, the men's voices are raised in argument.

'Wait till the authorities get wind of this. Your next abode will be Norfolk Island!' shouts the missionary. 'Mark my words, if any harm should befall me, the girl or her brother, you'll swing.'

'I'll swing, will I? Well, you came willing enough. Have you told her that? All too eager to convert the heathens, jabber in their tongue, explain the parley to me and my coves. Trifling chores you'll do for me to feather yourself a pretty nest. Five rundlets of rum and chicken so fresh you could wring their necks.'

'Stealing children was not part of the arrangement.'

'Hark at this, my coves. Stealing children is best left to the experts. Only missionaries can steal children. Only the mission can whip them, starve them, grind them down, make slaves of them.'

'We gave them slate, taught them to write,' shouts the missionary. His mouth contorts; losing, he is, a battle with the wind as it grabs strands of hair, scrapes his scalp. He should know, Bridie thinks. The wind will win and so will their commander, Robbie Fitch.

'Taught them, all right. Taught them to serve the landed ladies, the landed gents. Whipped them to submit to a life without fun or sin.'

'They're too young for such ill use.'

'You were a ship's boy yourself at what — nine, ten? — an experience that apparently failed to turn you into a man. Turned you instead into a mewing waif.'

The men laugh. Robbie whirls around.

'Adzooks! Show the man some respect.'

Whirls back.

'The dimber's nigh on what — fifteen? If I lay off, she'll become a thornback. It's all such a great fuss about a little corn. And I'm puzzled, Mr Sky Pilot. Age didn't trouble you none in Kororāreka, that great hellhole — the purgatory, you might say — of the Pacific. I remember your dusky maid seemed none too old. What were her years? Fourteen? Little less? Very little?'

'She was well into her womanhood, not a girl.'

'What would you rather clamp your chops around? Brown lamb or brown mutton? Quite the expert you'd be, Mr Sky Pilot, on—'

'You're vile and disgusting. The marriage increased my understanding of the language and people — to forge a relationship for—'

'Fornication? Did your great language learning extend to finding out her age or were you none too troubled with that while you were drilling for knowledge?'

The missionary's face closes. Sermon over.

Wind-whipped waves lash over the starboard gunwale of the ship. Once Bridie would have called it the side. Starboard causes her to think of a leap to stars, a leap from the bulwarks of the ship to eternity. She loops the rope that binds her to this mast, feels the wet and cold straw of the rope. Looks to starboard, likes the sound of the words run together, star and board, would leap over it if she could.

The missionary is mumbling, crying.

'There, there,' says Robbie, mocking sympathy. 'Mr Marsden was none too impressed with your original sinning, sent you to purgatory, didn't he? Demoted you to a mere flaybottomist. I've bowled you out, oh aye, indeed, I have.'

Bridie dares not look at the missionary for he would be loath for her to witness his humiliation change to shame. Let it end here, she thinks. But the ropes rattle, the sails crack, the sky scowls.

'Entertainment will resume at sun-up tomorrow. All men on deck.'

Three men she can hear when she is returned to the captain's cabin. Three men on the deck beneath the cabin, or possibly, four. Shingle sound of coins shaking in a fist. Fancies she even hears the slosh of liquor, tamping of tobacco, strike of a tinder, but these could be her imaginings.

She lays her ear to the deck. Words rumble, indistinct. She takes from Robbie's crate an earthen bottle, unlatches a reluctant porthole and pours the liquid into the sea. On the wooden floor she turns the vessel to her ear and listens. This she has seen the whalers do, listening to the deep song of the ship, checking whether she holds tight or has sprung a leak.

Bets float up from dank darkness, men speculating on instruments of torture. The voices are clear.

'I've not seen a ducking. Seen plenty of floggings.'

'A glorious gory thing it be, a jolly game-ho. Strap a commode to a man's arse, run him around the deck and duck him in a cask of tar.'

'Depends on the captain, whether he wants to drown the sky pilot or scar him with the claws.'

'Does he not himself fear the wrath of God?'

'Not as much as God fears the wrath of those he serves.'

'So what will it be, lads? Lay your bets. Dunking or flogging?'

'Cat-o-nine or the sennet?'

'What's the odds he'll scourge the missionary himself?'

'Captain's a scourger from way back. I've seen him turn men to dog-meat then feed the dog-meat to worms.'

'He should scourge the missus. Bad luck it be, bringing a dimber aboard.'

———

Morning brings the creak of sails, cream canvas, edges weather-slapped brown. Twisting between her fingers the rope that links her to the mast, Bridie wonders at Tom in his over-sized slop clothes, how he runs to Robbie's beck and call. On the sea-soaked foredeck Robbie, naked to the waist, parades hardened muscles like a boxer stamping across the ring. Flexes an arm to swill and slosh morning ale. Hollers at Tom.

'Fetch the salted eel.' On seeing the boy's mystified expression he yells again. 'Oakum lash — the sennet, not the cat — you blithering crab-sneak. Adzooks! Regard how the boy gallops at pace-of-snail.'

Entertainment to himself once more is Robbie, declaring the foredeck an amphitheatre, offering front-row seats. The entertainment comes at the expense of the missionary and her brother. Arms low, Tom passes the weight of rope to Robbie, shifts his eyes to her, her brother does, quick and quick away. What is it that shows so brief? Sorrow? Shame? Fear?

Stripped of every inch of cloth, hands shackled to the mast, legs dangling under him, Cuthbert reminds Bridie of one of the scraped carcasses that used to swing in the stinking yard of Craddock, the butcher.

'Our Mr Sky Pilot is a rantallion man,' says Robbie.

Quartermaster Mallet picks up the thread of crude ribaldry.

'Oh aye, right you are, sir. Look, men, his shot pouch is longer than his barrel!'

Turning her eyes from the mortified missionary, Bridie sees that the skies are dark, as though the devil has come to regard Robbie's theatrics, his skill in bringing to life the lifeless rope. Trained it he has, to flap and turn, lure wind, fill sheets, tighten and bulge. By equal measure he can bring closure to life. She has heard him boast that the sennet rope will flay flesh from bone, suck the life out of life.

He heaves himself up, laughs at the ripple flowing through the missionary's body as the man flinches.

'How's about I mark you with the cross of Christ? Oh yes, the criss-cross row.'

He cracks the rope, raises himself. Drives fury and force at the missionary's back. White skin slashed, sluices blood. A scream shrivels inside her. The missionary's body shudders. Robbie's lips tighten under his salt-tangled beard. He coils the rope as though one stroke was enough, dangles it, untangles. Plays with the rope, a gush of wind and he strikes below Cuthbert's left ribs, whirls the whip vertical and horizontal so that the skin is divided, sectioned into squares. Meat is what the missionary becomes as the rope storms down.

Robbie turns to the crowded deck, the amphitheatre.

'Regard, my coves, here he lies, a beast like the rest of us.'

A beast beaten and ruined, Bridie thinks, a cowering dog whipped into wretchedness.

Robbie wrinkles his nose, mocking.

'Smell it, coves. Is it not the stench of fear?'

'God's son Jesus Christ rose, saved us.' The missionary's voice is a whine and a whimper.

'What do you think, men? Shall we slice him up with the flensing knife? See if the Christ-crossed sky pilot rises like bread?'

'No, no, please,' Cuthbert begs.

'To whom do you address your plea, Mr Sky Pilot?'

Bridie wishes the missionary would stop all this pathetic pleading. Robbie, eyes rolling, rope furling, is more likely to spare the wicked than the weak.

After the sixth stroke the missionary collapses. Robbie heaves himself up for a seventh. Cuthbert begs for mercy, is rendered a slobbering, writhing form.

'Who's your commander?' Robbie yells at the man of God.

'You, you, you!' The missionary is blubbering. Tears from his eyes, snot from his nose, dribbles from his chin. Robbie nods at young Bill, the son of old Bill, to cut him down from the mast.

'And who speaks for the dimber and her ninnyhammer brother?'

Gulp of silence. She can hardly bear the sight of him. Sweat dripping from his bowed head, quivering forearms, knuckles clenched, heaving chest. Blood splashing over knees. Should she pray? Would Christ remember his own suffering and sympathise? Would her namesake, Brighid, flood the missionary's body with healing light?

'Shout it loud you stiff-rump, you spoil-pudding, you humourless grumbletonian. What man is their protector, you or me?'

'You sir, you.'

Once the ropes are hacked down Cuthbert crumples, draws his knees to his chest, cradles himself, rocking back and forth. Gaping, he coughs bile, blood-streaked yellow, into his lap. Raises himself to stand, hobbles toward Bridie. Imploring hands stretch towards her, his weak, cold fingers slithering over her wet, cold hands.

She wants to escape the dismal state of herself, of him. Escape from Robbie and his leering crew. A cold trickle of hopelessness, she feels, from the missionary's hands all the way to her frozen heart.

CHAPTER 7

The voice Robert Fitch uses now to write the words he will not send is different to the voice of Robbie Fitch, King of the Coves, who two days ago flayed the missionary. Different to the voice he used a short while ago heaving himself up from the net he had swung himself over to dump, balancing over the edge, holding the taffrail while opening his arse into the shit-catcher net. Feeling the waves rise up to laugh at his bum as he emptied his waste into the sea. So much fun the men have with this act when a lesser man than himself uses the net. Standing on deck urging the man on or unfurling the fingers of a man whose bottom is straining, roaring with laughter as he falls into the shat-on net, into the shitted webbing. On one ship he'd served on, a man's hands were prised away and the net was cut while he opened his bowels, despairing screams as he fell.

It is a risky business serving on ship. It's important to be liked, but not too much; vital to be loathed and feared, but not too much. Risky being a captain, too — not a toff or a swell, not a cove neither. Robbie is tired, bone weary. He has to roar some days so he can believe he exists. He squares himself at his desk, spreads his arse on the bolted-to-ship's-floor captain's chair. Picks up his quill. Prepares to flourish and flow.

Mister Justice J. Wells,

Sir,

My impression is that you are desirous I forever suffer your judgment without pardon. You profit from my feats and yet you sneer with disdain when I am in your presence.

I spend my winter commanding a ship, seizing and skinning whales and seals, felling forests of trees and flax. You yourself would be deeply embarrassed if you could not send your gentlemen the fine heads and skins I procure, the heads and skins of women, men, infants.

T'was on your demand that I learned myself the art of preservature. It was under your orders that I tortured a New Zealander to teach me the task. This was the only way we could be certain of procuring the chiefs you sought for their fine faces, their artful lines.

I had to work devious hard to meet your requests. It served you well, did it not? For without their leaders the people become unruly, and that unruliness serves a purpose, does it not? The fighting, the 'who killed who', the revenge, the affrays neatly side-stepped, these all create opportunities. I am a master, sir, not only at whaling and sealing but at provoking war and preserving the spoils.

The surgeon's skill is mine, sir, the removal of the brain and eyes. I have learned how to gut and skin a man, how to fill the orifices sealed with flax and gum. I've steamed more heads than I can count, smoked and dried skins in the sun, deprived people of keeping these heads to weep and mourn them in artfully carved coffins — you should hear their weeping, sir, for you would laugh mightily at the sound of them in the depths of their grief.

The profits are yours, sir — yours for sitting on your silken posterior while I spend the year reaping the ocean and land. Autumn I shore up the harvest. Spring I clean and repair. Summer, I admit, is a festive season when I reap the rewards of hard endurance.

I deserve a season of respite, sir, a season after the season of pillage. Yet your latest proposal is to deny me this, to deny my men as well as myself. Your suggestion that I run your store on your farm estate during my season of rest is a suggestion I resist. You require me and my men to work your land, you might even require me to direct the planting and toiling, to administer the flayings. Am I supposed to be gratified by this instruction, this new notion of yours on how to best employ me and my men?

Should I grovel, should I feel the double shackles burned on my legs once more, to please you? Should I be more measured, less boastful? Sturdier in my morals, not sway at all? Is it only you and your kind who have the right to quaff and chaffe and spew, fart and shit and vomit?

Are you finer than me, sir, because your gravy sweeps across fine china, across a blue bridge to blue trees, rather than puddling on a glaze made from a mix of blood and piss? Why does it irk you when I deign to wear the same garments as yourself, sir? Why do you refuse to allow me to drink and eat from the same fine vessels?

I am not nor will I ever be your humble servant, sir. I will indeed have my own ship, my own fleet of ships. I will look out on the sea from my rocking chair in the lounge of my own four-chimneyed mansion resting in the basin of a valley, I will . . .

The quill trails a dribble, black drops of drool from the mouth of a dying man. He has felt words rise from the ink and spill back from the quill so many times. But always, always he screws the parchment up. Wishes he could stuff this balled-up letter up the arse of the lord, so far up into the darkness of the man that he could pull it out of his so-called Lordly Judgly Lordship's horrified gaping mouth.

A rustle, smell of female. He turns. Finds the dimber watching from the corner of the cabin. Has he been stating these words aloud? Most likely. Saying the words on every breath as he wrote them down.

Pity she has in her eyes, pity with which she eyes him now, as a mother would look at a sick infant crying in the dark.

Seizing the quill he reaches across, hovers over her chest, grabs her wrist. Stabs her right arm, stabs, stabs as she kicks his shins, tears at his hair. He fastens her arms behind her back.

'Spying on me?'

'No.' Fury, he feels, at the anger in her whisper.

He wonders if his strength could plunge the quill deep enough to stop the pumping of her lungs, to still the beat of her heart. Shoves her from him, lest he be tempted to test the move.

'You come down here when I bid you and not before, you prying whore, and you do not speak of this letter to anyone. You hear, you hear?'

'Who could not?'

'Excellent then, good. Mind how you go. Accidents happen more often on ship than shore. Now back on deck. Tie yourself to the mast and do not come down until you have my say-so.'

When she has gone, snuffling, sniffing, mumbling curses, he lays the quill down. Could swear the feather lifts a little. He stares at the quill, the feather, the weapon. Something stirs, an uneasy sense. He shakes it off, the stupid notion that there is something in the quill that sees him more clearly than he sees himself.

———

There is a strange happening in the way the blood and ink mix in the grooves of the wound, the shapes that appear in her skin. She sees that she can choose to endure the pain, for surely what has appeared is the shape of a turtle in her flesh. A scene, a story, a picture, in her wound.

She alone does not have to empty her bowels into the net over the side of the ship. This convenience enables her to retreat to privacy, to dip the quill and carve more ink into her skin, turn a pattern from the wound.

During the week she clenches her buttocks and squeezes her thighs, pulls the inside of herself taut. Selects times when Robbie is most occupied in tense discussions with Mallet on the quarterdeck, or when he is dishing out a punishment, a rowdy entertainment or keeping a fight in check. These are the opportunities when she asks to be untied, feigning a frequent need. Time and again her plan works and he lets Tom or Bill or Jake unbind her, lead her to the ladder steps to descend to use the pot.

Two days she does this, two days of chiselling with the quill, of dipping the ink, of feeding the blood, of using her arm as a palette, a canvas to create a living scene.

———

Eight days later, on a morning when the sky is bleached of colour, she twists the ropes that tie her to the mast. Surveys proudly the welts on her arm. The wounds had oozed blood and black ink at first, and then became scabbed. Knows well enough, she does, to keep a wound clean, to not scratch or pick no matter how hard or loudly the scabs scream. The ink has become a permanent stain in the wound; she is tattooed. Watching her running her fingers over her arm, Robbie approaches, grabs her arm, turns it over.

'What the fuck you gone and done?'

'Funny the shape of it,' she says. 'The main puncture mark is a little turtle and the marks around it have the look of a moon and stars.'

She smiles, for it makes her smile, the turtle at the centre of a circle of pretty light.

'Who fucking did this to you?'

'You yourself, Robbie, gave me these pretty marks.'

She wants to curse as he curses, call them fucking pretty, but it is risky to use the words he uses himself. His response is measured, his expression confused.

'You've gone fucking flaming mad. I did bloody not.'

'Oh aye, when you stabbed me with the quill.'

She delights as the cloud of knowledge crosses his face, makes him stomp off, infuriated. Proof that these are not marks he would choose. A mystery wrought by misery, welts of survival these tattoos, a sign the skin can heal. Unlike the wounds she feels inside.

———

She steps back as Bill the younger heaves a pail of dirty water over the deck. Strokes the turtle tattoo as she watches Tom, her changeling brother, proudly swagger on deck before he climbs. Smug he is, for his light frame leads to dangerous work. A tiny spider dangling unsteadily in the rigging. The web won't hold the spider and the spider won't climb back up the web should it fall. But he spends long days on the watch to spy a spume.

She waits for the fall as he scans the horizon with the spyglass, feels herself filled with thrill and fear when he shouts.

'There — thar — thar she blows!'

'You sure, boy?

This from Jake, the master's mate.

'Yep, yepeee.'

'He's sure, sir,' Jake shouts to the quartermaster, who shouts it to Robbie, who shouts for all hands to get themselves on deck.

The action is fast. The harpoonist, lancer and other whalers lower the longboat over the side of the ship and cram in, hugging the boat. Bridie strains on her rope, sees that the boat bears a similarity to a child's cradle, one filled with new life sweet and soft, but the boat is filled with men grown, men she cannot imagine as squalling infants in need of a mother's comfort.

She shades her brow with her hand, casts a shadow to avoid the harsh light of this nautical noon. Never before has she seen a whale, not on her first voyage out as a convict child of a convicted mother on a convict ship travelling to the shores of Sydney. She knows without doubt that such a monster can swallow men and carry them from one place to another. Could probably swallow the whole longboat if it chose. If only it would glide through the water, open its huge mouth, swallow this ship and carry it to the far side of the world, to Éire. There, it would spit the ship on the shore and all the people they left behind would come running to the shore with pitchforks and spades, to claim her and Tom. Let them save the missionary too, but she would keen her mother, sob and sing. Give witness to the damage done to her by Robbie Fitch.

Wafting her thoughts are, as she sees the longboat grow smaller, her gaze following the white wake, trail of it like the trail of spittle. How little they seem, the men straining on the oars. She sends her gaze beyond them, over the wide, flat ocean, to white sails on the horizon.

———

Shrieks within herself at the force of it, fancies it spins, fancies it sings as it heaves out, spewing dazzling water. Between the white sails on the horizon and something else — a longboat that is not their own — the whale lurches out of the ocean. She cannot fathom why it brings her such happiness, the sight of it. Somehow deep inside and outside of herself she senses it is not a monster, not a beast, but a creature so much more amazing than she could imagine. A whale, soaring from the water, shaking with water, astonishing.

The creature gives her hope. It is as though the whale is displaying itself, sending a message to the tiny humans who see it only as a creature to pursue, to hunt, to kill for their own selfish use.

Then it becomes clear that the other ship's longboat is nearing the whale. No matter how hard their own men row, strain and shout, they cannot win. Dazed they are, the crew, in the long swallow of disappointment as the other ship draws down from the horizon towards the spuming whale. Robbie trains a spyglass on the ship.

'American colours. Stars and fucking stripes.'

A man from that ship's longboat steadies to strike.

'So fucking fast.'

Robbie's coves spit and swear as the enemy's harpooner strikes the whale. They spit and spew as the whale drags the longboat and heaves like a huge black wave. They watch the chase until the whale falls into an exhausted surrender. Finally, they curse and jeer as the Americans drive into the whale their fluttering little victory flag.

Robbie inhales. Exhales.

'Yankee fuckin' doodle fuckin' doo.'

No singing. In solid silence the crew watch the return of their longboat. Like a theatre it is, for the sky grows greyer, a mirror of the glumness of men. Mallet is the first to make it over the taffrails while the others are still scrambling up the net of ropes at the side of the ship. Strides straight up to Tom, grabs the boy by the chin. Spits.

'I'd drive the harpoon into your nuts but you don't have any.'

Tom pulls his kerchief to his cheek, wipes the spit from his face. Robbie grabs the kerchief, pulls it tight. Bridie screams as Tom is pulled off his feet, choking, spluttering, cheeks bulging.

'Tell me, you ninnyhammer, how you can be leery to a whale but not the ship that thieves her? For how fuckin' long has that Yankee shark been tailing us?'

He drops Tom, whose hands scrape at the deck as though the planks could suddenly proffer a trapdoor.

'Never saw that Yankee ship before, sir. I swear it popped up like magic.'

'Magic?'

Robbie looks at his crestfallen crew.

'We've been caught on the fly, boys. Magic, not the boy, is at fault. Magic would bring us to our ruin.'

He turns to a big beef-faced man, Nob, the cook.

'We're halving the rations this night, Nob, and the morrow. You hear me, coves? Stay leery to other ships and keep watch for whales.'

'Stay leery, aye-aye. To ships and whales.'

Robbie places his thick hands around Tom's neck. Squeezes.

'Billy, fetch me another hempen cravat so I can stretch this little bastard's skinny neck.'

She learned it from the stray cats in the streets of Sydney, how to pour the power of herself into her gaze. He turns. The look drives from her to him. Sends him the power of her love for Tom. He unhands the boy.

'Just don't — don't you ever dare let it happen again, you weak little crab-sneak.'

His face struggles to summon a scowl, fails. He pushes Tom away. Turning from her regard of them, Bridie crouches under the great crack and slap of the sails, wanders her gaze over the vast churn, the grey sea, and wonders. Wonders what caused the light that shifted the shadows that live in the deep well within Robbie. She would like to think it was her power caused the change, but did it come from something else, outside him, outside her? She senses a presence hanging over the ship, something not of men or women. Wherever it came from, whatever it is, it stirred within that walking devil, Robbie, a rare show of care.

CHAPTER 8

The calm of night is torn down by screams that rise and rise from the whare. People roll, tumble, sit up, their sleep destroyed by her, Manaia. All the sleep of the whāea, the mātua, the rangatahi, the tamariki, woken by her screams.

She has no idea how to stop the vivid dreams that seem to roll out like life. Each night a long wriggling worm rides the sea, slithers up the beach. She holds out her hand to the creature, gives it gifts, places a necklace of shells around its neck. The creature's response is to rear on its tail, sway its small head. When she tells her whānau about the dream, the women tell her to stop now, stop scaring the children.

The second night the creature comes closer, has grown larger. Prepared now, she drives forward, leading her whānau in a hīkoi, marching forward, striking with their patu. The creature shrivels and shrinks. She cheers with victory. Shrieks as it breaks, multiplies.

The third night multiple worms writhe out of the large worm. They wriggle into every crevice, suck streamwater, strangle trees, crush birds, devour fish. Now when Manaia screams, Manutaki mutters to Rima. Tenderly Rima takes moss, dips it in a bowl of water, squeezes moss water over Manaia's head. It trickles into her mouth. She wants to sit up and cough but feels she could break something important if she moves. Manutaki shifts over to sit beside her.

'Go back to sleep and back inside your dream,' he says. 'Do not welcome the creature when it appears, then it won't breed. Don't give it food or water, or rest. Command the worm to leave,' he says.

Determined to remain awake while others sleep, Manaia scrapes her fingers down the woven tukutuku panels, sings to herself the oriori her mother sang to her, the song she has sung to all babies. Presses her eyelids open with her fingers. The worm towers above her.

'We want it all,' the worm says when she tells it to leave. 'Land, forests, birds, fish and all the water.'

'To what purpose?'

The worm laughs until Manaia screams. Manutaki groans and, as if everyone else now has permission, the others follow. Rumbling, grumbling.

On the fifth night she tries to find the worm in the darkness but it has gone. She tries to find her people. They have gone. She shivers as though her skin is a korowai that no longer fits her flesh. Her mother holds her.

In her fever she hears Manutaki tell her mother that the dream is a premonition, an ill omen.

'You must take her and impart this to Te Rākaunui,' he says.

'I promised him I would leave him alone,' says her mother.

'Manaia has his skills. He needs to know. He won't be angry — you will see.'

The moon is restless, skimming in and out of night cloud as she and her mother brush past wet fern fronds, feet pricked by the sharp white shells on the path. Tī tree leaves rattle dark laughter, but the sound is a warning. A young warrior steps in front of them, brandishing a flaming stick that stinks of pigeon oil. Mata pūkana, rolling his eyes. Drowsy, tired, bewildered, Manaia listens as, firmly and fearlessly, her whaea bids the man to call the tohunga.

When Te Rākaunui arrives she wants to run. Surely she is just a foolish girl who has had a foolish dream? Steadying herself, she breathes in slowly. Hā ki roto. Waits. Releases the breath. Hā ki waho. Inside herself she asks the tīpuna to give her strength, to guide her to find words that have the best intent, so they find their mark and land safely in the ears of this great man. When her breath flows steadily the words are ready.

She tells him about the worms.

'They will crawl out of the sea and over our land, devouring our fish, our water, our birds, our forests, even our sky,' she says.

The old man looks at her mother.

'You should have sent Manutaki with this message.'

Rima pulls his eyes to hers and looks at Manaia.

'It is time,' she says, 'for you to listen to her.'

Te Rākaunui turns to the warrior at his side and speaks in a low voice. When the warrior has gone, he turns to Manaia's mother.

'I have told you not to speak of that,' he says.

'She cannot disappear, she is your daughter, yours.'

She hesitates, softens her voice.

'Manutaki believes that she is like you. She has the gift. That those who have gone before speak through her.'

Manaia tugs her mother's arm but Rima pushes her off. The tohunga raises his eyes and his arms to the stars. Breathes in, breathes out. He keeps his eyes closed and does not look at them as he speaks.

'You should not encourage things you do not comprehend.'

Listening to his lofty voice, she feels sick. Sick that this man, Te Rākaunui, does not greet her as his own.

She watches in shock as her mother stifles a sob, as her mother's fingers reach towards his arm, as he gathers his cloak and departs. A sound like feathers in the wind. Darkness folds around him as his torch moves into the forest, brushing light on leaves, trunks, branches.

Rage and fear rising, Manaia turns to Rima.

'He is my father?'

'He can help you — you can help us, Manutaki and all the others and those to come. You must see the sense of it. He is a great man. A powerful man. I wanted him. You understand?'

Manaia tries to shake free of the hand grasping her chin. Her mother's hand is hurting, her nails digging in.

'I wanted him.'

'What about my dream?'

'Now we have warned him he will lead our people out of danger.'

'How?'

'He will talk to the others and decide. Move the people up the hill inside the palisade of the old pā if they deem that necessary.'

———

The whare is calm, the people sleep. Only Manaia is awake, wrestling with the way one of the most esteemed men in the village has treated the whaea who birthed her, how he failed to see the wisdom and strength and humour of the woman who has been at her side every day of every year, every night at the end of every day. When she does sleep she does not dream of the worm. When she wakes in the morning she tells herself her dream was not from the other realm, it was not a warning of things to come.

CHAPTER 9

Wings stretch, wings fold, wings cup the wind, make no headway against the rage of the black sky. An albatross, as gallant a bird as she ever saw.

'Bad omen,' old Bill calls up to Robbie on the quarterdeck.

'My fucking oath, you're wrong,' Robbie harps back. ''Tis a good omen. If it weren't, we'd shoot the bugger down.'

If she weren't so afeared of Robbie and if the future didn't look like a dark slab of slate, Bridie would laugh at the bad weather galloping over the horizon to prove him wrong. The steep dark waves draw high as the ocean folds back on itself, becomes a black mountain. The sky groans, the ship shrieks. Rain is a thousand blades. High above in the black, the source of anger, is the eye.

Heard, she has, Robbie's talk of the eye, but what does he mean? The eye of God? Here it is in the one clear swirl of light. Peering down. All-seeing, all-knowing. What does this eye make of these devilish men, what does it make of herself now, staring up in fear? If this is God's eye then she should shout at Him, for He has done nothing for her, has wrought nothing but pain and punishment on her mother. He didn't stop the English from taking the land, the stream, the sea, the croft. The wrath of God: it makes her laugh with spite.

With the freedom of her sea-legs — for Robbie has at last released her from the mast — sodden to bones, she climbs the steep deck, straddles the hatch. Slides and bumps down the narrow wooden steps as the ship thunders down. Lands with a thump on her bottom.

Trying to steady herself, pained by bruises that will show on the morrow, she pounds so hard on the missionary's door that the door seems to pound her back, driving new pain into her knuckles.

Cuthbert has been wallowing belowdecks since the lashing. She must impart the talk she has heard through her upturned bottle, the festering grumbles rousing a plot from the galley.

Belief, there is, in a curse on the ship, that the pair of them are double bad luck — a woman, a man of God.

She pounds on the door again. The door cracks open. Cuthbert, bent, bleary-eyed and bedraggled, as though he has spent the nights and days weeping. She bursts past him.

'They haven't caught a whale. There's a storm. They blame us. Claim we've hexed the ship.'

Inside the fetid cabin she falls to her knees as the ship heaves. He joins her, the back of his nightshirt bloodstained, his hands pressed for prayer. She would like to ask him how well God has served him thus far. Surveys the room as the ship slides. Manages to grab his bowl of cold gruel, tip the contents into his pail, scraping the lumps with her fingers, keeping her face turned from the shit and vomit inside the pail. When the ship has dipped over another crest she presses the sticky empty bowl up-down to the wooden planks, the way the men listen for leaks in the ship. Bends her head and listens. Nods. In truth, she can hear no sound of them above the wind shrieking through wood, but she must convince him.

'They're at it again now, jabbering about us being Jonahs. Plotting, they are, to throw us over. Planning to do it at night. They blame us for missing the fish the Yankees caught, and now they are about blaming us for the storm.'

'They should look to themselves.'

She shakes her head.

'Something else — Tom's changed, he's different.'

Cuthbert shudders and the ship joins him. Sighs as it strains to find the strength to mount another heaving wave.

'A cabin boy is ever the captain's whipping boy,' he says.

She meets his eyes and steadies her expression. She must not let him see that she remembers his own naked humiliation and the whipping. As though he is suddenly aware of her sex, the missionary pulls his nightshirt down over his thighs. Voices rumble from the deck below, rumble through the boards; Cuthbert clutches her shoulder as the ship heaves once more.

'If we survive the night I will speak with him on the morrow,' he says. 'There must be some Christian soul among the men.'

'Bill the older hates Robbie — the loathing blazes out of his eyes.'

'I'll ask Tom, see who he trusts.'

Silence as they grasp the rails of his cot bed, fall, gasp, then silence again as the ship heaves, as they hear the call go out for all men to head on deck.

'They're too occupied to kill us tonight,' Cuthbert continues. 'Tomorrow I will talk to Tom. Fear not, we will find allies to talk sense into the men. Perhaps even Fitch himself would see sense.'

'You would trust him to save us against the men? The lowest of the low we are, Mr Cuthbert.'

'We must pray.'

'Pray for what?'

'That the storm abates soon.'

An answer comes from the ship — another long rise, fall and shudder. What does she make of this folly?

'Or that the storm is so strong it drives us to Éire.'

'Sadly, that is impossible. The best we can pray for is that God will speed us back to Sydney.'

———

A summer storm his mother would have called it back home in Ireland — swift to arrive, swiftly gone. A term for the squabbling squalls that passed between his mother and his father. His mother chiding, goading and demanding they keep the faith. His father bawling that the landlord would only allow them to retain the croft and field if they turned Protestant, and then they might even acquire a horse and a cart. To escape the sparks, the thunderous brew, the portent that something worse was on the horizon, Cuthbert joined the navy, for the navy was taking Catholics and boys of nine years old. Tried and failed he did, to follow his mother's prayer and find a way to join the French. Came home seven years later bearing the hurt, humiliation and pain of ill-use. By then his mother and sisters were corpses in the peat, his father a drunken convert. The glow on the horizon was not a storm, his brother assured him, but evangelical Methodism, and so he joined that society to become a missionary. An Englishman's boy after all.

The storm on the ship left as quickly as it came, but this is winter, not summer. Alone in his cabin, Cuthbert opens the Bible. Stabs a finger on the page. His finger tugs pain, the way a string pulls a bell, only this string pulls pain that screams and screams again. He reads aloud.

'Now, therefore, kill every male among the little ones, and kill every woman that hath known man by lying with him. But all the women children that have not known a man by lying with him, keep alive for yourselves.' Numbers 31: 17–18.

Wrong one. Stabs his finger on another page. Sways with the ship, with the sway of the light from the lamp and sudden shaft of shadow. A swell is rising — please, Lord God, may the weather not turn again to a storm. He prays aloud before looking at the God-ordained open page. Let this be your message to me, God. Looks down to the passage his finger stabbed.

'There she lusted after her lovers whose genitals were like those of donkeys and whose emission was like that of horses.' Ezekiel 23:20.

Some moral compass this. He slams it shut, the Bible, lest that image of women yearning for men who shoot ample semen should penetrate too deeply in his head. On a ship there is no moral compass. Time shrivels and expands into latitude and longitude, north, south, east and west. The tiny quivering needle, the exactitude their captain seeks, a fixed point in time. But the ocean is not fixed. To think it so is false.

Every wave is eternal, has a life before it reaches the shore and will fold back on reaching its aim, to return to the shore from whence it came. There is no beginning or end, all life does is revolve, waves and stars, plants and trees, creatures of the sea and land. This is what the sea has taught him. Yet forced he has been to find income. With no land or home of his own, he found in religion a hook to throw his cloak upon.

Warily Cuthbert makes the painful progression down the steps to the bowels of the ship — best avoided, the bowels, for this is where all creatures become rats, deprived of light and air. Stinking, wretched and wet. Rapid his breathing. Memories grow, light shrinks the farther he descends. The glass lanterns shielding candles are sparse down here. Light is the brief flicker of the strike on the tinder, the spark in the bowl of a pipe. One flash from a tinder shows four pairs of rats' eyes staring at him from atop a puncheon. The stab of light on a man's face reveals the scowl of brow, grimace of sharply crooked teeth. Every utility is strapped and bolted to the ground or buckled to the roof. He ducks under a dark beam, almost slides on the slippery floor.

Whispers Tom's name into the darkness and darkness returns laughter. Men locked in the rudeness of their low thoughts. The boy reluctantly shuffles forward and trails after him back to the cabin. Cuthbert lifts the blind covering the porthole. Allows light to enter. Tom does not look at him, will not turn to face him, averts his eyes. Left to right. Scowls.

'What the fuck do you want with me?'

83

The change in him so abrupt, the shadows pushed down, burying deep.

'Whatever they have done to you, Tom, please know it is wrong. You are a child and the things done to a child do not make a man.'

Should he say it? The image comes to mind no matter how hard he drives it down. For he was a cabin boy on the *Indefatigable* when the English navy raged against Napoleon and his men. On account of what the English officers did to him, he nurtured in his wounded Irish body the secret hope that the French would win. Perhaps if he reveals this experience now it will open a way for trust to resume, create a bond? He studies the boy's furious expression. Remembers the jeers, the shame, the smear on his name.

'Nothing,' Tom says. 'Nothing's been done. I don't know what you're supposing.' His voice is high, insistent and indignant. 'You don't need to be pothering yourself about me. It's yourself you should be pothered about.'

So many bad men, this ship is full of them.

'Are you aware that there's those on this ship who are blaming your sister and myself for the ship's troubles? For the whale, the loss of her? That they entertain such nonsensical superstitions they are plotting to throw us over?'

Left to right and back to right, the boy's eyes. To the porthole as though he could squeeze through and cast himself into the sea.

Cuthbert tries another tack.

'I want to know — I demand to know — who these men are that say such fanciful things. And who might be persuaded to a sensible view. There must be a man among this lot who could inspire and lead us out of this miserable muck-hole. Wouldn't you like to return to Sydney?'

He had not intended to imply, to suggest himself — and yet he knows much about ships . . . perhaps he could, with help, seize the ship and take control.

'I was a boy myself in the Royal Navy, from the age of nine to sixteen.'

Tom shows no sign of interest or surprise.

Cuthbert coughs.

'In more recent times I was on the survey of the Torres Strait, the Dampier Archipelago and a circumnavigation of—'

'Why should I care what you did? You're a sky pilot now, not a sailor.'

Cuthbert finds his hands on his face, rubs his eyes. He will not confide, then, in the boy. Will not mention that even out there (even out there, at sea) he was the butt of ridicule for not sharing the sinful tastes of depraved men who took what they wanted, when they wanted, in whatever manner they wanted. Will they ever leave him, the shrieks of women pleading for help, beseeching from shore, reaching him on ship?

'So you brought me here not for that other thing, but . . . but because you want me to spy? To find those who would turn on the captain? It's more than my life's worth. He would strip, gut and quarter me.'

'It's a risk, yes, but the Lord will watch over you, protect you.'

Feels miserable for pulling at this last resort, invoking the name of a Lord he himself has doubts about. Why invoke the name of one whose brief return to life as a gardener might be myth for all he knows? He pushes the doubt down, for doubt will not serve him well now.

'I need the names of those who speak against us and those who would speak for, who we could employ.'

'What will you pay me?'

'You will have the comfort of knowing you chose well — the right path is the Lord's path.'

All the way to the olive garden.

'I've been down the path to Hell already and I don't fear it no more. I want coin.'

'To spend on what?'

'Not saying till you give me some.'

Cuthbert lets out a long sigh, a wheeze in the sigh, damp in the sigh.

'God shows no mercy to mercenaries.'

'Use all your fancy words but I need coin to help me pay them off when I lose.'

'Lose in what?'

'In the games. All night. The cards, the dice, the flipping and betting. If you give me enough, I can pay them off. Might even stop them . . .'

So here he is, close to it.

'Which men will you pay if I give you say, Spanish—'

'Mallet, Jake and . . . no, forget I said it. Please.'

He is a boy now, whimpering. The hardness gone. As the missionary instinctively reaches out to hold him the boy stiffens, raises a fist and in a flash he lays a hard right hook to Cuthbert's jaw. Then he withdraws his fist, shock in his face, apologises for hitting the Church. Puts his head in his hands and weeps.

'Make them stop, please make it stop.'

CHAPTER 10

Endless, the rain. Māwake pā roa. Drowning the hillside and the valley, rain splats from the kahikatea to the ponga and whekī trees down to mānuka scrub, and the ground ferns, the aruhe and the manamana.

Under the dark eaves of the whare, Manaia hunches over a half-plucked kererū, tugs hard. Another colourful feather to add to the pile for a fine kahu kererū. Her back hurts, her fingers ache, and the mound of dead birds seems no smaller.

Running along the path around the whare, in the outside world of fleeting shadows, someone slips. A boy. In the fall, one of his pārahi-rahi harakeke shrugs loose from his foot. Shoving the dead bird from her lap, Manaia rushes to assist the boy.

Cold rain dribbles down her spine as she holds him steady and straps the pārahirahi to his foot. Looks up to find a man behind the boy. Kauri, his soft gaze on her. Something shifts inside her like a boulder falling from a cliff. She sends him the beauty of her smile, hopes that poetry will now float from her lips. Instead she utters a damp greeting.

But it isn't a good morning. His tone to her is the fond tone a man uses to address a younger sister, not a lover to a lover. Tears hurt her eyes, sting her cheeks as they fall with the rain. She wants to scream out that his body knows hers, hers knows his, but instead she stands and watches him trudge away from her along the watery path.

The breath at her back is Rima, coming to her from the shadows inside the whare. She lays an arm around her daughter's waist.

'Shame his korowai hides the carvings on his body, all that fine artistry.'

Manaia turns, sees the smile, Rima taking such pleasure in teasing her.

'Now, back to your mahi. Pluck, girl, pluck.'

Crouching, Manaia flops the dead pigeon into her lap. Wishes Kauri would return, give her the chance to make him be with her. Cold nips her skin, but the rain has eased and the swollen clouds are rolling away. She holds up a feather to test the direction of the wind, feels a change. Puts the feather in her hair. Feels the stir of desire inside it, the urge for flight. A breeze parts it from her hair — Tāwhiri-mātea is playing with her, holding the feather aloft as she runs and reaches until it is carried out of reach. She runs, smashes, falters and is held.

Kauri has returned, and she is behaving like one of the tamariki. He is holding her steady. So close, he is, to her. She looks up to his face, shining from the slick of rain and the stroke of light. The sun breaks through cloud — the gods are surely conspiring, playing with her, lighting him up, increasing her desire so that as he turns and walks away she shouts at him to wait.

'E tatari!'

Frantically she lays a boulder on the pile of plucked feathers. Ignores Manutaki, who shouts for her to return to her mahi because the wind is rousing and he himself is always working, is right now laying rocks on the roof of the whare to hold the rushes tight. Ignores the tamariki carrying gourds of rainwater. Ignores the women removing the wet mats from the steaming food pit. Ignores all the fastening, straightening, tying and tending. Worst of all she ignores Rima, the whaea who laboured to bring her into this world, who stands in the doorway scowling at the wicked daughter who runs after this man.

In a state of bliss she grasps his hand as the wind — which seems indeed to be playing — turns again. She squeezes his hand as the clouds shed the great aching weight of rain. Tells herself that the falling rain is a tohu of approval from the ancestors.

Under the splayed branches, splattering rain slides down a path that has disappeared into gushing, streaming mud. On the beach they tear down the dark, wet sand and across the small black stones at the far end of the beach. Around overflowing rock pools to three large boulders that mark the entrance to the cave. Clamber past the boulders, laughing as they crawl, drenched, inside the cave.

Inside they huddle, still laughing as they lean against the walls of rock, under the roof of rock, rock that muffles the roar of the ocean, rock that holds the thrashing rain. His laugh is young and easy as he unties his korowai, lays it gently on a rock. So happy, she is, to hear him laugh. He has come back to himself. He unties his topknot and shakes his long hair around and over his wide shoulders, splatters rainwater on Manaia, on himself. She lays one hand flat against his shining chest and with the other she pulls the string that binds his maro. Pulls the string that binds hers. Soft rustle of harakeke, whisper of the life of leaves — leaves soaked, dried, woven. With their strings untied, the inner garments shed and dropped, nothing between them now but skin, she draws a long breath inside herself, hā ki roto, releases her breath, hā ki waho. He pulls her wet legs around his waist. Pulls again as her legs slip. Adjusts. He holds her firm with his strong arms. Their nipples tight. His taut penis stroking her belly, pressing further down. She touches the tip and giggles.

Her giggle breaks a spell. He shifts her lower, thrusts. Shriek of the shrieking wind, moan of the moaning trees. Shudder. Shudder. Silence. Even the rain has stopped. He drops his arms, lowering her, stepping back. Wanting to stop him from pulling away from her, she presses her hands flat against his mouth to stop the words coming out, stop him from causing her grief. He takes her hand away, firm. The boy, deep within himself, cannot possibly know what he will lose by becoming the serious man.

'We've grown so used to each other, Manaia. Tired.'

'We are still learning. There are plenty of other ways we can try.'

'I am sick of the two of us, Manaia. I need to be free.'

Her voice is a whine, a desperate sound, sickening her of herself. She slaps her hands against his hard chest, borrows his toughness.

'I need you. Kei whea te tau ō tāku ate?'

Firm, insistent and stronger, her voice.

'It's over.'

'You don't know me fully. I have special skills.'

'There is nothing about you I don't know.'

'If my father was Te Rākaunui would you still spurn me?'

'Āe, I would, because he is not. You have many possible fathers. Not one of them is a rangatira.'

Before she can respond he is at the mouth of the cave where laps the mouth of the sea. Seems to hesitate, turns to her.

'Don't stay too long or the ocean will rise and swallow you.'

She hears the waves slapping his legs as he leaves. Slap him hard, she thinks. But now she is alone and he has gone. She clutches her ears, feels the wrath of the tīpuna at her boastfulness. She will be tested for speaking in such a way. If only her gaping mouth were like this cave, and words were like waves; if only she could suck the words back the way the sea sucks and spits. Water rushes over her ankles, reaches for her knees, the great crash of waves sounds from the rocks, the call of the seabirds, the cry of her heart.

Wading around the rocks she sees it, struggling against the sweeping rain, like herself. In the sky she sees a toroa blown off-course from the south, fighting for flight against the fierce wind. Realisng the tide is coming up, Manaia jumps from a boulder into shallower water, gulps back a mouthful of spray, stumbles up the beach. Standing on the seagrass she faces the ocean. From inside and outside her it wells up, a long karakia to Tāwhiri-mātea, an appeal for the source of the unrest to rest. Soften the rain, steady the wind, ease the struggle for the passage homeward. Then, weary in heart and heavy in tread, she clambers up the hill. Like the toroa, before darkness falls she must find the path that is her thread home.

CHAPTER 11

All around the cabin, light is trapped in cages. Behind the bars on the lanterns, flames flutter like birds begging for release. On the table, pewter platters have been arranged by Nob, the cook. Robbie suggests they play-pretend.

'Rather than salted pork and dry biscuit, what we have before us is turtle soup and beef and carrots in rich gravy. I am the king, you be m'lady. Here, my dear, aren't you partial to cake soaked in apricot syrup?'

Taking from him the weevil-ridden sea biscuit, she had declined to play, smile or laugh. In return he called her a hoity-toity fusti-lugs. A decanter shifting light reminds her of the back room of the rumbling ken where this nightmare began. Would that she could sink herself into the amber liquor. Swallow the drink, let it swallow her, give her its shine. Following her gaze, he fills her goblet, grabs his tankard.

'Here's to the change in you, my dimber, for I dare believe you have come to fancy me a little.'

Her shudder is inward. Has he no sense of himself? Even if he were kind or handsome, he is old enough — just old enough — to be her grandsire.

'Come now, my darling, what awaits you in Sydney? Return to life as an aspiring flaybottomist, wiping the slates and arses of orphaned waifs?'

He raises a hand against her protest.

'Do you know the best way to quell rebellion?'

'I'm sure *you* do,' she retorts.

He laughs, bitter. The laugh turns into a cough, the cough to a rattle, a choking gargle.

She wishes he would drop dead before her.

'Your Church is more adept at it than I,' he says, wiping saliva from his cheek.

'Supplication it teaches — be content with your lot, do not dare to rise above your station, work the plough so the clouds will roll back when you reach Heaven.'

Moving from the table, he opens the tap on a puncheon and fills his tankard with the slosh of evil-stinking dark liquid. Sloshes the ale into his open mouth. Burps. Laughs.

'You don't need to chain men to make slaves of them. Delay the reward for the next world and threaten them with Hell if they don't comply. Convince the people that the big man at the top is God and they will come willing to be enslaved. Ask yourself why the Church would take you from your mother, then ask you to serve the Church.'

He bangs the tankard on the table. Brushes his elbow, flings a pewter knife to the floor. The light inside the decanter shifts. He seizes the dull pewter bowl, holds it to his mouth, slurps the remains of salted beef stew. Stale crumbs of ship's biscuit stick to his greying beard. One crumb may be a maggot. Sour his grin at her critical scrutiny.

'Me? Oh, I'm scum, my darling. And you know what scum does? It rises. You fancy a better life — the gowns, the finery, the flumdiddlery. Come and rise. I'll be the king of our new town, you'll be the queen. We'll keep the company men at bay — at bay we will, in a bay of our own. Choose otherwise, rebel, and I will sink you like a stone.'

Keeping emotion from her gaze, looking him straight in the eyes, passive her face. Hard and black his eyes. Spark of mockery. Jaw set, the hardness showing even under the bristle of beard. The crumbs on his beard make him look foolish. Anchors under his eyes. Tired, wakeful, wary. Around his wrists and ankles are scars where manacles were burned on to contain his flesh. His broad shoulders, his thick thighs. A man made for the cutlass he so often carries at his side.

A gust, a draft from the shore wind that whistles into the sails above and burrows between the cracks of the planks of the deck that is the roof of this, his cabin. She looks to the flames of candles bowing inside the lanterns. The way she sees it they are birds, the flames, straining against the bars of cages. Light longing to fly to freedom.

———

By morn the sails flap a lighter mood. When the storm abates he appears, the missionary, beside her on deck. Bible in hand, thankful to God, praying aloud no doubt so she hears him, believes in his God.

Bruised and beaten, the clouds have slunk over the horizon. The change is as swift as the sun breaking out over the water: greetings are cheery, the cursings subside, talk of Jonahs on board seem to have flown, fleeting as gull shadow.

Bridie watches, waits. A storm abated is a storm lurking somewhere unseen. Wonders how to plan her rescue — perhaps if she could see another ship, a ship on the return to Sydney, a captain and a crew whose manners don't change with the weather. Perhaps, somehow, she could convince Robbie to move this ship alongside that, let the ships speak, lift her across on the gamming chair.

———

He does not sleep till he has had his way, has poured himself into her. All the while she is cursing his wretched flesh, cursing her own flesh for not repelling his. When his moans turn to snores she wriggles from under him. Waits as he coughs, splutters and sinks, as he rises and gushes another shuddering expulsion. She counts ten of these before sliding carefully, trying not to rock the rocking gimbals, trying to time her movement with the ebb and wake of his stinking breath.

She reminds herself in the swaying blackness that she knows every shape, can count each step to the desk. When the ship lurches she resists reaching to steady herself on the swaying ropes of their bed but rocks on the bare heels of her feet, lurches with the lurch of the sea, feels the roll and rides it.

Slides the drawer in the desk. Slowly. Dares not breathe. Takes hold of the cold spyglass before the drawer is properly open. Is aware that there is no sound of his breath, not a snore. Wait. Wait. His voice causes a surge of fear to shoot from her feet to her calves, to her spine, to her neck where it tingles.

'Aim for the forehead so the ball enters smack in the centre.'

'What?'

'The pistol. That's what you're after, is it not? Shoot the fool who taught you to use it, to prepare yourself for where we are headed.'

She could almost laugh. How sweet that would be, to take the pistol and kill him. But if she did, who would command the ship, guide them to safety when she herself is considered a Jonah? No, they must wait, must plan, must find among these men some friends.

'It's the spyglass I'm after.'

'What in Hell's bells for?'

'To see the stars, Robbie. To make them closer.'

She does not say that she may find the star where her ma has flown.

'Take it then. Go.'

Has she heard right? Is this his trickery?

'You mean it?'

'Before I regret it. And Bridie?'

Here it comes.

'Don't go falling overboard.'

———

Here she is on deck, here she is at the prow, the salt stinging and the singing thrill of the winds of the night, her hair flying up to play, the spyglass hers for now, her treasure. Sea stronger at night and night is stronger at sea. She shivers under the huge embrace of winds that stir the night. Her eye on the spyglass moves back and forth, squints, blinks, and her finger twists the tiny wheel until her gaze traverses the dark sky and finds the moon, finds the shadows of that luminous globe, shadows on it like moths plastered to the globe of a lamp.

Travels her eye now to stars. Jumps from one star to another. Removes the glass from her eye and looks up and around. Far away it is but she knows it is still there, all the life she cannot see. Tears of the sparkle of all this life prick her eyes until the tears fall; the taste of the water that rises from a well deep inside herself is the taste of the ocean.

———

Squinting and blinking from lack of sleep, Cuthbert answers the rapping on the frame of the shuttered door, is surprised to see Tom. Wind-blown, the look of him. Small and scared but meeting his eyes in a way he did not before.

'You kept your vow, paid them off. I will try and find — bring you the names of those you can trust.'

To deal with the debtors, Cuthbert had bolted a fierce flash of rum down his throat — physic, he told himself, for God seemed ill-equipped to assist his second descent to the bowels of the ship. He needed sturdy stuff to face that particular darkness where lay black-hearted creatures with round, bloated eyes. Had lingered and insisted — as though he had some clout — that the man he met, a greasy scurvy type, pass the coin to pay Tom's debts to Mallet, Jake and any others who had claim over the lad.

'Avoid their games, feign sickness of something,' he advises Tom now. 'I cannot pay them off again. Now the storm has eased, danger has passed. Soon they will leave you alone. Once we're landed, they'll be busier by day, and by night will find . . . other amusements. Can I offer you—'

But the boy is gone. When he closes the door Cuthbert wonders how he is again on a ship, why it is such a difficult thing to stay landed. It is not just the horrors of boyhood but of manhood that he presses down. It is the screams that have followed him these past twelve years. Screams of women, children, men, people who had been happily splashing about in boats, fishing. How stupid he had been, forsaking the Lord to join a sloop to navigate and plot the parts of the Australian coast Flinders had failed to record.

Far off that dazzling coast now but the screams follow him. Nothing he could have done differently, nothing. Those sailors, that captain, had fallen about in mirth when he beseeched them to behave well, to take gifts, not weapons. Mocked him for refusing to accompany them in their so-called entertainments. Are they all the same, sailors, whalers, even the English gentry? It seems to him that they all treat women and children — anyone physically weaker — as creatures to be disciplined or devoured.

———

Shortly before the sun labours over the horizon, Bridie hears Bill the younger shout. Confirmation, the shout, of the change of smell and that signature of land — white, circling, black-winged coastal birds.

Shout-screams, the boy, that phrase reeled off by so many boys and men.

'Land-land-land ahoy!'

On deck she finds men rushing. Tom's mouth twists; he wishes no doubt he had seen it first but is forbidden now to climb so high, to have work of importance on which others rely. Failing to sight the Yankee ship is still a wound rubbing raw. The pang of sympathy

Bridie feels for him will find no home as he marches around the ship, ignoring her or cursing her sex.

The chorus of huzzahs sinks into shallow grumbles.

'Disappointment inlet,' says Mallet.

'No smoke, no signs of a township,' says Jake as the ship slides along a green coast to a green cove.

Trees seem to float out of the water, shifting between shreds of sea fog. The smell of moss and moisture, leaf-clogged soil, but the main smell that comes to her is that of water free of salt. Different to the smell of Australia, which is of dry grass heat, ancient creatures, leathered skin.

On the quarterdeck, Robbie is lord of all he surveys.

'Virgin land, my coves.'

The men respond with moans.

'Looks nothing like Kororāreka.'

That shout from Jake, directed at Mallet but intended to reach the quarterdeck.

'Change of plan,' says Mallet. 'Lost our time for rooting and rum on cause of the storm. Bloody woman, fucking sky pilot, 'tis all on cause of them!' He points his finger at Bridie, traverses it across to Cuthbert, who blinks and bites his lip.

Watching Tom as he works beside these rough men, Bridie sees her boy of a brother shouting vile curses like the men who surround him. Pale and thin, he scampers from under the quarterdeck towards the bow. Bumps her. Instead of begging pardon, he curses.

'I pulled you out of our ma.' Her voice is low, her anger is not.

He shrugs. In the careless curse on her — the sister who aided his birth — is a curse on the mother who bore him into the world and the mothers before her. The mist floats hands, drapes hair, gape of eyes, cavernous mouths. Wishes, Bridie does, that all the withering wisps are women come to claim what bad men snatch from them.

Clenching the taffrails, she stares into waves that roll the jade and teal green gem colours of the orient into this South Sea cove. Pours her gaze down, finds a darker green, almost black shadows. Looks past the ship to the cove, the land itself. An ache and a tug, unlike the punch and jab of Sydney. The slow unfolding. The land is hidden. Mist pummels the hills like a troop of ghostly warriors tumbling down the valley to fight along the beach.

She wants to detest it but something moves in her. The familiar chorus after the unfamiliar verse, a refrain so deep it is deeper than words. Feels it unfold, the creep of the known into the unknown. Somewhere a girl is unpicking a badly sewn seam. She must unpick herself to start again.

Behind her the grumbling of the rabble is growing louder. Three months they moan, like a song. Three months stuck here. Chasing whales and seals. Were they false, the promises Robbie made, that they would call into the wild northern town with breasts, booze and song? A reward they reckoned deserved after the rigours of the storm.

When she had asked Robbie about the town they were headed for, he had crushed her flight of questions or answered rough, vague. Not as many stores as Sydney, not as lively as Kororāreka, no. Not many horses. Now she sees what this place is not. Absence of smoke, lack of wharves, paths, lanes, kens, storehouses, dwellings. For her, the deep loss of a town that promised the company of women.

'I know what you're after,' Robbie calls down to the men.

'Cunny fresh and sweet as the flesh in a shell prised open by a knife!'

Laughter. Roars. Huzzahs.

Robbie holds his hand up.

'The flesh to drive yourselves into. The sweet release. Oh aye, you shall have it.'

Someone barks like a dog. Argh. Argh. Argh.

'Nothing beats the pleasure of native flesh, but the pleasure is so much sweeter when it is artfully acquired. Go greedy, rape, murder and the natives won't stand for it, see — you will all be eating your own cocks in the fires of Hell. I forbid — yes forbid any damned one of you to pop your cocks before my say-so.'

Moans.

'We have to cast out a line, see? Most chuckle-headed sea-crabs would not catch my drift. But you lot aren't mere sailors. What are you?'

A mumbled response, not quite audible. Some call themselves tonguers, some whalers, some declare they are coopers, others say sailors — stupid to the core — and one man calls headers. Robbie spits twice, draws breath and stirs them to remember that they are here to catch the most whales, boil the most blubber, sell the most oil, make up for time lost in the storm or — as he has warned them countless times — he will lose his stake in the ship and their names will be dead men's names for no captain will take on a man who cost him his ship.

She notices that he makes no mention of the outlawed trade. The missionary has never spoken of it. Should she ask Cuthbert if he knows that Robbie trades in human heads? Would he challenge Robbie, risk a thrashing? She scans the faces of the men, listens intently to the grumbles. Stores the knowledge of this man or that who is most disgruntled. But it is changing now; if anyone knows how to turn a tide to his advantage it is Robbie Fitch.

'And what else do we hunt?'

'Cunnies!'

That from Tom, who knows the word now if he never did before. She watches young Billy the cooper's son give him a slap of praise.

'What do hunters do?'

'Kill!' yells young Bill.

'Listen, you addle-headed cove cock-suckers, there are other ways to master what we want without causing merry Hell to break lose.

His tone is harsh now. The men fall silent.

'A man hunting a fish or laying a trap, he casts out a net, see? The prey thinks she is being fed, see? Gets all eager, goes in for the bite. Utu it is called. If we aren't artful on this shore we will all be for the pot. So, lads, go easy, you hark my drift?'

A chorus of aye-aye from the men.

All theatre now, Robbie. Bridie watches him lean forward as he did all those weeks back on the flunkey's rumbler and in the Shipwright's Compass. Grown more in herself now and so used to his habits, she waits for him to cup a hand to his ear, and so he does.

'Say what?'

'Go easy!' the men shout.

'So, no rooting yet.'

He cups his hand to his ear, waits for the echo.

'No rooting yet.'

That from Tom also. Was her brother always like this?

Robbie isn't done; the quarterdeck has become his stage.

'Let the fish think you are feeding it and you will get more than your fill.'

He parts his greatcoat, dangles his pale cock, displays to the men who have not seen it that yes, he is a man who can withstand pain in any place, for climbing up his cock is the tattoo of a snake. He gyrates his buttocks, rotates his cock, round and round the climbing snake. Bows at last to the hails and huzzahs of the men. Raises his face ever so slightly, catches her eye and winks.

CHAPTER 12

The night is full of terror, for the worm has once again invaded her dreams. Cowering behind a thorny mānuka bush, she screams as the worm divides itself into multiple worms, shakes its small heads and calls. Waking, she sees shapes rising and hastening.

Outside in the cold air of the new morning she stands transfixed, listening to the eerie sound of the wind in the shell. Long call of the pūmoana warning of danger. Three times it sounds, then is followed by feet pounding on the shell path. The pūmoana bangs against Kauri's chest as he runs past her, followed by Rāwhiti.

Shaking her head, separating from her dream, Manaia stirs herself awake and joins the flow of people heading to the marae ātea. In that courtyard Kauri huffs loudly, waits for the flow of his breath, waits for silence. Beside Manaia, Manutaki grumbles.

'He's likely only seen a beautiful wahine in his dreams when he fell asleep while he was on duty.'

She is used to him speaking like this, but he has been harder in his criticisms of late.

'Remember when that silly boy you lust after thought a school of fish was only the shadow of clouds on the sea? An arrogant fool, Kauri, who cannot tell the difference between fish and cloud.'

She puts her hand on her uncle's arm, appreciating his loyalty to her in her heartbreak but urging him to stop talking, for others are motioning him to quieten. The rangatira draw forward, long-feathered cloaks falling around them like folded wings waiting for flight. When even these birds have fallen silent, Kauri speaks, and as he speaks Manaia observes the twitch-twitch-twitch of a muscle working his jaw.

'The mist was so thick last night it would challenge the eyes of a bird hunting its prey, yet like the ruru hunting the kiore I saw something unsettling. Saw that unsettling thing before the first show of light.'

He takes three deep breaths, drawing the air inside, huffing the breath out. Listens to the tamariki whose excitement is like a fire trying to jump out of a circle of stones. Waits until they have been hushed to quiet.

'We have seen before these foreigners sliding along in their waka, in deep water past our cove. But now such a waka — a waka of tauiwi — is out there and it rests. It rests.'

The silence that follows is ominous. It is as though Papatūānuku is holding herself still, to keep the calm inside herself so the unborn child deep inside her womb will not shake with terror. Then, stepping forward, drawing a space around himself with his right hand, Kāhu Kōrako shows the patient wisdom that has earned him his name as the pale-feathered bird, the great leader. He congratulates Kauri, assuring him that such clear-sighted vigilance protects the people from harm. Stretches out his hand towards the rangatira.

'We will consult with the tohunga who can read the signs to determine whether the manuhiri come in peace or whether they come to wage war.'

The wind gasps — such a serious word, war. After the gasp it rises, the wind. Ruffles then strokes the feathers on the korowai of the rangatira. Women sing as their rangatira stride to the wharenui. Grey clouds that have been drawing close draw closer.

———

Chatter and speculation. Rima, Keteiwi, Manawa, Manutaki, all the mothers and fathers, sisters and brothers, older to younger are experts on the tauiwi. Bad spirits they are, goblins with pale skin and narrow feet who drink strange potions and eat disgusting food. The tauiwi only worship one god, a god who has no wife. Much laughter at this, and Manaia herself laughs, imagining a people who worship a god who has no wife, no sisters or brothers. The stories deepen and darken, like eels crawling into a swamp where the water turns to mud and no longer flows.

The tauiwi have powerful weapons that kill many people, and other tools useful for digging and cooking and hunting. But they have captured and violated wāhine and tamariki, stolen them, taken them on their boats and dumped them in the wrong places.

Manaia slips away. Outside of the talk she watches her mother gathering leaves from the trees that shelter the gardens. Watches Kauri and Rāwhiti and their brothers flick their taiaha, catch the weapons from behind, spear in one direction and another, throwing and catching. She sees the tohunga Te Iho o Ranginui walk down from the veranda of the wharenui to kneel on the ground. He touches the soil, he listens to the sky.

It is the āniwaniwa that decides matters, appearing where the grey sky darkens to the darkest blue. The āniwaniwa, a bridge of colours aglow in the rain. Stretching from the hill over on the next bay to the sea. She would like to feel happy and excited that this rainbow is the sign that leads the rangatira to decide that the tauiwi come in peace. She would like to put her faith in them, in their superior knowledge, but she cannot shake off the foreboding, the whispering of her tīpuna in her ears. She cannot ignore the kāhu, her guardian, as it flies nearer and nearer, circling great arcs in flight. Silent, this guardian, yet screaming to her heart that all is not well.

———

At the whare an argument is taking place. Holding herself high, Rima reminds Manutaki that he is her younger brother, not older. That as a respected weaver she knows how to lay out the whakapapa, the pattern, sing the threads of the whānau into the pattern.

'What finer craft is there than weaving the mats and cloaks that are worn next to the skin of our people? We study the pattern, lay it out before we weave. We think and plan.'

Manutaki bows his head like a boy, mumbles that what she is saying is not relevant, that he plans to be part of the welcome party to greet the tauiwi.

'You are our heart. The outer leaves cannot live without you,' she replies.

Manaia wants to say something but finds she cannot, does not know why not.

Her mother tries again.

'Please do not do this.'

Time and again she has told Manaia that the threads that start the pattern are the threads that finish the basket. Yet she does not seem to see the pattern that starts with herself, where it will lead. The more she implores her brother not to do something, the more likely he is to do it, to board the waka and paddle out to meet the tauiwi, ignore her fear, ignore her anguish.

'It's an honour the rangatira have bestowed on me,' he says. 'We will make pets of these strange new men, play with their tools, take their prizes, prize their gifts. They will entertain us, bring comforts.'

'Not if they slit your throat.'

So quickly it happens, Manaia feels the change and her own helplessness inside it like a storm, but there is no way to push back, to stop it. Necklaces of shell and stone are handed around, mats and gourds are laid down. Taonga. The best gifts will be reserved for later. Weapons — patu and mere — are tucked inside cloaks, close to the skin.

The welcoming party has gathered. Against the blue and black of the sky and the arching glow of the āniwaniwa, the high tohunga, Te Iho o Ranginui, intones a karakia to Tāne-mahuta, to Tangaroa, to Ranginui and Papatūānuku. Atua of the forests, the ocean, the sky, the land and all their offspring, all creatures, gods of all the elements and the life force therein. The tohunga asks the atua to guide and protect the welcoming party as it travels forth, keep the people safe.

———

After the welcoming party has left, Manaia joins those who remain, standing by the fire. Comfort flows from one to another in the huddle of men, women and children. Darkness swirls the clouds, stirs the trees. Deep is the stir of listening under and over and around. She pushes a tōtara branch onto the fire, watches the flames gobble the wood. It amuses the tamariki, this, for as the tōtara cracks, it reminds them of a patero bursting from a bottom.

'Ka hemo anake te tou o te tōtara,' a boy yells, breaking into giggles.

'Āe,' says his mother, and all the huddling people, young and old, share laughter.

Shortlived, this levity. Mist rolling down from the valley lays glistening webs over their heads; damp sinks into their bones. A waiata is sung, in a tune of sadness and hope. The sky is devoid of colour; Tama-nui-te-rā, pale and distant, is trying to disguise himself as Marama, the moon. A tree becomes a warrior, a branch is a weapon. A tiny black pīwakawaka weaves a pattern in flight. Descends to settle on a flat leaf, tiny head cocked, tiny black eye watching them.

Manaia clasps her mother's hand, draws it to her chest.

'If only I had the courage I would run after Manutaki,' she says. 'Implore him and the others to turn back, not to run to these tauiwi and invite them here, but to send them back to wherever they came from.'

Her mother tries to smile but fails. Their eyes meet, the shine of tears. Her mother's voice is full of regret.

'I told him that he is my heart, but I could not survive if I lost you.'

Her words make no sense. Parting from her mother, to break from this whānau, this world of aroha and manaakitanga, is more impossible than anything Manaia could ever imagine.

CHAPTER 13

'Their state of nudity will shock you at first, but you will grow accustomed to it,' says Cuthbert, stepping beside Bridie.

Sucks her clay pipe, she does, and chugs smoke out. Taps the bowl. Dried leaves spark inside the carved pipe, the bowl a dented hat on a lady's head. Not pretty like her mother's figurine, that loved thing. Perhaps the hat was bashed in by a man. Perhaps the lady would like to bash him back. Not pretty, the story of so many things shaped by men.

She shakes her head. Should she anticipate danger or delight? She has no idea. The notion of thought is dizzy-making. Ahead, in the direction Cuthbert points, she sees them. So many — too many. Parading out of the dark of forest, through tussock, under trees waving bladed leaves. Over their shoulders the men heave long intricately carved boats. Women are armed with baskets and gourds. Children juggle infants.

Bridie finds her gaze cannot stray from the varied stages of nakedness. The strength of the men ripples as they take up paddles, push out boats. She has no word for the state of her mind. Mist seems to have drifted inside her, clogging her body, fogging her thought. Is this shock?

'They don't shock me.'

Remembers, she does, Ma and others wagging tongues in Sydney, about how the missionary was rescued from a beach in the north of New Zealand wearing not a skerrick of clothing. Whisked back to Parramatta to serve penance under the strict eye of the flogging parson, Samuel Marsden.

'These Middle Islanders have yet to learn that the way we come into the world is not how we should remain,' he says. 'It is beyond their comprehension, the notion that nudity should be reserved for our most private moments.'

'As our captain and commander so aptly demonstrates.'

She would like to ask him whether these New Zealanders differ in nature from the New Zealanders who stride the criss-cross paths in The Rocks at home, gather along the wharves and stores in their cloaks, smoking clay pipes not unlike hers. Walking tall, leaning in the shade, selling mats, baskets and capes. Flax and feathers. Sailor caps. Beyond the route around steaming horse dung piles and the whine of a dog in the shadow she had spoken with one of them. He had smiled at her in a way that brought heat to her face. His eyes on hers, his smile on her.

'They will find you arresting,' says the missionary, breaking the spell. 'The natives in this part have been left to themselves. Never seen a white woman, I dare say. Will quite likely find your colour distasteful. Evidently our skin looks sickly to them. Doesn't look like skin.'

Laughter. She laughs at the bizarreness of it. That the paler she is, the less attractive she would seem. A new thought, this — is this how the aboriginals see her? How funny that the settler ladies wear hats to protect skin that must be fairer than the lightest wheat flour. She cannot suppress her giggles that here the settler women who never do a day's work would be considered ugly. Pats her face, feels her skin patched and peeled by salt and sun. Is her skin still pale?

'What's your reckoning? Have I caught the sun enough to be considered a beauty?'

She laughs again and her laugh is wild, is a thing apart, a beast.

The missionary looks nervous, making her laugh harder.

'Show some decorum.'

The snap of him shakes the child out of her, draws from her a snap in return.

'Decorum?'

'Please settle yourself.'

'You mean affect good manners in front of the natives? Should I deny and hide the truth of my station?'

Cuthbert twists the chain that leads to the cross at his neck. He wears a nervous face, worried, no doubt, that the men will hear in her shriek the wayward strands of a wandering mind.

Drawing her gaze back to the busyness on board, she scans the scurrying crew. Stacking wood and blankets, dangling cheap trinkets, opening tins of dried tobacco leaf, rolling a battered puncheon of Bengal rum. Drawing the scene to herself and ensuring Robbie is not in earshot, she turns on the missionary.

'Not long ago, no man had known me. Now two men have wormed their way into me, one a high gent in Sydney, the other that man, our captain. A conniving monster who keeps boring his way in, and I can do nothing to remove myself.'

The sick taste in her mouth turns to spit. She taps the pipe, hoiks a glob over the taffrail. Caught by the froth it dissolves in the great sputum of salt water. The missionary's hand hovers over her shoulder, then drops. He cups her chin, a little too hard.

'Concern yourself with the trial at hand, Bridie.'

Points her face towards the shore, where more small figures are scrambling into boats. Not only men but women and scampering children. The women who are not cloaked expose the drop and droop and swell of breasts. She hears the sunlight songs of birds, the lap and thrash of waves on the shore, a chorus and a verse.

'Singing — a good sign, surely?'

Out from the mist the sun is showing a shy face — splash of light from paddles, light striking waves, light splashing on forearms. Strong forearms. She sees white feathers struck into topknots on men in the first boat. Bare tattooed bodies, tattooed faces. As the boat draws near she hears women singing from it. Men enter the chorus but one man does not. She tries to read his expression. Does he wear a smile or a scowl. She cannot tell, sees only the ripple and swell of his body as he drives a paddle into the green trough between waves.

'They can be friendly and full of charm but so quickly it turns.'

Cuthbert has taken so long to reply his voice surprises her.

'Prompted of course by the actions of our sailors and captains. Up north one fool of a captain brandished a burning torch and tipped a chief overboard. When Robbie is drunk he is also a danger—'

'You talk as though I don't know.'

'He has a temper fit for the Devil and needs us to keep him in check.'

'So the path forward depends on us teaching him how to behave?'

She struggles not to laugh as she remembers how Robbie reacted when Cuthbert tried to challenge him.

'The men are tired, cold and foul-tempered,' he continues. 'All they want is to get on shore, drown themselves in drink and things I cannot mention, but they must hold back. And I must pray — pray for guidance and the New Zealanders, that with the aid of their medicine I might make a full recovery.'

'Medicine?'

'Their science, knowledge about the healing properties in plants.'

Seeing Robbie coming towards them, his voice under the cover of his hand becomes a feigned cough.

'As long as Robbie doesn't upset them, they will help us, help me, end this insufferable suffering,' he all but whispers.

A skip in it now, in Robbie's stride down the quarterdeck steps, in finest blue frockcoat. Someone — not her — has polished his buttons. Beaver crouching on his head.

'Beau nasty,' she whispers to the missionary. 'He could fell the natives by breathing on them.'

The chortle in her voice is blocked by the missionary's hand, hovering. Almost a slap.

'You must hold your tongue and still yourself, or one way or another this day will be our last. Think upon your brother. You have a duty to Tom and yourself to behave and keep your mouth shut.'

She pulls her hair, twists and plies it, rope over rope, ties a knot. Today she might die, so what to do? Catch the sun, present as fit to live?

The deck is awash with light now the mist has cleared, but Robbie's body casts a shadow from an obstinate cloud. Coming down the steps of the quarterdeck, he takes the pipe out of his mouth.

'Look at the New Zealanders clamouring to greet us. Think us gods, they do, and no wonder. This great ship of ours, all our fine implements. And look at you, pretty as an English peach.'

'Sod your rotten peach. I am not nor will ever claim to be one of the sodding English.'

'If you don't dampen the fire in your temper, I'll do it myself.'

He takes something from the inside of his blue coat and drives it hard to the side of her head. Flash of it so quick. Sharp and deep. A knife? She remembers the comb he gave her in the Shipwright's.

Eyes on hers now, the darkness in him expands. No gold specks in this deep well. No crouching tender thing inside. He does not know that to kill a thing is to increase its power to destroy. Groping for a way forward, she sets her mask to meet his; if a man can turn a turtle to a comb, a woman can turn a comb back into a turtle.

———

Robbie has given the order to lower the gamming chair. The chair that might have passed between ships, fetched Bridie over to the American ship to meet the captain's wife had Robbie availed her of that social enterprise. The chair is swaying and tilting towards the clamour in the sea below. It tips a wave, dunks into the water, is quickly hauled up and lowered again by Mallet and Jake, the men who only a short time past would happily have cast her and the missionary overboard. All grins now, Mallet adjusts the rope and calls out to the missionary to tell the women on shore that their carriage awaits.

The missionary explains that there is no word for carriage. Waka might do, for that is the word for a boat. Perhaps the chair is a small waka — there is no word for chair. Robbie tells him to shut it; he is dulling the excitement of the hour.

The New Zealand women push, laugh and shun the chair, leave it swinging. One following another, they haul themselves up the sea-soaked ladder against the ship's flank. Hand over hand, arm over arm, until Robbie offers his hand. Small his hand seems, compared to the hands of these people. The younger children are skittish, giggling, caught between the urge to survey the ship and their curiosity about herself, Robbie, the missionary, the crew. The older children raise their faces gradually, cast their gaze cautiously, arms around arms, protective of the little ones. A woman calls from the ship back to the people on shore. A long wavering song coming out of her to float above the roll of the waves. It is a familiar song that seems to Bridie to thread earth, rock, sea and sky. Threads of webs woven by those who remain and the spirits who have left.

The empty gamming chair is noisily landed on deck by Tom and Bill the younger. The tallest New Zealand child tumbles the youngest into the seat, rocks it as a cradle. Their giggling pleases the crew who seem, some of them, to remember their own families. Shoulders drop as smiles form. Tom kneels beside the boy, rocks the chair like a boat.

'Waka,' says the boy.

'Boat,' says Tom.

Surveying the New Zealand men, Bridie notes the strength and height, wonders about the New Zealander she met in Sydney. What it might be like to have his face above hers.

Mist rain turns to real rain, falls hard. Slides down their bodies, seems barely to bother the New Zealanders. Smiles in their eyes and on their lips. She who would never trust this crew is touched by this. She who would never trust the man who rules the ship wonders now if she can even trust herself. Her gaze turns to the missionary, Cuthbert, man of God. She knows him well enough, but can she trust him? The look in his eyes is raw, open hunger, his eyes on a woman's breasts. Catching Bridie's look, he adjusts his expression to one that says if only these women would cover up.

A stab of envy as she watches the women climb the ship with ease, no need of assistance. How stupid her gown, the hem that hampers so many dreams. Etched in her mind, an afternoon after she had been returned from the orphanage to The Rocks to live with her ma. Forgetting she no longer had the girlish freedom of her wide, high skirt, she had jumped a crevice. In the dizzy shock of the fall she had grabbed the edge of the rock above, felt its softness turn to clod and the clod splinter away. Snatched till she clawed onto one part that held. Hauled, kicked, clambered to solid ground. Knows now that the long tight outer skin does a woman no favours; the change in garments from girl to womanhood had nearly cost her this life.

She wonders how it would be to stand astride like these women in their woven feathered linens. Catches herself staring at a woman who smiles, taking her for friendly — which in truth she is, but less sure as the woman steps forward, arms raised in embrace. Eyes shut, noses press in the sharing of breath. The sureness of the woman, the hesitance on her own part. A shroud of soft darkness. Something gives in her. Breath rises from deep within, in something akin to the way of a prayer to Brighid.

In this meeting with the woman there is the deep and rising comfort of shared strength. In the darkness under the closed blinds of her eyes, in the soft press of a nose to hers, Bridie smells the sod of soil, salt of waves, the rain of sky. Some timeless passage has found her. A shiver of delight. She feels herself safe, clothed in the warmth of breath, protected in a way she never feels with the man who gives himself the name protector.

Opening her eyes as she and the woman part, she catches Robbie's wry regard. Sees his expression shift as a boy reaches for the dangling chain of his pocket watch. Robbie wrenches the boy's hand away.

'You won't be having that. Savages have no sense of time.'

As he tugs the watch from the boy the chain snaps.

'Hell and damnation. See what the little bugger's done?'

His hand is raised now, about to come down on the squirming boy. Is the hiss the wind or the breath behind teeth? She does not detect the movement of lips. The hiss rouses into a ripple around the ship, stirs a wind, causes Robbie's hand to falter.

'Stop!' cries Cuthbert. 'The New Zealanders do not hit their children.'

Robbie looks around, sneers.

'How in the Devil's name do they teach them?' he says.

Bill the older snaps a button off his own coat. Gives it to the child, avoiding Robbie's glance.

'Going soft, you old moll.'

'Just heeding your own advice not to rile them, Mr Fitch.'

Revelry, delight, children laugh and talk in their own tongue. Tug at the crew, searching out more buttons. Robbie calls to the missionary whose gaze is still on the woman.

'You're very quiet, Mr Sky Pilot. Pussy got your tongue?'

Cuthbert, caught off-guard, steps back. A comedy of theatre. Sticks his boot in a bedpan, which spills a stream of shit.

'What the . . . ?' thunders Robbie.

'Sorry, sir, I meant . . . sir, to throw it over earlier like but . . .'

Bill the younger, the cooper's son, is all apology. Robbie is all wrath. Bridie struggles to stifle her mirth.

'Your butt belongs in the ocean. Over you will go, like this.'

The basin hurled, the contents separate in the sky. A gull swoops, beak agape. A shift in mood as the New Zealanders shout at Robbie.

Removing his fetid boot, Cuthbert speaks to them in their tongue. 'Mō tāku hē.'

Turns to Robbie. 'I'm taking it on myself to apologise for you. The natives would never dispose of fecal matter in such a manner. You might recall pits outside their villages where they defecate. They lean on a pole over a deep pit.'

The first thing Bridie hopes Robbie will build is a dunnekin with a private door, not a pole, and a seat over the pit, a pit into which she could surely fall.

The missionary continues.

'The sea is not for the disposal of what passes from — out of — you know where, for the sea is where they catch the food that enters their stomachs. If you transgress their laws of nature, well — that probably is not the best plan.'

'Aye. Forgot about that.'

In an attempt no doubt at distraction, Robbie orders the men to open the puncheons. Brings out an array of tools and hands them around. Turns over an empty puncheon and shuffles with his sleight of hand, a pack of cards. Runs a card into his palm and produces it from the boy's ear. The boy laughs and passes it up to the man who holds him. Robbie starts to shake his head, decides better of it, shrugs.

'Won't be much of a game if they deign to keep all the cards.'

Taking all this in, Bridie wonders who will win and who will lose. Sees the measuring up of them by Robbie. As he did with her. Measuring a New Zealander, heavily carved with tattoos. Measuring the worth of the man even as he holds a boy, tickles him under the armpits.

Watching from the deck as some of Robbie's crew row their own longboat to shore, faces to the stern, backs to the bow, the New Zealanders talk rapidly, gesture.

'Reckon we must have eyes in the backs of our skulls,' Robbie guffaws.

The missionary answers, dismissing the merriment.

'They think us a goblin race, full of strange but useful magic.'

'Why *do* we row back-to-front?' she asks. No one replies, not a one.

After she is lowered precariously — squealing — from the gamming chair to the boat and rowed to shore, her arms can go nowhere else but around the wide shoulders of the New Zealander who wades the waves to plant her on shore. Picking up her wet skirts, laughing at the feel of sand, she catches Robbie's expression. Laughter silenced.

She squeals as rain from dark clouds stings her face. Pulls the hem of her gown, bunches it high, bends to swat a tiny black speck stinging her ankle. She shivers in disgust as it spurts blood. Turns and finds three New Zealand men have been enjoying the view of her rear. Drops the gown, wondering how much she exposed. Judging by their nudges, too much.

Fearing Robbie's wrath, she shifts her gaze, feels the wet drag of the gown as she unbuttons her sodden boots. Her red swollen toes, finally released, dig for freedom, clench the sand. Refreshed she is in the cold from the rocking waves, soft the sand as her toes dig holes and scuttle crabs. She wobbles and sways as she did on deck, on unsteady sea legs. Wades, her gaze on the ship, tired now the ship, skirts bedraggled. Alive and young when her sails were set, at anchor now she looks sullen and bereft like an old woman in yellowed undergarments.

Bridie feels a kinship in the separation, a yearning. Like herself, this ship. Driven by men from past battles and dangers, towards future battles and dangers. Will she give up, wreck herself on the rocks, seek the peace of darkness? What if she could sail her own eternity, come ashore where she desired, bathe with turtles in the gold of soft sand, sail an ocean blown by moon and stars, follow maps sung by whales? What if she could dream her own future outside the machinations of sailors and settlers, of men?

Pointless, such entertainments, dabbling in dreams. The ship, like herself, is a vessel to be dressed and battered, broken and repaired, not a free spirit. No way out of that, ever.

———

Turning for her boots, Bridie sees them struggling up a bank of seagrass under the legs of a sprightly New Zealand boy. He crouches, picks at their buttons. Kneeling beside him, Bridie removes the boots, returns them to her own feet.

The New Zealanders are assisting with the unloading of the ship, using their boats to ferry supplies from the ship to the shore. Puncheons of rum, pease and biscuit, kegs filled with lamps, harpoons and adzes. When the supplies have been laid on shore they hoist oiled skins over branches. Bivouacs are pitched from other branches. One for herself and Robbie, another for the missionary, others for the crew.

Striding towards her, Tom tries to look bigger than himself, carrying a bundle of branches so wide and high it disappears his face. She knows better now than to laugh at her younger brother. Somewhere over the sea his senses lost their humour.

———

Lying on her back under the makeshift canvas tent, Bridie watches dusk turn to dark. Blissful in her aloneness, drifting in dreams to the lapping tongue of the ocean, dry smoke, men singing. Through the flapping roof of the canvas, flapping open, flapping closed, she catches a glimpse of an Indian-ink sky. A dark forest smell like a wild animal taking a pause before it pounces. She tries not to breathe the stink of this roof, the dark stinking skins — skins that still smell of old blood turned black.

She tries not to think on the round-the-fire feast of a few hours earlier. Six terrified chickens hung upside down for the slaughter, her hunger gnawing even as her stomach sickened at the impending kill. Tries to wipe from her mind the expression on Robbie's face after he passed the axe to a New Zealander who rapidly swooped and sliced. Robbie's unease passed to the crew, the missionary and herself. Blood spraying, birds trembling, her fingers itching to touch her own neck to keep it safe.

She wriggles now, feeling the comfort of the bed created for her by two New Zealand women. Robbie would have had her lay a single skin on sand crusted and cold. With kindness and care the women laid rushes soft as a horse's mane, tufts of tussock fine as silk. When the bottom layer was springy they placed ferns over this sponge, topped it all with a woven mat. Motioned eagerly for her to lie down.

Sinking into bedding firm yet soft she squealed — so real her delight. Watching them as they grinned back, she was reminded of the ease of being she felt when she met the New Zealander with the earring in Sydney. She was among people who had refined senses, who could feel the waves of emotion beneath the surface of the skin. These women would not hide their own feelings; would surely know if hers were ever hidden behind a mask.

But it is the men she thinks on as the wind mews and scratches at the skin roof, stirring life from death. In the twixt and tween of restlessness she cannot rid herself of the flitting images of the naked men. Wide shoulders and chests and tight ripples below their chests. Stomachs flat and — when they turned away — buttocks taut. Men whose skin is the colour of soil — lighter than peat, darker than sand. Men moving in the strong thrust of action; ferrying and unloading, stretching and reaching.

The cough of a bird or otherworld being. Sound of it calling, poor girl, poor girl. The sky holds back the rain, bush rattles and whispers. Water laps a lullaby. Men who laugh and embrace their children and who dance. Dance. Laugh. Men whose tattoos remind her of that beautiful New Zealander back in Sydney. How might he have touched her, held her, if Robbie had not captured her? She remembers his hand drawing hers towards his stone. Pounamu.

She reaches down to the softness of herself, touches herself. Hips rise, her finger gentle as a butterfly on the moist tip of a flower. While Robbie and his crew roar and jostle and jest outside, she moves her finger in slow circles, circles faster until it is almost unbearable. Withdraws and touches again. Tender strokes bring her to throb with the thrill of herself breaking open. When her shudders subside, she slides into sleep and, for the first time in such a long time, sleeps content.

CHAPTER 14

Grey fade of night into dawn brings shouting, stomping. Bridie rolls over. The mound that taunted her awake in the hours before dawn, the mound that fired putrid air from both his mouth and buttocks, has gone. In his place a welcome hollow. Louder than the crackle and flap of the wind in the skins of this makeshift house is his sound. His voice is a bell tolling them all to rise. She stretches herself up as far as the skins and branches allow, reluctant to leave the comfort of the bed but eager to move towards the crackle of wood, smell of smoke, signalling warmth.

All over the land Robbie stomps, pausing only to fetch sticks, lay them down, draft out their base. The kingdom of Fitch. Long hut for whaling weaponry and more besides here, the rumbling ken here — not like the miserable one-storey Shipwright's Compass in Sydney but handsome buildings. He heaves some large dead branches for two hotels — no, four — at the crossroads. Each facing the others with coach-houses adjacent. The finest local wood — he casts his arm around the forest — for parquet floors and masterful balconies. His own home will have four chimneys with bricks imported from Sydney, passages upstairs and down, four bedrooms, an attic storey over the whole to bed servants; the road to his house will be named after himself.

His kingdom extends to the sea. A fine port he sees in the pale water — a wharf to the left of the cove, stores housing the wares all along the edge. Wharf Road there, which takes you, of course, to the wharf. Main road here up to the hills — and a man may stop at the crossroads to survey the choice of accommodations at which he can suck and suckle. The rocks that mark the curve of the bay will be ground down for—

He sees her watching him.

'Very well then, a park with proper grass. For the common folk, markets, sports and the like.'

Eyes light on hers.

'Look of you is more gypsy than captain's wife.'

Up he races to the fire where her hands are warming. Swoops her in his arms. Plants her on a field of shells. Her toes curl. He bows a flourish, his eyes willing her to curtsey. She will not.

'Welcome to the ball, your majesty.'

'Majesty,' she dares correct him. 'It ends in -tee not -tree.'

'Captain's wife starts with C,' he replies, 'and so does cunny or whatever the fuck you may be.'

Jigs her around. Sings at the top of his voice and is joined by the crew who form a circle around the two of them. Bending knees, raising boots, swinging arms. She cannot help herself. Minds not even the sting of the shells under her feet. Laughter ripples through her like a stream running towards the open mouth of the ocean, natural like; it can do nothing but be released. Clap-clap jig, the jigging that was forbidden in Ma's country.

Then she sees them.

High up on the small hill above the tumble of rocks. Scanning the stick plan and the merriment. Three New Zealand men and a younger one, a boy — yes, a boy by the shape and size of him. The boy who wore her boots. The men are wearing toppers given to them yesterday. The boy wears, like a gown, a red soldier's jacket from a stash Robbie purloined from the Sydney barracks.

She waves at them. The boy waves first, the men follow. The boy bends his knees, lifts a foot, lifts his arms. She lifts her leg, he lifts his. She raises her arm and twirls. He does the same. She claps, he claps. Everyone claps — New Zealanders on the hill, Robbie's crew on the ground. Sky turning from grey wash to blue. She raises her face towards the sun, this change in weather is a good sign. A mirror reflecting light. Surely it bodes well.

———

Rising in the rain, floating mist, above the foreshore and estuary, between the flax and swamp, meandering from the rained-upon forest, is the fern-furnished freshwater stream. On the pebbled shore of this, crouched on a rock, is Robbie, perfectly naked.

His hands a bowl, fingers sluice cold water. Splash of the water reminds her of glass breaking, a looking-glass shattered. His blib-blib-blib water noises no different to a coach horse snuffling and coughing in morning fog. She crouches beside him. Traces with her gaze the whiplash ridges, the trail of tattoos. Seven stars on each thigh, eagle wings spreading his shoulders, petalled pansy on his chest, quite the dainty, a sun splicing rays of light, its face a smile. Down his belly her gaze trails, and under. Climbing up towards his foreskin, the forked tongue, the tattooed snake.

'That on your cock must have hurt like Hell.'

'Booze-addled I were, for the pain. Look, he's going into hiding, needs a snake charmer.'

The jester in him, wit and fool; she almost smiles. Shakes her head, no. He raises his fingers over the coiled cock with its bashful snake. Plays an imaginary flute. Hums an air that rouses the perfume of musk and carpets, gems and baskets, that is Egyptian, Romany or Oriental, not of cold roses in spring, not of England. Drops his hands.

'Disappointingly slow he is today, on account of the cold. Or perhaps he is lonesome, needs to stick his head in a nice warm basket.'

The snake hovers and recoils as she reads the other tattoos. Eagle is power, flower is remembrance — for his mother he has said, though she doubts this. Dots and crosses are maps to troves of fantastical treasure. Hieroglyphics, the secret codes of tribes whose ways and words are kept by sailors. She ventures into this manly kingdom with her voice, firmly shutting out the melancholy warning cry of all the long nights. Poor fool, poor fool.

'Robbie?'

'Aye.'

'If the market for skins and heads was for yours, would you have got all these adornments?'

Judges by his expression, jaw grinding, muscles working, that she ought to have tried another tack. Trying to unsay the unsayable, she ventures further, says more.

'Would you? What if your skin was slung up for viewing in the galley of a smoking room at a gentlemen's club in Kensington? What if the toffs were after your tattooed pelt?'

Splashes water as he stands, spraying drops from his black mane.

'There isn't a padlock —'

Braces herself.

'— big enough to lock away your stupid fucking thoughts —'

Clouts and curses break the bough, crack the twig, fell the whole damned tree.

'— inside the cunny-addled stupid fucking moll head of yours.'

No place to hide. The man leaps up and the blows descend. Rises, she does, sheds her own skin. Floats above the shelter that was her body, floats high until she can see the husks and hulls of creatures that spun and turned and spumed and sang. Dimly hears the thump of his fist pummelling face bone.

Circles, she does, above the cove. White horses are kicking blood. Red is the foam. Black is the cauldron that cooks the flesh. Black smoke, black sand, black dead stench from chunks of flesh hacked by all the whalers who have chased down whales. Peeled-back skin flensed into lumps, dumped into a giant iron cauldron. In the cauldron float bricks of flesh, bubbling, boiling to oil. Flesh prodded by little men in aprons, singing killing as they pitch and stab long iron forks. From this she flies. Past the dead land up the green valley. Where birds cloak trees and hear her song.

———

He had dictated the list the previous afternoon. She scratched them down as he reeled them out. Fetch wood, brew tea, wash garments — not the stinking rotting garments of the lowest men, for they can wash or stink their way to Hell, he cares not. She must wash hers, the missionary's and Robbie's own evening attire, his best long shirts, his stockings. For he is on his way to gentryhood and the lady by his side will have her own fine gowns when she has earned her worth.

So here it is arrived, the wash day. Grey clouds hesitating at the line where earth drops to sky. Stay put, she tells the clouds, as she would tell a dog. Fancies they withdraw a little to obey. The dumping of the keg startles a bird. Flight of it is light falling from a cathedral of trees, a pearl-fastened mourning glove brushing a black fan to hasten the breeze.

The weight of the washing could be enough to bring down the rigging between two felled trees. A mixed wash — barrack garb, pea jackets, raven duck jackets, pants and shirts with the line of dark anchors, Guernsey greatcoats. Her underskirt lonesome without female company. The missionary's cambric shirt is also a thing apart. White turned dull grey, the shirt buckles and drips in the cold shiver of a breeze.

Should it fall, rigging and all, Robbie will surely shout that it is on cause of her being a fool, a dimber, a crack, a bint, a moll, a mot. It will matter not that she has wrung the load until her shoulders strained and her arms pained, her fingers grew red and still the water swelled inside the wool, the worsted, the cotton.

Behind her the forest watches. Past the sea of flax, at the thick entrance of the forest, from sodden roots trunks rise, withdraw, coil and hunch like Bonaparte's men retreating from Waterloo. Hunch under cascades of mist that might be smoke from cannon fire. Like men these trees, beaten pale ghosts. Here is a dark place where the monster himself, Boney, could rise, crawl through the undergrowth and suck the life out of a man. Dead the dead are, but that Boney would never be dead enough.

Her fears are broken by the missionary wading through the flax sea. Into view and across her mind he strides, like a finger navigating a map. A rescuer of sorts he was in Sydney. Back in the orphanage he had protected her from the flogging parson, Samuel Marsden, had helped her teach the younger children, white and copper-coloured children, to read and write.

A spark of fervour in his eyes he had, until he went to the North Island of New Zealand for ten months and returned in shame, with a stain on his name like a blotter mark. Once the hope of the Methodist mission, he had returned to lesser work, stacking Bibles with her, teaching with her, had never spoken of it. Here he is just Cuthbert, wearing a holster, fingering the trigger on pistols hanging from his right and his left.

'These aren't for killing,' he tells her. 'Robbie — Captain Fitch suggested that I should equip myself for the trade, just in case.'

'In case of what?'

'In case something goes awry.'

She waits, knowing him well — too well perhaps. Her mother's voice in her ears. Ná bí róbheag is ná bí rómhór leis an gcléir. She wonders though how it is possible to be neither too big nor too small with the clergy.

'Wise man, that Captain Fitch,' says Robbie, joining the conversation as he stretches himself down beside the small fire, pushing his voice out over a fart and a grunt.

'A bullet is all they're good for — a bullet for every mother's son.'

She dares enter the pause, risk a fist or a scowl.

'Why do you call the New Zealand girls titters?'

The missionary answers. 'It's another word for giggling, for laughter. They do laugh a great deal.'

Robbie looks set to guffaw. She tries to force her mouth shut but the words find their own way out.

'I know well enough what tits are.'

Robbie slaps the missionary on the back with his farewell.

'She's got you there, blush and all.'

'First light, then.' Robbie gives the blushing missionary a swift wink. 'Bring some bloody Bibles. Fat lot of good it'll do, but you're not to overdo it. You're here to translate their gibberish and to lull them into a sense of trust, do you hear?'

But Quentin Cuthbert does not hear. His eyes are not on Robbie but on the rigging, where hangs the washing, where hangs Bridie's forlorn underskirt. Robbie hoicks a small bloodstained splash on the missionary's left boot.

'Right on target.'

She unties the knot on her neckerchief, hands it to Cuthbert. Watches him wipe his boot.

'One has to mind where one steps,' he says.

She answers him with silence.

'Not unlike Ireland,' he says.

'What know you of Éire?'

'Born, bred in . . . only turned from my mother's religion so my father could keep his land.'

The sound of him, different now, is green, cloud-rinsed, rain-soaked, ocean-rolled. She kicks the empty keg with the toe of her boot. Hurting herself. So he has buried the wonder and knowledge of Éire deep inside, forced all the magic underground. Wonders, she does, whether he even believes in the magic conjured by the clergy.

Flappity-flap say the garments, flapping back and forth, ghosts against the grey gusting sea. The missionary's shirt sags on the line, the first to drop.

'See that?' she says. 'When one goes down it drags the rest.'

CHAPTER 15

Thoughts weigh Manaia as an anchor weighs a waka. She is afloat but unable to drift. Wishes she could be like them — the mātua, the rangatahi and the tamariki, join the sleeping journeys of her whānau. She envies the soft sounds they make in their sleep. Warm, the whare. Comforting, the smells. Embers. Dry ferns. Fragrant flowers. Fur of a sleeping kurī.

In the wharenui others will be awake too, figuring out the meanings, the signs, forecasting what should be done. How tempting it is to follow the path to them, to listen under the window or put her face to one of the cracks between the wooden poles that support the wharenui, which is the finest, largest whare in the village. The urge to follow the path is strong but where might it lead her afterwards?

Earlier that morning she had been among the women who drew water and poured it into nīkau bowls. Plucked and prepared tight curls of pītau, a decoration imbued with meaning. The tauiwi did not seem to appreciate the floating new frond as she did, like a newborn baby, the coil before growth. They gulped back the water, made loud unintelligible noises and spat out the fronds.

The problems began at the gateway before they even entered. The tauiwi rangatira — she must think up another title for him, for he does not deserve to be called a rangatira — talked through the karanga.

It was the mother of Kāhu Kōrako who had stood and sung out the welcome. Her white hair blowing behind her ears, the kiwi feathers on her korowai stirring from her shoulders as she sang in long wavering threads the call, the cry for those who had gone before, remembering and paying heed to these ancestors. Her call addressed the ancestors of the manuhiri, honoured these visitors too.

The tauiwi leader who did not deserve the title of rangatira had ignored trouble caused by his men during the speeches when two of them walked blithely in front of the tangata whenua.

At this point Rāwhiti had risen, had angrily cried out.

'See that man and that? They do not understand the rules of tapu and utu that protect the mauri in all living things. Stones. Trees. Bones.'

Only one of the tauiwi men seemed to understand, and he had apologised in her language.

'Mō tāku hē.'

But the mistake was not his to own; it was one of many mistakes made by the men who accompanied him.

Their leader who was not good enough to be called a rangatira had not moved, head held high, eyes darting. Te Iho o Ranginui had whispered to Kāhu Kōrako, who rose and spoke.

'We will forgive these mistakes only if they are not repeated. We must teach these people to obey the rules of tapu.'

Manaia was one of those who spent many hours preparing the tiers of the pātaka with roasted fernroot, pounded hīnau berries, the soft steaming flesh of kūmara, and the array of kai moana — all the pātiki, the pāua, the pipi, the tuangi. The tauiwi grew restless while the rangatira were served first. When it was their turn they grabbed and snatched.

Some of the young hungry rangatahi slapped and pushed the tauiwi in a friendly-casual manner and the tauiwi slapped back. Sometimes the slaps grew hard. The laughter grew hard too. Like the first cut of the young axe against the old tree.

When the tauiwi were taken to the whare harakoa for the entertainments she and the other workers were able to sit and eat. After clearing the mess they sucked on the bones, the scraps the tauiwi left behind.

CHAPTER 16

After the dances and feasting they had been shown to this round sleeping house, their long beds separated by black logs. Their voices are low as they retrace the events of the day. Hopes to himself, Cuthbert, that Robbie will consider the day's disasters and tread more carefully on the morrow. The mistakes of the day could have cost them their lives.

'Did you see their tattoos?' says Mallet.

'Aye, they'll all be grinning in glass cases by the end of the season,' says Robbie. 'Cuthbert, you must find out where the heads of their ancestors are stored. You need to mingle more, talk to them, earn their trust.'

Cuthbert risks venturing a protest.

'I caution—'

'And I caution you to shut your gob and stop being a grumbletonian. We won't do nothing now, that would be stupid. The big raid we'll make shortly before our departure. When we return next season the only people left will be slaves who do our bidding.'

A low whistle, then someone starts clapping slowly. Others take it up.

'Fairhaven,' Robbie says. 'That's what we shall call it.'

It doesn't sound fair to Cuthbert's cold ears. But his employers back in Sydney and England would favour the name as long as a steeple was planted at the centre of a square — a square given a name like

Waterloo or Trafalgar. Nelson's empire. Sprawling parishes, plots of fenced land. Rows of crosses above the dead.

Fairhaven, the word repeated, a mumble, a rumble from Robbie, followed by a snort inwards, a long shuddering snore outwards.

Stews, that is what Cuthbert does; he stews it over. Thinks himself the only one worrying that they might become meat in the morning. He regrets so much of the day. For the New Zealanders had made every accommodation, had prepared the finest delicacies, accorded the motley crew of whalers the respect of esteemed guests. He might have cherished the experience if it weren't for Robbie. How could this shipping man have failed to learn from the ship herself? Keep the cannon tied firm, for a cannon that rolls loose can wreak havoc on a ship. But here he was, Robbie, a cannon rolled loose, senseless to the sensitivities around him.

When the New Zealand men had danced, stamping their feet, sunlight shining on oil- and ochre-streaked muscles, their chests, their thighs, their flat stomachs, Robbie boasted that all the dancing strength of them could be felled by a volley of bullets. When an elderly woman had called the karanga, her long crying song calling out and beyond, Cuthbert couldn't help but think of his mother keening in Ireland and the other women who keened for Bridie's mother. Here at this kāinga, this village, listening to the karanga sung by a New Zealand woman, he did not dare or even care to stop the sound. As the spirit of it shivered down Cuthbert's spine, Robbie in his brash bull-headed manner spoke so loudly he virtually shouted. Told Cuthbert the woman should stop crowing — the only value she might serve in his view being due to her fine tattoo, which had a place inside Lord Aglionby's curiosity cabinet. Her head perched on a shelf.

So relieved he is, the missionary, that their hosts cannot understand English.

Cuthbert had felt an uneasy portent back in the cove when Robbie insisted on a musket as the gift to the New Zealanders. A killing tool is an ominous gift. After laying it down, playing the part of the important captain, Robbie Fitch had turned his back on their hosts. Diminishing himself in their eyes. Always the expert, an expert in foolishness this day.

Topped this off, Robbie, by demanding that the missionary enquire whether there was a slave who deserved to be felled so he, Captain Robbie Fitch, could demonstrate the power of the musket. Wouldn't that impress them, if he could put a bullet in the leg of a fellow. Or perhaps they could tattoo a slave so Robbie could shoot him in the carcass and take the head as his prize. Robbie insisted the missionary pose these offers but Cuthbert had feigned deafness.

Unthwarted, Robbie went on to demand Cuthbert talk to the children, for it is well known, Robbie had said, that children spill the beans. Give them gifts, ask them where the natives store the heads of their dead. Seek the whereabouts of precious boxes that contain these artefacts that would sell for a pretty price in Sydney and in turn in Europe.

Exasperated and exhausted, Cuthbert had wondered, as he does now in this pleasant reed-lined, thatch-roofed guest-house, how much longer he can keep the brute at bay. It was all proving too much, this translation business. He had feigned inattention and deafness, feigned tiredness, feigned that somewhere along the way he had lost his ability to comprehend his own language.

But the captain did not give up.

'Tell them I want a New Zealand wife.'

'But you have a wife.'

'Aye and I want another. A winter wife. A titter, a — what's their word for virgin?'

'Puhi.'

'Aye, one of them.'

'But the puhi only marry the rangatira. They are treasured.'

'And I'll be unlocking some of that treasure.'

If the New Zealanders had known that Robbie had been transported for stealing, that he was a ticket-of-leave man who only had a half-share in the ship he commanded, they would have deemed him a servant. Cuthbert could have enlightened them, but this might have put them all at risk. Instead he had waxed lyrical, referred to Robbie as a captain of high esteem, requested formally, humbly, in the politest way possible for his captain to be presented with a New Zealand wife, as a special honour, a sign of trust on the part of both parties.

Robbie had interrupted — said he hadn't heard mention of the word puhi. So he said the word quickly while telling the rangatira that no, no reperepe, no dowry would be needed, the gifts of food and accommodation and all the other treats had been ample, thank you.

'And tell them to give her a tattoo,' said Robbie. 'A fine face tattoo.'

Turns all this over, Cuthbert does now, to the tune of Robbie and the rest of the ruffians snoring. If he does not serve Robbie he will be dispatched, and he has no wish to test yet whether he is fit for Heaven or Hell. Of Robbie's destination there can be no doubt. When he first set eyes on him, in the dingy court of London and then later in the North Island of this country, he had looked into the soulless eyes of a killer. Robert Fitch would surely not hesitate to kill him. If he crosses him, he must do so with the utmost caution, for loyalty is what Fitch values. Loyalty he pays to those above him, and loyalty he prizes from those below.

If this is my last day, Lord, send my spirit back to my country, Éire, for there I wish to lie. Bury me in the black peat, from where my soul can rise over the sea.

'Mr Cuthbert.'

It is Tom who squeaks and touches his shoulder. Fearful, Cuthbert checks the other mounds. Still asleep. Sweet relief. The boy has crawled to his side while the others slumber, untroubled by the day's disasters.

'Captain Fitch says they eat people. Would they have treated us so kindly if they wanted to eat us?'

Heavy-terror silence: the boy needs him to respond with certitude. 'Of course not.'

'If we was to die now and our heads and bodies devoured, would we still rise to Heaven?'

'Of course, my boy. Heavens, yes.'

Entertains for himself the thought that if they die here their spirits might depart to a different realm, for the New Zealanders believe that the spirit dances after death, dives off a cliff, clings to the branches of the pōhutukawa, descends into the river underneath the ocean, rests, eats, drinks. Rises to soar into the overworld of stars.

'Their spiritual world encompasses every living thing, streams, rivers, the earth, the forests, the sea, to the creatures that belong to these. Even mountains and rocks. Sometimes I wonder, is there something to it? Are we — people — threads in this fabric, rather than the main design?'

A soft outward breath is Tom's answer, which is as well, Cuthbert decides, when he himself has turned into a running brook babbling blasphemy. Fear it is, doing this to him. Night has lifted away the border between him and them. But he felt it in the day as well, as though he had entered a gateway he had been through before.

During the festivities he had taken account of the geography of the village as best he could. Sleeping houses of the tangata whenua to the left of the gates through which they entered. Naked, bowing low as the prayers were said over them, after which they were presented with fine mats. Made Robbie laugh, the nakedness, the mats. The wharenui, the meeting house of the rangatira, was past that, further along and in front of the large, shell-paved courtyard. Diagonally opposite the entertainment house, he thinks. The guest sleeping house is somewhere behind the wharenui. Somewhere. The kitchen houses and dining houses are on the right. He needs to find the path to the wharenui, for it is the way of New Zealanders to hold council on important matters long into the night.

If he were to venture to their meeting house and listen to the great debate of this night, he would learn their plans for him, for Robbie, for the others. If their lives are threatened, he would earn merit with Robbie by warning him. They could sneak back, row the boat out to the ship, every last man and the Irish girl. Leave and never return.

As he walks the shell path that should take him to the main meeting house he rehearses the phrase, asks where the area is where he can relieve himself without causing offence. Yes, this is what he will say, should a warrior challenge him.

———

Manaia takes the back paths to the wharenui, skirting behind the whare where the tangata tell stories and act them out, dance and laugh. The black night flings itself out like a cloak that has caught all the sparks from a great fire. Sound is the wind wrestling with the wall-posts, the rushes and the rafters.

She presses her face to the crack between post and wall. Spies the listeners, faces fingered by hungry smoke, their toes almost — but not quite — touching the searing pit of house-warming stones. The speaker rising now is Te Mārire. Though he is not a master of warfare he always offers winning words in the battlefield of discussions.

'If we fail to establish an alliance with these tauiwi we will be crushed like moulding leaves under their feet. The tauiwi will bring us more guns, or would it be better to succumb to our enemies who are already so armed and be roasted alive?'

Rāwhiti, who is named for the rising sun, begins with a tribute. This is his way of winning the sympathy of his audience, just as the karoro — the black-backed gull — drops the small fish to catch itself a larger meal.

'Your words are poetic, Te Mārire, and may prove to be prophetic. You think the tauiwi are strong. Personally, I think they have a sick look, but what do I know?'

He is huffing, as is his custom, letting it be known that his argument is so powerful it might require more breath than he can possibly muster. Some of the rangatira shift uncomfortably at this kōrero.

Rāwhiti continues.

'This day I have seen a disgusting sight. I have seen pale fools stamping over our whenua and removing the tapu on our sacred places. Today we sat with men who don't even know how to keep their bottoms out of the food. Wherever would we be without our tapu places? The tapu guards the mauri — the mauri that preserve the life of our trees, stones, birds, mountains, rivers, men and women. I say we should kill them now.'

As Rāwhiti settles back on his mat, Manaia feels the urge to sing a waiata to commend his speech. To stop herself, she steps back, holds her breath before pressing her face to the wall. Kauri shifts and stands. The younger men rival each other for the attention of their fathers and grandfathers but Kauri always seems most popular.

'It is true we cannot take them seriously, these men with their blue veins for moko,' he says. 'They are not men but wētā.'

He pretends to scuttle in the manner of the insect. Laughter drums from roof to floor, causing those who have fallen into sleep to stir and grumble.

Manaia wonders what she would say to them now if she were sitting among them. Would she agree or argue, take one side or the other, or use waiata as a device, singing at a pause to end a speech.

She realises she has missed something for there is a change inside. She presses her eyes hard against the wall, to the finger-space of light. Kauri is swaying his weight from one foot to the other. Behind the embers of the stone pit, men are sniggering and whispering. Kauri addresses them directly.

'If you think such a brave girl sent to live among the tauiwi would not want to return to her own people, you are wrong.'

He pats his taut stomach muscles.

'She would return to marry a man with real strength and true mana.'

Realising the talk has turned and that Kauri is describing a woman who would earn his high esteem, Manaia is all attention. Desire for him causes a soft waiata to pour unbidden from her lips. Longing stirred by the same wind that causes a fern frond to unfurl towards the sun. . . . She is startled out of her reverie by Kāhu Kōrako. Swinging his weapon, a great taiaha, he causes several young men beside him to duck their heads. For one moment the weapon seems to point straight through the crack between the walls to her.

She pulls back slightly as Kāhu steps forward, tucking the weapon to his side, staring into the silence of his audience.

'Te Rākaunui advises me that the girl Manaia has gifts that could be used to our advantage. She is alert and senses trouble. We should send her to spy on these visitors.'

She feels a spider tickle her chin. Casts her eyes around the room. She must have misheard. It cannot be her name he has uttered. Kāhu Kōrako cannot mean that she should be the one who is to be sent to live among the tauiwi.

'If these are good men, men of integrity and honour, the marriage of their leader to Manaia will please Rongo, the god of peace. We will trade with them and they will respect our rules. We will be good hosts and they will live under our protection.'

He pauses, casts his gaze on each man in turn.

'On the other hand, if they are bad men, if they ill-treat her, she will report to us and we will rain the full force of a great taua down upon them.'

The terror inside her is colder than the night wind and rain. She should rush in, demand that they listen to her, but this is the seat where decisions are made and it is not her place to speak. Some of the older men present are guided by the tīpuna and draw from a reservoir of knowledge. Others like Kauri and Rāwhiti are little older than herself. She wonders how they can know the difference between what is good for themselves and what is good for her. She would force them to stop thinking of the good of everyone and pause, think, protect her and only her.

Arguments drift into agreements, the strong voices merging to become watery murmurs. As the meeting closes, two men linger. Kāhu Kōrako is instructing Kauri to tend to the eel weirs first thing in the morning. One of the many fences across the river has fallen over and the eels have been slipping through.

Fearing they will see her, Manaia retreats back into the shadows and becomes a shadow herself. A shadow fleeing — but to where? She tries to imagine herself married to the ugliest man among the tauiwi, sleeping in his whare, cooking food and serving it to him. She feels māuiui from her stomach to her chest. Sickness rises from deep inside her. She stumbles over a log, falls to her knees as the sickness that is fear tries to leave her body. The wrenching sound from her throat is loud and she knows they will hear, will come looking for her, that she will be revealed as a girl who spies not on the tauiwi, but on her own people. She is not the girl they think she is — not brave, not clever, not willing.

She runs, stumbles and looks back towards the men still talking under the eaves of the wharenui. It is then she notices a form scuttling away on the other side. As he dashes from the fiery light of torches straining against the wind, she recognises the tauiwi who has shown some skill in speaking her language. He is a man who listens under the eaves to plans crafted in the night. He has learned what she has learned, and she has learned that, in some small way, he is like her.

CHAPTER 17

Light spreads over the sea, the cliff, and into the plateau where the village lies. In the whare, light separates one body from another. Manaia feels sad, wonders at the light that separates Papatūānuku, the earth goddess, from her husband Ranginui, the sky god. Sad in the knowledge that light separates, darkness binds. Sadder today, and fearful.

Makes herself small, lies on her side, knees to chin. Refuses to talk, refuses to move. The women come, lean over, whisper, talk over her head. She must give them a reason but she cannot reveal the truth. Not yet, not before the news is conveyed by those who have the right to share it. Instead, she complains of a sore puku and they offer remedies. Hard work rather than rest, and grubs that will eat anything bad in the belly. Some shake their heads, declare her sickness the fault of the tauiwi; perhaps the foreigners poisoned the water and food with their foul actions.

As their voices fade she remembers that while she has been malingering, Kauri is working at the eel weirs. Hastening to be alone with him, perhaps for the last time, she rallies. Hurries past the rangatahi standing over the cooking fires, past racks of dried shark and eels, vats of kina pākira, past three women pummelling pāua, past the tamariki playing tī rākau to learn their numbers, past the whare for weaving, the whare for healing, the whare kura for learning, the whare takiura for higher learning. Round through to the back of the village, past the pākoro and the pātengi where the cultivated foods are stored. The season of gathering is coming to an end, the season of huddling by the fires, of rest, is almost upon them and her heart is sobbing. How can she leave all this?

On the bank she stands under a sad tree. Strangled by vines, this little tree still manages to squeeze out sweet-scented flowers. Thanking the tree, she takes a small white flower, threads it behind her ear. Composes herself. Licks her lips so that they have the shine of seaweed. Walks in the manner of a girl who values herself, a girl who is the pride of her village. Feels the flow of her body — her hips, breasts, buttocks, thighs — the surge of life down to the soles of her feet. The full force of her abundant self marches past the traps. Kauri calls out.

'E hine!'

She smiles. How to catch a man and land him. He dangles before her a scented purse hanging from braided flax.

'E iti noa ana nā te aroha,' he says.

Even if it is true that this gift of 'little worth' was shaped by love, the love was not intended for her. His other lover must have picked the tītoki berries in the season when the fruit is harvested. That woman would have crushed the berries and added a handful of piripiri, mixing and blending until she was satisfied with the fragrance. Manaia does not want to think how it came into Kauri's possession.

He hangs the necklace around her neck, in the trough between her breasts — breasts that have risen from her since their first far-off playful days. She lets her breath fall lightly, without the weight of care. Chewing his tarata gum, he looks at her slowly; his eyes are like a net pulling her towards depths she does not wish to enter.

'There is talk of a special girl,' he says at last. 'A girl who will marry the leader of the tauiwi. This girl will learn much from these ugly visitors and return with all their baskets of knowledge for the benefit of her own man.'

He brushes a lock of hair that has fallen loose from his topknot. She reaches up past his wide shoulders and binds his hair in place.

'A girl might prefer to keep her baskets to herself,' she says.

Her fingers find the thread of a little wind, let it glide upwards. She trails her fingers so they do not quite touch — almost stroke — his chest. Lets her fingers float and fall with that thread of wind to almost touch him, further and further down. Walks away, leaving the fish to flap his mouth in wonder.

———

As she crosses the kūmara plantations she sees the kāhu wheeling, summoning the wind in her wings, soaring over the raised branches of a kahikatea tree, and down, down, so low and close Manaia is forced to step back. The bird must have spotted a kiore. She bows and, as the bird flies by, she hears the whirr of its wings, has the sense of forked claws and glaring eyes. She clutches her ears as the bird utters a long karanga so full of pōuritanga, spreading over her the cloak of sadness that is felt in the lament for someone who has died.

The tamariki quieten their chiming. Tahi, rua, toru. As they cease their number games, the sticks and stones clatter and fall, abandoned. Inside the whare she finds them in a huddle of weeping. Fear and grief suffocate like the dust on a stinking hot day.

So it is true.

Barely able to draw breath, Manaia takes her weeping mother's hands. Above her mother's head Manutaki smiles, but his cheeks are marked by tracks of tears. He pulls her from Rima and leads her outside. She turns on him.

'So, I am to go with the tauiwi, live with that strange, ugly man?'

'Āe, you will watch their ways, learn whether they are good or bad. If you like him you will stay. If not, you return.'

'They are the victors in this situation. We are the victims. I will be a wife in captivity.'

'This is not so. You have been chosen because you see things others do not. You are descended from the tohunga matakite. You have the sight, special skills. If there is not one path out, find another. We will remain here waiting, all of us.'

He takes her hands, tells her now that she is the ngākau, the centre, the heart of the whānau. She could remind him that this is how Rima feels about him, that he is the heart of the family, but perhaps it is true of them all. No one can survive without the other. No one should be plucked out. If the heart is taken the body dies.

She opens her mouth, their eyes meet. He silences her with a heavy look. The heart has no mouth.

———

Her whānau have gathered in the creeping light of dawn, heads bowed as Te Rākaunui works on her moko. Her head on the log where Kauri's head lay not so long past, Manaia tries to swim herself away from her mother's words. Words that hurt like the chisel, the chisel that is now piercing her flesh like the pincers of a crab. She swims away from the pain, up and under, in and out of each wave, hears the whispering of the tīpuna who have gone before her, who have lain in this place and swum from this pain. Around her, kuia breathe over her, carrying and releasing the strength of their breath. Hā ki roto, hā ki waho. As Te Rākaunui cuts her skin, the women wipe away the blood.

Te Rākaunui's eyes meet hers, and his spring tears. Rima reaches across Manaia's body, touches with her finger the finger of this man. Poised, his finger, like a bird poised above a shadow in the water. Manaia gargles tears that have fallen from the back of her eyes to the back of her nose to the back of her throat. Tears she will not let fall lest they blemish the beauty of her moko.

———

Silence on the morning of her departure, silent, all of them — all her mothers, all the fathers, brothers and sisters. One by one they creep outside. Only Rima remains, jiggling a baby on her knee. Manaia crawls to her, longs to push the baby off, to be a baby again herself, but she must not let her mother see her fears. Her mother seems changed.

'Our ancestors tangi,' Rima says. 'Last night I had a terrible dream. A crowd of tattooed faces. Our tīpuna. Tangihanga. The tīpuna lamented because they had been stolen. So lonely they were. So far from us, their tangata, their whenua.'

'That could never happen.'

'The ways of our tīpuna will be buried by these people. The tauiwi will make you void, empty like a useless shell. They will poison your mauri. Hear me? You will be empty and useless like the tree that stands idly by while its sap dribbles away.'

'Is this your dream or are you cursing me?' Manaia cries. 'This is how you greet me, e whaea? When I am honoured with this fine moko? When my father, who never respected you, respects you now and respects me at last?'

The sound in the space between them is of rain falling on the rush roof of the whare.

'You are right,' says Rima, finally. 'This is something we cannot change. But be careful. Protect yourself however you can.' She slides Manaia a kete containing supplies.

Others come to console her, console one another. The tamariki climb into laps and over shoulders. The women sing a waiata about a girl who is like a small wave drifting far from the other waves, drifting up into the dark hills of rattling trees, far from the ocean of aroha, far from her whānau.

———

The tauiwi are slow — they do not quicken their pace and lengthen their stride, they do not run-fly. By the time they have laboured over the hill and down the stream near her secret pool, up and over the second hill and down past the ocean of flax, she feels she is drowning. Fatigue, wave upon wave, tries to fell her. Staying awake to danger causes the world to spin, her feet drag to the place she does not want to go.

She alone sees it. The pounamu stone that drops from the hand of the man she is to marry. Ropi. Stolen, surely. Quickly she picks it up and warms the stone in her hand. A stone from a man's ear but not a man she knows. As she lays it inside her kete, she feels rather than hears the words passing from its owner. Whakamārōtia atu, ka whaka-hoki mai ano, ki te kapua whakapipi.

Stretch out but return to the sheltering cloud.

———

She sees who he is by the state of his whare, which is worse than the worst temporary shelter. Absent of carvings and the ridges that represent the back and arms of the tīpuna. There is no protection here; she is not inside a sacred body. She tries to crawl out but, taking up the small doorway, the man who is supposed to be her man pushes her back. After roughly stripping off her garments, he tears her hair, grabs her throat, pushes his fingers into her eyes. As she turns her head he forces her under him, grinding his horrid stinking body all over her. When his hand reaches her mouth she bites. Savagely he grabs her neck with one hand, thrusts the other hard between her thighs.

Outside the wind screams high in the trees, whistles through the scrub. He has seized a handful of her hair, pulls as though he is pulling grass from the ground. She feels pain like roots screaming into the earth when a tree is hacked, but she fights with every limb, fights with every tool that can wound. Kicks, bites. He punches her eyes.

Sobbing and praying, she begs her tīpuna to help her fight more strongly. Make him sick, this man, make him dead.

He grabs a leg and pulls as though she is a bird. Her teeth and nails tear, her feet kick. He is stronger than she expects. The sickness inside her rises as his finger touches the softest part of her flesh. Her flesh. Hers. Not his. She tries to push the sickness down, make it enter him when he violates her.

He moans. Rolls over her and lies at her side, his legs drawn up to his chest. She waits until his ragged breath slows, seizes her discarded clothing and kete and gropes her way through the darkness until she is outside and she can rise. She runs until she feels the soothing edge of the sea.

She wades into the water where baby waves suck and spit, where the thunder in the belly of the ocean is a mother's song. Her karakia to Tangaroa is an appeal for an end to this loneliness, this feeling that her wairua has left her body, this sense that she is broken. Slides into the sharp yet soothing sting of cold. Washes into the waves.

The ocean knows the hurt caused by this man. She cradles her hands in the moon's reflection as old waves lick her body, caress and soothe her wounds. A sliver of the moon's light floats over a wave. She reaches out, picks it up. In her hand is a white feather. Tired from its journey, cleansed by the salt water. A tender breeze lifts the feather. The feather stirs, stretches for flight.

———

She considers running, returning to the kāinga as fast as she is able. It is her imagination that blocks her escape. She imagines Kauri's face when he realises that she has failed in her mission. All the fuss, all the tears at her departure and then she returns with nothing. Such a girl would not be so special after all. She decides to wait, to hide, to watch the tauiwi and learn their ways, to spy on them from afar.

Turning from the waves, staring up the beach into the black hollows under so many canopies of leaves, she prays. Prays to Tāne-mahuta, the god of the forest, seeks in her prayer a place to hide from the tauiwi, where she can build a house that will protect her from them and from where she is still able to watch and learn. She walks into the darkness, through folds of shadow until she finds a space where the trees have moved aside, a space where light falls not too bright, soft and gentle. She breathes the forest into herself, hā ki roto, pulls inside herself the cool, soothing breath of thousands of trees.

All morning she gathers wood and shells and stones, makes tools of the shells and stones, scrapes soft branches and dry logs, gathers dried fern leaves and harakeke. All the while she communes with Tāne-mahuta, listens to the trees and asks that the protection given to this forest be spread over her also, and this, her whare.

Finally, she stands back, looks at the outside and the inside, the roof and the floor. So pleased she is, so proud — and so alone. She misses all the whare that should stand next to hers, and all the whānau who should stand with her. But the trees are here. She strokes the bark of the tree next to her. What is this tree? A brother or a sister? A mother or a father? Now all the trees are her family.

Inside her whare she crawls, curls into herself. The smallest sea creature seeking the biggest shell. Gives the shell all her pain and longing, the aches of her body, her desperate need for manaakitanga. She floats in her dream journey. Dives, breathes, and in her breath finds the gushing song of life. She is the tohorā, the giant of the ocean. A film of water slides down her eyes, skewed against the wind and waves of the ocean. She sees a waka steered by Ropi and his crew of tauiwi. The terror she feels fills the ocean.

CHAPTER 18

Shouts wake Bridie. Robbie, ever disturbing the peace, is hollering for Cuthbert, the sound harsh as the bitter wind that picks and pecks her skin.

'There you are, you bastard, you traitor. Used goods are no bloody good to me. Did the word "virgin" fail to penetrate the dingy hollow of your brain?'

Peering out of the makeshift bivouac, she sniffs the salty air, decides the sky has the look of poison. Waves that travelled to this shore seeking warmth are recoiling in horror. Clouds, like burnt paper, crisping brown at the edges.

Such sweet relief it had been to sleep alone, to not feel the bulk of him behind her back, wrestling himself into her at night. To not hear him shouting, mocking, any tempered mood, any show of good humour an hourglass waiting to be turned. Standing outside the shelter she listens, for his anger this time is directed at Cuthbert. The missionary, his back a little hunched as he responds, remonstrates rather pitifully.

'Puhi means virgin or feather. Same word, two intentions. I find the grammar befuddling. Seems aspects were wrong between the verb and the noun.'

'Grammar my arse. Fool. Simplewit. These people don't have proper language. They fight, they sleep, they work, they eat. Like animals.'

'Beg pardon but I lived in their midst. Their life might appear simple because they are for the most part content, peaceful. Treat life as though there is a god inside every living thing from trees to fish. But they have schools — schools for astronomy, oratory, fishing and gardening. Schools with teachers who are experts in these disciplines.'

'Says a man converted by the natives, who still does not know the word for virgin.'

'When I told them you sought most especially a virgin it seems they gave you a chosen girl esteemed with a white feather, bestowing honour on yourself.'

Robbie's laugh is so harsh the missionary takes a step back.

'When you're at the cockfights laying your bets—'

'Sir, I don't bet.'

'Everyone bets, Cuthbert, but you would never ever lay a bet on a game cock sporting a white feather.'

Bridie stifles laughter, presses her hand to her mouth so hard she fears it will leave a bruise.

'A white feather is a tohu,' Cuthbert pleads. 'It is a sign to you from them — it imports honour, peace, on you, on us.'

'It could have been a feather from the bloody angel Gabriel for all I care. Send her off, tell her to be gone.'

A loud silence follows. She hears a noise, sees Robbie hoiking phlegm at the missionary's feet.

'You see I can't help but wonder if this white feather flim flam is one of their gammy games—'

'An artful act of trickery, Captain? Be assured, it is not. Deceit is a habit of the English. In mariner speak, the New Zealanders sail a straight course.'

'You don't reckon they'll be sitting around their fires laughing at . . .'

Bridie follows the sound of a rumble from up the hill above the cliff. Sharp yells from men as rock after rock tumbles over the cliff, a dust cloud rising from the sea. Men who had stepped back to escape the rockfall cheer, link arms. Sing a chorus about boiling up whale tongues.

'Back to work,' Robbie yells.

'They are honourable, the New Zealanders,' says the missionary. 'Be assured.'

As he turns from Robbie, she sees the flicker of Cuthbert's mouth, almost a smile.

———

Robbie's displeasure stirs pleasure in herself and the missionary, but the captain's moods dictate the season. His square shoulders and short back appear to be fuming as he walks towards the mound of fallen rocks and trees, to the torn branches, the spindle fingers of roots, to yell at the men who have yet to resume their labour.

She wonders about the New Zealanders and his plans for them. Her trepidation had melted at their friendliness. She knows their village is far off, out of sight. She is glad they are far from this menace, but is it far enough?

Wishes, she does, that instead of being forced to wash the men's smocks she had been permitted to venture with the others to that village, see their houses and the gardens Cuthbert has talked about. She looks up at the sky. In that great ocean, trouble is brewing. How will she get back to Sydney if she seeks the protection of those who belong here?

As the sky scowls, she wonders where the New Zealand girl is now, and whether she is suffering the same distress as herself, in agonising silence.

———

In the smallest hours of the night, Bridie wakes to Robbie's groans.

'Fuck, fuck, fuck, the fucking agony.'

Curses, he does, the New Zealand girl, babbles that she must be a witch.

150

In the darkness she smiles. Composes her expression as she turns the light, as he cries for rum to ease his plight. In front of her, waving in front of her eyes, his forefinger is swollen and tight. Such difficulty she has swallowing her smile, for the thing that pains him so much reminds her of his ugly, standing prick.

———

Blubber finger, she hears old Bill tell Robbie in the morning, reminding him that the disease comes from the scratch or bite of a seal. Hears Robbie arguing he's barely touched fresh seal of late. Handled fewer than a dozen skins.

'It's not a seal that's caused this — it's a woman,' he snarls.

'P'raps a seal magicked into a woman,' says Bill. 'Or a woman who magicked into a seal.'

Listening to him, Bridie knows. Her mother's hair was a sign, some said. A sign that a woman is a brief thing — that she might be found, washed up, even rescued by a man, but she can never be owned. The 'ownership' he believes in is fleeting. She will always find her old skin and, when she does, she will leave.

Cursing all women now, Robbie trudges back to her. Seeks her sympathy. His finger pains him when she touches it. No pus will come out of it — there is no open wound. She wonders whether the disease will spread through his body until all his flesh is fat and his skin is pulled taut. Entertains the thought that he could be skinned himself, become a pelt.

In the afternoon, as she plunges her cold hands into the cold wash, she laughs to herself for she has heard others say it may spread to the rest of him, for this is what it does, blubber finger. Imagines the whole of him becoming a fat sausage. She is lathering the washboard when he comes up behind.

'What's cracking your ribs?' he says.

'Nothing.'

She tries to stifle her mirth.

'It's this, isn't it?' he says, swiping at her face with his finger. 'This bloody thing. It's fuckin' burning and besides, it's growing. Is that so funny?'

She makes her face solemn.

'Watch yourself, woman or you'll be spending eternity in the bush.'

If there is any bush left, she thinks. For all the trees under the watchtower have been felled, the scrub burned so nothing disturbs the hunter's view. Sound is no longer a deafening chorus of birdsong but log-screech as trees torn are shorn to planks, to spars, to casks, to huts. As the bush retreats like a subdued army, the foreground is shadowed by ghosts.

———

Manaia hears the night warning with the crack of a branch. The clumsiness of this man. Preparing for his arrival, she unwraps a parcel of pigeon fat from her mother's kete. Smears the fat on a large stick, pokes the tip into the fire until it catches. Splashes the fire towards Robbie as he advances, parting the bush with his cutlass. Legs astride, she is ready to fight. Seeing her, he stoops, lays his cutlass down.

He rises, wags his outstretched finger. Under the light of the fire it looks grotesque, reminds her of the stretched skin of an eel, like that other part of him — the worm, the snake that coils and grows. She spits laughter, brandishes her stick of fire.

It is the same finger he used when he so roughly explored her tara.

Her laugh sounds hideous even to herself. Ka pai: she is doing well. Using her power, she whirls the burning stick until the flames are a circle of fire. He looks up and around himself, as though he is aware for the first time that the forest is watching him.

A look on him. Puzzlement, fear. He shakes the finger, cannot flick away the trouble that bothers him. His finger is huge, bulbous. He babbles at her, the words an anguish and anger she cannot comprehend. There is power in seeing this pain, but he has caused this damage to himself. Even if she wanted, she could not remove the poison his actions have caused. He repeats the word he knows, shows his fear.

'Mākutu?'

He waves his finger; the sickness could spread. His face crumples, but his gaze is wide, staring around the forest as though it hides an enemy. It is good for him, this pain, she thinks. If he lets himself feel it, he might learn.

He lays down a tool and backs away, leaving as he came, showing he has learned nothing, for he does not even stop to consider whether he should drag a stick behind him to remove his footprints. In his weakened state he should take care to wipe away his footprints in case someone steals the mauri he leaves in the sand.

She picks up the tool he left for her. Black cloud scrapes the moon, the sharp glint of the white light on a scraggy branch. She moves to the fire and holds the strange tool to look at it. Is looking at her own face. Her breath hurts as it breaks through her chest, and her face disappears behind mist. She licks a finger and pushes it around. Round and round, sees her own eyes, her own nose. The moist cold surface is not water or skin. This is not the self who shifts in ripples in the beauty of water. Pūkana. She grimaces to ward off this evil, so that the mauri that is her essence is not snared, cannot be violated. Hurls away the weapon.

One more task, most important. She moves to one of his large footprints on the sand and plants her burning torch beside it. Holds her head above the print of his foot. Smells the rotting fish stink of him, from the stink of his bowels to the rot in his mouth. Stands astride his footprints and squats. Her thigh muscles clench firm and strong, the warm trickle slides down, sweet relief of release. Dribbles down her thighs into a warm, hissing pool. Makes his footprint disappear.

CHAPTER 19

'Fish! Fish, fish, fish.'

Young Bill — Billy Boy — it is who gives the call, high up in the watchtower on the hill. Spyglass to his eye and view trained on the horizon. Robbie's sorry-for-himself funeral march changes to a jump and a skip. Bridie thinks Billy wrong, for she cannot see any blowing, any spume, but Billy has a spyglass and she does not. He is up the hill and she is not.

All around men are running, hauling weapons from the half-made long hut, heaving the longboat over shoulders down to the shore.

A breeze that is not a breeze, as though a hand is brushing the land. Bridie gasps as for the first time she sees her, the New Zealand girl, the source of the men's fear and consternation. Here she is in the flesh, striding long wide strides through the speargrass. Strides under the cabbage tree grove, past a pile of upturned abalone shells snatching rainbows in the sun. Hands clenched, face fierce, calls the men as though they are under her orders. Hers.

Bridie leaps back lest she be scraped into the wind that is the force of this girl as she walks, shoulders squared, past her. Cuthbert scrambles after her as she heads towards Robbie and the longboat crew. Waves hungrily snapping at their ankles, the men survey her, shaking their heads. Words drift back to Bridie, lost to the sound of the waves for the most part but some parts float, drift in strange sequence. Finally, Robbie barks loud enough for Bridie to hear clearly:

swears, he does, that of course the bloody woman cannot join them. What would a New Zealand girl know about whaling, and that is not, he says, a question.

'She is not fucking wanted. Tell her, Cuthy, to fucking fuck off out of here.'

Cuthbert shakes his head, mumbles. Bridie wonders whether he is more scared of the girl or Robbie.

Robbie gives the longboat a shove, wades back with the tide. The keel scrapes sand, legs splash water as the men leap in, settle and haul oars.

'Best harpooner, Robbie,' Bill says as the whalers pull away on their oars. 'Would be on that boat today if weren't for his finger.'

Facing the ocean, hair ruffling in the wind, the New Zealand girl begins to chant. Words Bridie cannot understand spear her soul. The sound floats out and out, above the boat, above the sea, rises in mist that lifts and shifts towards the whales.

'It's a karakia — a prayer, to keep them safe,' says Cuthbert when she joins him nearer the shore.

'Charitable of her.' Bridie feels confused, betrayed.

'Not the men — she loathes them,' says the missionary. 'She prays for the whales.'

———

When she sees the girl walking towards her Bridie holds herself still. Should she step towards her as she did with the woman on the boat? The girl comes close and, her eyes fixed on Bridie's, fingers the weave of Bridie's shawl and the weft of her gown. Taken aback, and struggling not to blink, Bridie sees the shadow of sadness in her eyes as the girl steps back and sweeps herself away, taking back with her something that is like the wind. Bridie's eyes follow her, the flax linen cloak, the strength of her striding-away legs.

She rounds on Cuthbert.

'He harmed her, didn't he, like he harmed me?'

'Yes.'

Bridie shakes her head. The familiar rising fog of it, the sadness she doesn't want to feel, the sorrow she wants to push down, fly far from.

'Where does she live? What does she eat? How does she manage? Why doesn't she return to her people?'

'Shame? I don't know. We shouldn't speak of this. In matters of Robbie's business, it is dangerous to enquire and deadly to interfere.'

She knows this and feels sorry, for he still winces from his wounds, an ever-present reminder that Robbie should not be challenged.

'What is her name?'

'Manaia.'

'Man—'

'Mon as in Monday, and eye: mon-eye-ah. In their world, in the world of her people, it means . . .'

He seems to reconsider, holds his tongue.

'Go on.'

'Pardon?'

Toying, he is, turning it over, she knows not why.

'The meaning of her name?'

'Guardian,' he says.

———

It plays out, the kill. Surveying the men, she sees they are all, except perhaps Cuthbert, enthralled. Bill the elder has stepped up beside them, his eyes on the sea.

'Two whales. An adult and a baby,' he says. 'See them blobs on the water, that's the milk.'

'Like—'

'Aye, like cows.'

Like mothers, she had been about to say. Like her own. Like all mothers who fear for their young. Like the mothers of babies taken from the Parramatta factory — mothers who had no man, no protector, no one to stand up to the thieving government.

The long, sleek body of the whale mother moves towards the longboat, nearer the shore.

'Why doesn't she flee?' Bridie asks.

'She's tricking the men, trying to sacrifice herself to save her young.'

'Why not attack?' says Cuthbert. 'She could surely kill the men with one strike.'

'Happens, but rarely,' says Bill. 'Might be fact, might be myth. Creatures that don't feel anger don't seek revenge.'

One man has taken his place in the prow, seems to be shouting at the other six.

'Pull on the long white ash, boys!' shouts Bill, for the sake of his audience. 'Haul on them oars for all you're worth.'

The longboat steers carefully towards the huge hump. Balancing on the prow, the harpooner is poised against the burgeoning clouds.

'Steady, Jake,' says Bill, though Jake is out of earshot. Nudges Bridie. 'Danger coming up on them now.'

A dark shape, Jake. Harpoon held high and straight. All breaths held as he balances his weight and bends forward, almost off the boat as he sinks the harpoon into the whale's flank.

'Watch the fluke,' says Bill as the whale lunges.

Sure enough, the great tail arches, thrashes and thumps the waves. The figure that is Jake has resumed his place as they row out towards the far side of the cove.

'Ride of their lives now, you watch,' says Bill. 'The rope attached to the harpoon will unwind until it is taut. Will unfurl so fast it burns.'

Bill reels off the way of it, for he has seen this, he says, four-hundred-and-eighty-two times. Misty-eyed, he is — missing the action, he says. Bridie says nothing, choosing to keep to herself doubt that he ever chased a whale, for the cooper's job surely is to render wood, make vessels to store the oil.

She wants to question Cuthbert further about Manaia but Bill is still talking, full of fervour, sweating as he describes the action they can all observe for themselves. At the far end of the bay the whale tows the boat high and fast over steep waves as tiny men cling for their lives.

Further off, rounding the cove, they are gone. Gone far out and away towards another horizon.

'The whale will tire after a few hours and they'll tow her to shore,' Bill continues. 'That's as long as she doesn't dive and pull them down.'

Now he serves up a story of men who haunt islands and coves, all on account of them being pulled down to the bottom of the ocean — to the cemetery of whales.

'If only,' she thinks.

'Beg pardon?'

She must have said it aloud.

'If only they will return safe and sound.'

———

Almost two hours pass before the waves flush red as the longboat returns towing the mother, towing the babe. Under a dusking sky they sing as they enter the shallow water of the cove. A back-and-forth song.

The men from the shore and the men from the boat merge in their singing. Slap their hands on the sides of the whales. Come all ye tonguers, they sing. Victory in the raised voices. In the drift of words and the thump of the tune, a story about men boiling up the tongues of whales like the whales lying before her, Bridie, now.

Men thump each other, hit each other, smash hands and huzzah each other. But she is a thing apart from them. Blooded red are the waves washing over to spit on rocks, red the waves that lick the sand, blood washing up the bark and blossom, flotsam of the felled forest. Gone the green of this sea. She strides into the water herself, not heeding her skirt ballooning in the sea's drag.

Strokes the mother whale's face, sees in that one eye a whole planet, milk of the moon, last spark of the sun. Not dead yet. Loud, Bridie cries out, a long wavering song sob. A lament drawn up from sky and sea and wind. A song for her mother, for all the mothers. For all the lost children with a penchant for longitude, wandering towards Éire.

Pauses her song, for she hears a song coming back. Ghost or echo? She picks up the thread of her song and, as the salt of her tears mixes with the salt of the wind, she hears the verse of return. This song coming back to her is a song sung in the language of this water, of this land. A song sung by a guardian. Back and forth singing, one to another.

A meeting of laments.

CHAPTER 20

Inside her whare, skin drenched, Manaia is the tohorā whaea raising its fluke, plunging down, lunging up, screaming for her baby in waves of shadows and light, but the waves are not blue, the waves are rātā bright, waves and waves of blood. As she draws herself up from the agony of this dream, Manaia hears that all around, birds in the surrounding trees are calling warnings. She draws herself down into long, slow breaths. Hā ki rōtō. Hā ki waho. Was the whale an ancestor? Is it visiting her dreams to warn her?

Shuts her eyes. Listens through all her senses except sight. Someone is approaching, his boots almost soundless, trying hard not to smash the shells. He is careful, this one, not careless like Ropi. If he does not want her to hear him, he must be an enemy.

She pushes her arms out, pushes fear far from her. Crawls outside, crouches. With the strong force of her outward breath, she leaps. Pūkana. She will send him away in terror.

In front of her is the man who can speak her language. But before her now, he is a creature who is not inside himself. A man but not a man. Something has left him. Mouth gaping, body quivering. On his knees, head bowed, mumbling. She ventures closer, admonishing him. This is her space; how dare he enter without a proper invitation? Even if he is not like Ropi, he is clearly rude and ignorant, and worse he has done nothing — nothing! — to protect her since she was brought here. She tries to make out what he is saying.

'Mō tāku hē. Mō tāku hē.'

How easy it would be. Grab a heavy stick, step back. Surprise him with a great jump, then club him on his head. Utu. This would restore the balance. Or it would cause a retaliation. She wonders which voice is the wiser, which choice she should make. She takes a deep breath, wonders if it is the cold, or his fear of her that makes him tremble.

How thin he is, how wretched. So white, this one. She giggles at the bright-moon whiteness of his skin. In her giggle she is a girl again, almost forgets the pain, the sadness behind and before her. But there it was, here it is; sadness.

His eyes meet hers, and she sees in those strange eyes the colour of the great wide moana. And swirling in those eyes is shame.

'Kei te pēhea koe?'

How does he think she feels? Happy? Delighted to be forced away from her whānau, to be violated, isolated, so she can watch and wait and try to find a way to protect her people? Would he even understand if she tried to convey this to him?

'Kei te ngenge ahau,' she says. 'Kei te pōuri ahau.'

'E pukuriri ana koe?'

She is sad and she is tired. Angry? Her anger is a torrent.

'Āe.'

He rubs his face. Behind his hands he is crying like a boy, like a baby, like a man who turns into a baby when his mother scolds him.

'Mō tāku hē. Kei te pīrangi ahau ki te houhou rongo.'

He should be sorry. It is his people who have violated the hospitality of her people.

There is a shift in the air: something has been appeased. He has earned his life. She will not kill him. He may leave.

'Haere atu!' she says.

As he turns, hunched and slow, she sees that the blood on his white shirt is fresh. Strong the voices now of all those who shelter her, all the spirits of those who have gone before. Is it breaking a rule to help this

161

man who is himself weighed down by a cloud of remorse?

'Crush the roots of the karewao vine,' says the voice of a tīpuna, reaching through from the other world.

'I nei! First you must pack the wound with the heated leaves of the kopakopa,' says another kuia. To draw the poison out of him.

'E tatari,' she shouts at this man. Sees the relief as he turns towards her.

She wastes no time performing the mahi. Gently unties the strange bindings of his garments, leads him naked to sit beside her fire while she collects and cradles water in a dried nīkau palm.

Tenderly she washes the flesh that hangs like strips of harakeke. In the trench of the flesh there is blood and something else — thick pus the colour of kōwhai. She listens to the knowledge about the plants to pick, the soaking, the squeezing. She orders him to come each day, for she cannot turn away a man who is in need of help and healing.

'Kore rawa ahau, e wareware ki tēnei manaakitanga ā mate noa ahau,' he says.

He did not need to tell her, she knows already. He will never forget this kindness, not until the day he dies.

———

Powerful sunlight painting stripes. Throb and crash of waves inside his head. Inside Manaia's whare for the third time, Cuthbert's gaze traverses the rushes and panelled craftwork, wonders how she managed all this, and remembers the skills of his New Zealand wife, who, like this girl, learned the craft from the time she could crawl. He nods in admiration and she smiles. One leg is crossed beneath her on a bed of the inner fluff from seed pods. In the north so many of his compatriots boasted about their exploits with native women. Captains and sailors, whalers — even missionaries — almost always took what they thought was their due when a woman invited them inside her whare.

He knows from listening to the women that those men saw a mirror turned inwards — saw only what they wanted. He remembers the kindness, the warmth in the northern islands. Women who wanted to meet and observe, curious to see him speak and eat and drink. Invited him inside as Manaia has done, to receive hospitality and companionship, and sometimes love. Yet so many men — he cannot count them — took the hospitality as an opportunity to intrude, invade and conquer.

Cuthbert shuffles, ensures that in Manaia's house he is not in front of the sacred space that is both entrance and exit. Feels the sense, the presence, of others. The New Zealanders are never alone; the ancestors are always there. The only way communication with this young woman can flow freely is if he is respectful of her hospitality, her kindness and her authority.

When he, on one occasion, tries to do his missionary duty, tell her about Jesus and Mary and Joseph, she laughs. Looks at him and asks how any man could believe a virgin could conceive a child? Asks him over and again how this is possible. Tells him that when he tries to answer, his colour changes, as though a sun were rising inside him, spreading colour on his face. She pokes the fire, gently, turning it over like a mother turning a child who stirs in sleep. Turns eyes on him and suggests that there could not be one god if there were a mother, a child, a father and a ghost.

Her honesty and sincerity and her kindness remind him of his family in the north — the New Zealand woman he lived with. He had joined her family — her mother, her niece, her uncles — but then it had gone so very wrong. He worries the same thing could happen again.

This kind young woman's proud tattooed face could be her downfall. It is all such a conundrum. If he warns her, will he be saved? What will happen to Bridie? Will they pick and choose when it comes to utu? Could anyone ever be more trapped than he is right now, in this place at this time?

She is trapped as well, he thinks. On an island in an ocean where her people have lived for goodness knows how many centuries. Sailing, walking, working, loving, growing and being. The worst of trades are rife in the South Seas and Australia, in the Torres Strait. People of the land and water are pushed into the interior, pushed away from the coasts, pushed away from cultivated foods, pushed away from wild foods, while white men rape, pillage, enslave and massacre, invoking God as they do so.

He rubs his hand across his face but he cannot wipe away the frustration that what was done in Scotland and Ireland is being replicated here, and he is trapped in that savagery.

———

Looking at Manaia when he wakes, Cuthbert does at last feel rested. The pain that had kept him awake all the nights before has eased, has been almost completely erased since he started visiting Manaia. The girl is as good as any surgeon he has come across. Robbie had flouted maritime rules by not having a surgeon on his ship. Surgeons are apt to record observations, make reports.

He knows what he should do, knows what is right; perhaps that is why he was tempted to come here in the first place. Looking at this woman, this young woman separated from those she loves, still wearing the bruises of the man who violated her, he knows that even if it costs him his life, he must find courage.

Trembling all over he is, trembling so much it hurts. His face is wet, body contorted.

Ka pai, she tells him. It will be all right. But he is playing the wrong part in this drama. Cast among the villains.

———

Standing on the foreshore his gaze is away. Tranquillity is what he seeks from the scene. Scribbles on the water. A pleasant moment of quietude. But Bill the older scrambles to join him, munching the air with his mouth, planting his large boots right beside Cuthbert's own. Tells him they've spotted a seal colony on the rocks around the corner. Five whales sighted yesterday, three caught this day — not bad. Better than the day prior, but that was the first day, mind.

His talk turns to the long hut, which is still open and makeshift one end, but for the most part it is, well, a fine-looking sight. Cuthbert barely listens as the man babbles about the hearth pit, the mats on the floor and walls, shelves holding barrels of rum, gin and watered-down grog. Cabinet full of pistols. Locked, the cabinet, mind.

Still rambling, Bill. Keeps calling Cuthbert sir, tells him that he, sir, should join them for bowsing this very night.

'Oy, did the captain tell you he wants his finger hacked? Will you perform the job?'

'Can't think of anything worse,' Cuthbert says.

Allows himself, fleetingly, to consider the pleasure. Perhaps he could hack off more than the finger, but this is not what he wants to become. He does not want to kill. Not even Robbie. He has been resisting this shape for so long, the shape of the killer he is being urged to become, suffering the ways of men, not wanting to join but unable to stop it. Any of it.

'Settlers we are, not yet settled,' Bill muses, picking up his trail of thought. 'Off-cuts from another world.'

Cuthbert releases his breath, and in the long sigh feels all the sadness in his soul.

———

It is a sight on the horizon that finally stops the cooper yarning. A ship unlike any other, slinking into the cove. The sky complies, as if it senses danger, thunderous clouds rising behind the ship, a stage set for a theatre of horror.

'That ship's been pirated.'

'Are you certain?' asks Cuthbert.

Bill tends to be the expert on everything, but surely he's conjuring a fantasy.

'Aye, no sign of a flag,' says Bill, jolliness vanquished. 'That doesn't bode well.'

He has taken a spyglass from his frockcoat. Raises it to his eye. Proceeds to explain, before the missionary can frame a question.

'Her name's scrubbed out. Been replaced with another. It's rough painted, the sign, written most like by one of her crew who can write.'

They can't fool Bill with their new name, *Friends of America*. Nope, no fool him.

'Ah, she's striking the sail. Good. Paying us homage. Saluting a superior force. A sign they'll cause us no trouble. Must be the captain's coves come from their business in the north. Heads they'll be bringing. Nasty business if you ask me, but please, sir, do not ask.'

Up and down the beach, bells are ringing. The bell ringers, Tom and young Bill, leap and skip beside Robbie.

'Proceed with care,' Robbie says. 'That's the order. For here they come — the headers.'

Studying him, Cuthbert sees the man who stamped coin in the Black Lion Yard in London and pressed men in The Rocks of Sydney town, the look of a hard man looking out for hard fellows and something else. This is a man who can wear a mask, rein in his madness for a while. But the tell-tale sparks are in Robbie's eyes. Now the worst of his coves have arrived, Cuthbert thinks, the wildfire will be released.

CHAPTER 21

Bridie runs after the bell ringers to welcome the pirates. Grasping her shawl, boots scattering stones. Eagerly excited and excitedly fearful, she watches the macabre spectacle of the pirates' arrival. The back and forth of the longboat as it unloads a mysterious cargo.

'How did they seize the ship?' she asks.

'You don't want to know, miss,' says Bill the older.

But she does.

'Who had it before?'

'She's smallish, so a small crew, I'd say. Mix like ours, but smaller most like.'

She wants to ask if there would have been women and children aboard, stolen people, but Bill might embroider and report what she says. Safer to keep her fears to herself.

'To invent a future you have to invent a past,' says Bill. 'Give the authorities a story, even if they know in truth that it's a story. Robbie will conjure a tale 'bout natives killing the crew. The pirates will be heroes who escaped with their lives. Everyone wants to read about the savage deeds of the cannibals.'

'But won't people find out?'

'Not if there's no survivors they won't. And not if any left alive are too afeared to tell. I've suffered from Robbie's misdeeds myself.'

'So have I,' says Cuthbert.

'Me too,' says Bridie.

She had not imagined their lives could get worse in this hellhole, but it seems they just have. The beach is already a cemetery, whale bones rise like church rafters. Bodies that housed life are skeletons strewn against the rising tide. Sky showing through the bones. Black the sky, rarely a glint of light, mostly dark scraps of cloud and the smoke that rises seems to hold it, the deaths, the stink of all the rot.

Barnacle-caked, skin-peeled thick slabs of meat carted — the stink, the stink, the stink in the smoke and the black oil in her face and clothes and hair. The bay that once held beauty is a ramshackle row of makeshift hovels made up of broken spars, ponga logs, canvas and skin roofs swollen, slumped, heavy with rain, heaving a little in the wind.

Somewhere over that hill and down the valley and up the next hill and over, Cuthbert has told her, is Manaia's village. Surely it is a better place than this, and surely the people there will come and seek revenge, if Robbie and his men don't kill them first. She feels herself like a fox in a trap surrounded by hounds, not knowing where or how to run.

Even her brother Tom is not the Tom he was in Sydney, and this new ship has rolled in because it was ordained by Robbie. The pirates are his crew, to be made welcome. Once stories of pirates had enthralled her, but back then she had been able to keep them at bay, confined to fearful nightmares. Now they are here, in the bay, the arrow on the compass has shifted.

———

Down on the shore all the men gather. The pirates, the tonguers, the headers, the sailors, the sealers. Bridie must be lying low. Cuthbert does not blame her; would be doing so himself if Robbie had not come demanding he return, declaring that if the men did not kill creatures — in this case rats — they would kill one another.

As the fire strikes, the twigs seem to be fingers stretching for mercy. Flames grow rapidly from underneath, casting red shivering lights on stubbled and pocked faces. In the last span of the early winter sun the bets have been laid, laid on whose rats will flee farthest, be the slowest or the brightest. Cuthbert figures the men will be lucky to pay off their gambling debts by the end of the season. Their grumbles have the sound of bulls in the dust bowl of a butcher's back yard. Groggy, slewed, lushed.

Rats are plucked from a line of cages, struggling as they are held and oiled. Robbie offers him one. He shakes his head but cannot shake the look in the creature's eyes on him. That accusing glare at the spectator watching in sickening wonder. He watches as Robbie pushes at the straggly line, one man back and another forward until the line is even. Now he orders each man to strike his tinder and set light to the rats' whiskers. Cuthbert wants to protest, as he did when he was a boy among a crowd of bull-baiters. Feels himself helpless now as he was helpless then. Fire spreads from whiskers to fur as the rats try to outrun the flames.

Whoops and hollers ignite the air as the leaping men chase the rats up the shore, as the running creatures run to cinders. The fights, the arguments recede as he returns to his tent, hoping his absence won't be noticed. He would rather cower here with hunger gnawing his belly than drown himself in liquor to absorb the horror.

The crunch of boots on shells. Robbie pulling back the tent flap.

'Tonight, my honourable sky pilot, you are invited to a ceremony culminating in an execution.'

'Who do you plan to kill?'

His own heart pound-pound-pounding.

Robbie laughs, laughs till he chokes.

'Don't look so stricken, but you must put more into this. Prove yourself. You know how to deceive the natives, you learned from the best. Find that titter and interrogate her. You must learn where they store those ruddy heads.'

Contorts his face, Cuthbert, trying to feign willingness over disgust.

'But be wary, Mr Sky Pilot. The natives are good for a season but you need a distinction, a fence — what do you call it in Ireland? A pale. Go beyond it, spend too much time with them and, well, it all ended badly for you last time.'

Cuthbert flinches. Blamed, he was, for the trouble Robbie drummed up in the north, as no doubt he will be again. Has an image of himself running from the people who had cared for him, from the wife who had nurtured him, running to be rescued by the man before him.

'Aye, mark my words, Cuthy, if you aren't wary, if you get too cosy with them, you will find yourself being chased down the beach, only this time you will have whirly twirly carvings, bloody tattoos for your complexion.'

Laughs at this, does Robbie. Laughs, chokes again.

————

The rat-burning race is followed by dinner at the long bench in the long hut. Fish stew, rum and gin. Honoured guests, the pirates, take pride of place. Congenial Robbie blows sentimental with them over old times. Cuthbert shifts beside him on the bench in the long hut as he tries to drink himself under the bench, drown out the din and racket. The captain's voice drones like a mosquito in his ear. Actually deeper than a mosquito — less tuneful but mellifluous. If Robbie found God, became a preacher, he would be sure to find a flock to follow him. The man is master of his own universe on the deck of a ship or in a house built on sand. Perhaps this would be a good time to bring up the parable about building one's house on rock. But then, Cuthbert considers, perhaps not.

'Fairhaven is such a pleasant landed-gentry name,' Robbie is saying. 'Fair weather. Safe abode. Imagine it, Cuthy: my estate will overlook a fine town, a grand port.'

He gestures around the long hut with his rotten stinking finger.

'A fine ocean view, a four-chimney house. Served by my servants by day and by my lady wife at night.'

In the imaginative stimulation stirred by liquor, Cuthbert sees it quite clearly.

'I do see you, sir, all gentry attired. Robert Fitch standing before a bench like this, but it will be laid with china and silver.'

'My sons will farm green pastures, fish blue waters and become my heirs.'

Gulps, Robbie does, casts a teary, sentimental eye at Cuthbert.

'And you shall have your mission, Cuthy, though I sometimes wonder whether your faith has forsaken you.'

'Thank you,' Cuthbert mumbles.

'Indeed. But what other master have you? The old gods have buggered off. The native gods are entertainment but are monsters, don't you reckon?'

'New Zealanders see the spirit of life in everything,' Cuthbert contributes.

To this, Robbie stands. Roars.

'To the spirit of life. May it endure.'

Then he is off, telling the men that he needs to change his attire for the execution.

'You stay put, Cuthy. Don't move a fucking muscle.'

———

Flumadiddle, that's what he calls it, the gowns spilling from the chest. Pushes the chest into the house that is made of wood and skin and canvas. Takes up almost the whole of the house, the size of it. Tells her to stroke the garments. Finest quality. But the sheen in the gold and green are reminders of the night in the Shipwright's Compass, of the man who did not deserve the title of lord or gentleman, the man who violated her. Bile rising.

'Plenty of dimbers would be all over me for these,' he declares.

Turns out he wants her to play the lady for new mates and old, the pirates.

As they make their grand entrance, she the lady, he the lord, she holds his arm and longs to run. Fly free from men who clap and whistle, who thump the table. Robbie in his element, in his long red cape and high white wig, holding high the gavel.

In another place and time she would have cherished the garland of lace around her neck. The flowing field that flows from herself. The wearing of the green.

She scans the faces under the swinging cages of lighted candles. Hopes upon hope to find an appealing fellow — the smuggler, the rebel, the pirate who purges the bad to raise up the poor. Such a man is not at this bench.

A lump, hard-boiled tears in her throat. Hold back the lump. She will not release her sorrow or her longing. Robbie is pushing her, furiously whispering at her to use her toff voice. Gazes around again to be sure — yes, all these men, younger and older, are as devious and dangerous as Robbie Fitch. Men no better — possibly worse — than the crew of the ship that brought them here.

'Here, Robbie — where's these native titters you promised us?'

Robbie laughs.

'Remember how he promised us titters galore,' grumbles Jake, nudging Mallet.

'You will all be well rewarded at the end of the season,' says Robbie, 'but this is a hunting season. And what are we? We are hunters. We hunt for pelts, oil, heads.'

'And titters!' calls Jake.

'No titters yet. The festive season begins at the end of the hunting season.'

'Yet you got yourself a seasonwife,' says Jake.

'This is what I'm fucking telling you. Nothing but trouble that

New Zealand girl — worse than this Irish wench. A fly-by-nighter, a witch. A mad bitch.'

Seeming angered by the turn of the conversation, he storms outside.

'That blubber finger makes his foul temper more bloody foul,' says Bill.

Bridie is about to take her leave when he is back, making a great show of buttoning his pants with one hand.

'Listen to the bench,' he says, rapping the gavel.

Plays the part of the judge sentencing his finger to an execution. His crew form a parade of men begging to play the executioner's role.

Under Robbie's orders each must step forward to give an account of his most sinful deed, then the next man takes his turn. After careful consideration Robbie throws back his tankard, sloshing arrack over the long bench. Rears up with blasts of swearing pain and painful roaring laughter.

'Now who shall it be, my coves? Musgrove who killed a whore? Bill's son Bill who shot his dog? Cox who knocked the senses out of his mother? Gibson who hit a guard? Or Tom who's only killed a baby seal?'

Watching his sweating face, listening to his rancid ranting, Cuthbert regrets his own presence. Rather be cold and companionless, listening to the strange, lonely calls of the forest than spend the night in crazed festive antics.

Robbie lays his hammer down, hammers his tankard instead. Declares that the votes are cast.

'Tom who's only killed a seal,' he declares.

Watching the boy cheer, Cuthbert wonders whether Tom remembers that softness once dwelt in him, not so long past. The boy who was his mother's child seems to have disappeared.

A movement in the corner at the makeshift end of the long room. The missionary sees Bridie jump at the hook where hangs an apron. She drags the apron down from the beam, shakes it, and the hook falls.

'What the fuck are you about, woman?' Robbie barks.

Wonders himself, Cuthbert does. The girl is tying the apron over her green gown as Robbie hands the axe to Tom.

'I will have the honour of performing this duty,' she says, gliding forward, her tone queenly.

'Would you rob me of it, brother?'

Cuthbert watches Tom, who looks swiftly at Robbie. The older man raises an eyebrow. Over to you, boy, the eyebrow says.

'It's man's work,' says Tom.

'And women's work is giving life to men. My job here will yield less blood than when I pulled you from our ma.'

Laughter, raucous. This will please Robbie, Cuthbert thinks — that his mistress can entertain. But Robbie shakes his head, his hair splatters sweat, his beard splatters ale. He nods his head, shakes again, then nods slow. Smiles his most unpleasant smile. Cuthbert wonders whether he should intervene, decides best not.

'Aye, thy queen, thy executioner.'

Bridie grabs his wrist, holds the swollen black forefinger flat on the bench.

'Hold him, Tom, and press. No — harder. Press down hard as if you're in a wrestling match.'

As she raises the heavy wooden axe handle Cuthbert sees the wild white of her rolling eyes. Like a horse that breaks free from being shoed, eyes searching so far back in its head, hoping to find freedom. The axe hovers, seeks a mark.

Cuthbert feels the intake of his own breath joining the intake of others. Watches her eyes fix on target. Thwack, the crack of bone and there it lies, one part of Robbie's body separated from the rest. The long hut fills with a roar of huzzahs. What next, Cuthbert wonders as he retrieves his tankard from a pool of blood. Robbie motions to Bridie with his pulpy stump.

'Gimme your belly-cheat.'

Cuthbert watches Bridie make sense of the cant by passing Robbie the blood-splattered apron. Robbie's eyes are on him, he takes a manly swig and finds the taste sour, putrid. Holds the mouthful, forced to swallow but Robbie is still watching and Cuthbert has not mastered the manly art of spitting.

Bridie has taken charge of mopping up the blood. Brings out of her skirt a kerchief, lace at the edge. Scoops Robbie's finger, folds the kerchief over tender, as though she is swaddling a baby.

Wincing agony, mincing in manner. Robbie touches his left shoulder, his right, draws his hand to his heart: mockery of the cross over the shrouded lump of flesh.

'You should give us a prayer, Mr Sky Pilot,' he says. 'Bless the dead.'

'Requiem for a finger?' Cuthbert responds.

Feels the thrill in himself of making the men laugh. What Robbie does not see, what the others do not see, what Cuthbert *does* see is that during this revelry, Bridie takes that shrouded lump, slides it inside her skirt. He alone notices this surreptitious action. No one else sees as she leaves the company of men, out through the makeshift end of the long hut, withdrawing under the moon's light to canvas the solitude of stars.

CHAPTER 22

As Bridie leaves the long hut, Robbie the businessman returns, talks about a tally of heads, talks about quality. Calculates profits. Waves his stumpy finger and orders the boys to open a chest. Cuthbert wants to protest but to do so is to say goodbye to life. Robbie picks up a head. Waves this trophy.

Shaky, feeling the world turn, Cuthbert seizes a jug of ale and vomits into it. Parts of himself float inside the jug.

'More flashes of lightning!' Robbie says to him. 'That will harden your gut. Problem is you don't glug enough.'

He dangles a head by the hair. Talks to it, mocking.

'Evening, sir, meet your host, Mr Sky Pilot.'

He tosses the head at him. Appalled, Cuthbert leaps, catches the head, turns the face away, catching a glimpse of an expression horrified at death. He hurriedly takes it back to Robbie, then leaves, yawning, feigning tiredness, ignoring the men laughing at his departing back.

——

Curled into himself, knees to chin, on the cold sand, under the great wide heavens so empty and dark, Cuthbert decides he needs to change tack. Be clear and forceful — even, if necessary, unpleasant. He must warn Manaia so she may save her people. Unwilling he may have been and forced he was, but he cannot stand by and pretend he is innocent in this carnage. He can no longer deny the truth of this game he has joined.

Blind without candle or lantern, he stumbles to his makeshift abode. Strikes the tinder, sets a candle in the lantern. Kneels on shells and stones to pray and finds no answer, not in a god of war or a prince of peace. He only knows that he must warn the girl who has healed him.

———

He takes the gifts he had prepared, his koha: a patch box containing a flint, a fire starter, charcloth, sulphur-tipped splint and touch paper. A bag containing a knife, a looking glass. Packs them up and hurries towards her whare.

She greets him by the fire and they crouch together.

'Nā te aha koe i te tōmuri ai?' she asks.

Why is he late? He looks into her eyes, down her face to the moko on her lips and below. The swirl of the curve of the frond.

'Mō taku hē,' he says.

Such a well-worn phrase it has become, but he is sorry, he truly is. For the past, the present and the future he wants to prevent.

She points at a parcel of her own on a rock, a steaming parcel of kelp. Unwrapping the leaves, he smells the sweet fresh meat of crayfish.

'E kai!'

Afterward, using the phrases he has practised, he starts by telling her that she must have seen by now that they — the tauiwi, Robbie and his men — are plunderers and will not stop. They will take and sell everything.

Takes him by surprise, she does, when she shifts the conversation, like the wind turning from a storm. Asks about his seasons. When do the tauiwi rest, share, live on their harvest?

'Winter,' he says, thinking of all but whalers.

She tries to sound the word, misses the 'n' and laughs. Asks when this season will come.

He tries to draw a picture of their villages, the huge villages called cities, bigger than she can imagine. These cities want light, he tells her, and for that they need the oil from hundreds — thousands — of whales. Not for a family or a village but vast cities. He tells her about the huge markets for food. So much food is needed. The lords and ladies, the aristocrats, the rangatira of England, always want more light, more food. No amount is ever enough for them.

'Tēnei te ao o ngā tauiwi,' he says.

Then he tries to explain the trade in killing people with fine tattoos to sell their heads for ornaments. She laughs, and he wonders whether she cannot even conceive of such evil.

When she asks whether they take the heads of their own, he thinks of Bunhill Fields in London, Brickfields in Sydney. Any shallow graves will be visited by grave robbers who sell to the highest bidder. Even in death the poor are fair game. He thinks of Bridie's mother and all the others whose hair and bodies are desecrated. It is easy to fall into Hell and he realises he needs to climb back out.

He has no answer when she asks how the dead who have been so ill-treated will find their path to the afterlife. The silence is so long he almost forgets how to return from it.

A jeer from down on the beach, laughter, sound of something smashing. He shakes his head to bring himself back to the heart of the matter. There is no time to waste. He has to make her understand that her powers will not stretch to overpower all the bad men. He has to make her leave. As though she hears his thoughts, Manaia begins to shake.

'Kei te āngia haeretia e te tauiwi?'

'Āe,' he tells her, for only the truth will do, and the truth is that she and her people are being forced out.

Robbie and the other evil men in the crew, the new men, the sea beggars, chopping heads, trading them so they can be owned and admired by people far away. He tries to explain that those faraway people who buy heads do not work hard as the New Zealanders or think as deeply about the winds that move the constellations, cannot comprehend the deep world of Te Whānau Mārama, the family of light. They do not listen to the wairua. Realises suddenly, that he is coming close to trying to make her pity the foreigners. But they are not to be pitied. Not at all.

He feels his anger at his own people rising as he tells her that men like Robbie, and the men they work for, cannot imagine the lives of people who have earned the artistry of the moko. Such men will never understand the way the tattoos connect the people to the mountains, the rivers, the land and the ancestors.

She tells him that she is finding it hard to hear him because she is hearing another voice. She pauses, tells him she thinks it is the voice of the mother who birthed him. He stares at her in astonishment over the fire. Could his mother's spirit have found him across the oceans, all the way out here? Surely not. A log cracks in the fire, startling him.

'He aha te kōrero tōku whaea?' he asks.

She shakes her head. Kāore. She will not tell him what his mother is saying; he needs to ask her himself.

CHAPTER 23

Bridie wakes in the night. Through the skins and canvas of the tent comes a shiver of wind. On that wind, low and lonesome, a sad familiar call. Men who reckon that the owl calls for more pork are wrong. This bird calls for her. Poor fool, it says. Poor fool.

Outside on the beach she sees a lantern. Weaving precariously, veering beside the foam of the roaring ocean. Not much of a missionary now, Cuthbert, for he has proven himself partial to liquor. She has seen him before under the straggling light of his lantern. The tankard in his hand, the glazed look in his eyes, as he strives to be a man among men, sing a bawdy song, shout and curse. A man who pays no heed to the Bible, leaves it on his bed roll.

Poor fool, the owl calls. Poor fool.

Fear she feels now, fear of the coming and going. Like a tree whose trunk is scratched, she is etched by fear all the way down to her roots. Dread consumes her while from the long hut come laughter, stamping, whistling, singing and banging as the men continue in their revelry.

The raucous noise and the full luminous moon cause sleep to evade her. The only dreams she has are wakeful, stirring a stew of fear in the pit of herself. Morning arrives in tired waves, the sun labouring hard in the cold distance. Blood pouring towards herself, as Bridie watches. Blood pouring from the wedge, the edge, the horizon.

She holds his severed forefinger, still wrapped in her kerchief. The stink of rot merges with the black-veil stench of festering whale carcasses and boiling blubber. Black bile permeates the shore. Thick the grime that sticks in her eyes and hair, and the suffocating stink seeps into her skin so that she too smells of whale death. It chokes her, caused her in her first week here to vomit so much she feared she was with child.

Scanning the workers, she finds no sign of Robbie. Up the hill in the watchtower watching for whales, little Bill. She waves, he waves. At the edge of the forest men are dots bent over logs. Turns her gaze down and along the shore. Stubbled by carcasses, this shore. Tom cleaning the longboat. Bill in pause from arching planks. A raucous refrain from the direction of a whale. Robbie's coves young and old run back and forth in the creature's mouth. Bill abandons his craftsmanship to join the merriment, dance a jig. This would displease Robbie, who daily demands more puncheons made to store the oil. But of Robbie, she can find no sign.

She walks through scrub to the cluster of cabbage trees beside the open shed. Inside the shed a cauldron is perched over a fire, and over the cauldron stands the man who won't be moved from his task — or not lightly. Mallet prods his long-pitched iron, pokes boiling chunks of whale meat. The boiling oil drifts in a black mist.

Walking graceful as a widow in mourning, Bridie shades with her hand the tell-tale plan in her stinging eyes.

'Robbie wants you down at the long hut.'

This said to Mallet in her toffiest voice.

'What the fuck — why?'

'Don't rightly know. A net, or something.'

Sensible to stand watching him leave, and sure enough, before he reaches the long hut Mallet turns, scowls his rotten scowl. She waves, meets the grimace with the smile of a queen. Takes herself off a few steps. Turns to find him gone. Waits some more.

When she is sure, she hurries back. Unwraps the fat lump of Robbie's rotted flesh. Says a spell.

'The Devil speed you to Hell. May what you've done be done to you.'

Stands well enough back to avoid the burning splatter, throws the blob into the cauldron. Glow of satisfaction as it plops. Spreads to every part of her, the glow. Walks off, satisfied that this piece of Robbie is being gobbled by the whale's oil.

———

Watching Bridie drop the finger into the boiling cauldron is Manaia. So the kōhine has brought the curse to fruition. She feels drawn to find out how similar they are, this tauiwi girl and herself, and how different. Feels drawn in the way that all things search and reach for union.

She wonders if the girl is ignorant like the man who visits her for healing, or whether she knows that all things come from Te Kore, the space where all life is stirred. In the space that separates Papatūānuku, the earth, and Ranginui, the sky, are so many beings, related and searching for one another. The whānau. Welling up in her now, the aroha for all beings. She wonders whether she can teach this girl the rules, show her they must not be broken.

———

Bridie is on her way to haul water when she sees Manaia for the first time since the whale cull. Robbie has taken to calling her 'that witch'. Slightly nervous, but mostly curious, she follows when the girl indicates that she must.

Clambers up the steep part of the bank, where crusted sand becomes soil, then sludge of mud, into the valley of flax. Green and gold-edged blades catch the silvered light. Breathes hard inside herself the scent from the watery soil of the swamp and the deeper forever smell of oily darkness. Stench of a deep well where monsters sleep. A winter sun shrinks behind branches; the sky looks sad.

Tugs at her feet, the swamp, makes a hard sucking sound. She shivers with the thrill of fear. Surely the monster in this swamp would not want her, would search for better prey. Imagines that long green dragon flying up and swooping down, snapping at Robbie, throwing him up in the air. Grins as she imagines Robbie's squirming body, twisted face, mouth agape.

On a higher, drier patch Bridie grasps the black withered hand of a flax pod. Steadies her, the pod, as she unbuttons her boots. Wet they are, and weighing her down. Manaia comes forward, picks them up. Bridie tries a smile, says her own name with a hand to her chest. Would like to say there is a goddess in her name, a goddess men tried to erase. Succeeds only in opening her mouth and gawping at the New Zealander who has already turned back to the path.

Cold brushes across flax, like a great hand searching for something lost in the land. Black seed pods stretch cupped hands to the sky. Brown marsh blushes grey. A blue swamp hen, head startled up, feathers blue, beak red. Wings of it heavy, flapping slowly, body lifting for such a short spell. Bridie feels in it the frustration at not flying higher, lighter and further.

Bridie walks behind Manaia, talks to the retreating back about Robbie, about how bad he's been all her life, claiming he is a protector when he was not, ever. About him stealing the hair off her mother's dead head, about how she knows Manaia must have been stolen by him too for who would volunteer to be with that old brute? Talks about the New Zealanders in Sydney, the man she met in the storehouse on George Street, his good looks bursting at the seams. She prattles, even though she knows the girl ahead can understand little if any of what she is saying.

Ahead, Manaia strides alongside the stream that curves and widens into a river. Water flows faster, tumbles white over brown and down. Stones turned black by the wet water slap and stretch at banks and beaches.

Manaia halts. A tree fallen across one bank to the other is a bridge. A bridge she runs across, head high. Spins a dance of sorts at the far end, crouches slightly, legs spread wide. Cups her hands, calls loudly over the water, words Bridie comprehends because the missionary has taught her this much. Haere mai! Come, join me!

The log is long and Manaia seems so far off, the drop so horribly deep, the water so fast. She could turn back, leave, return. In not crossing the bridge, in refusing to shift herself from one place to another she might avoid smashing her head on a rock and gasping her last breath in gurgling, gargling water.

Hesitates and then, eyes on the deep green of the high trees, feeling their whispering courage, starts to run along the log. One foot in front of the other. Barefoot thrill courses up from the wet moss skin of the old mouldering tree.

At the other end Manaia grins, dangles the boots, an offer. Bridie forsakes them; her bare soles need to keep sipping the soil. Striding up and into the forest, she sees the fold of tree over tree. Each shrugs a different cloak, splays and sprawls strengths and weaknesses. Long, narrow, thick, wide, palm-leaved, falling, standing, bowing, praying. Forest smells of sun-dusted insects; rain-washed leaves.

Roots from trunks and vines from branches cross and coil like snakes frantically copulating. Quick, now, they say, while we have our chance.

Feels, Bridie does, the spirit of herself wakening. A song under her, an ancient walking song, a cold dark path song, a wending home to the hearth song. Always she has felt it, the unstoppable surge of it, the urge to wander to places secret, hidden from merchants and traders and hunters and missionary men, from all the struggling women and children, from all the toffs and pretenders and all the matters of business. Does Manaia sense this in her? That she is drawn to explore further, to venture inside wilderness?

She is a traveller, a wanderer. Wandering — the sound of the word, the ring of it. A crime in Sydney, wandering. It was on cause of this that she was taken. Because she straddled the sill and made the jump, ran with other running children who embraced the light, who roamed at night. Still has the urge to belong to a tribe of running girls. Would run back to those days if she could. Hammer her fists against the hard, closed minds of the so-called gentlemen, the men who are not gentle. Sew shut the mouths of ladies who scoured the skin, who raised the rod and taught her to use it on children younger than herself. Rebel against those cruel people of the narrow religion, of the raised rod and stolen sod.

She stops of a sudden, picks herself up and plops herself back in this Middle Island, for Manaia has halted in front of her, turns, opening her mouth. Makes no noise but mimes gabble, mute gabble, moving her mouth, contorting. Is this performance in imitation of Bridie herself? Has she been gabbling? Did her singing turn to talking aloud, which might, if you consider, be annoying to one who cannot understand the language?

Decides it must be so, hears now the quiet that is not quiet. Songs of the forest are so much more pleasant than the sound of her prattling, singing self. Songs of the stream trying to be a river and some other sound, trill of forest birds above the boulder babbling gush of the stream.

Manaia is reaching for her hand, is clasping her fingers in a tight grip, squeezing her to listen to another deeper sound. Hears the sound of something dragging. Sees solid bodies, thick fur on them. Silver-black. She has been assured that there are no wolves in New Zealand. Deer? Too small, and she has been told there are no deer either. Shadows made solid, these creatures who lie on the trail behind, the trail ahead.

Manaia shifts a hand to Bridie's shoulder. Do not move; hold back. One of the creatures, so very near, is now under the large trunk that stands directly beside them. Large, deep-as-night eyes. They wait until the creature moves. Pulls and slides. A rock shifting shape. In this strange spell of nature she sees that creatures of the sea are become creatures of the forest. Seals. Moving as part of this party of seals, she follows Manaia up a steep wall of rock. Breath drawing strength from the whirl and clamour of water on stones, eyes search for a resting place as the stream searches for a lake.

At last they stand on a platform of rock so large they can feel the wind of the water where the stream sheers off rocks and splashes into a large hole, pouring into and filling a lake. Water roars like a mountain hammering its chest.

Hands clasped, they leap. Hands clasped, they fall. Silver water under grey sky, sparkles of laughter as their heads break bubbles. Aching with cold, Bridie watches Manaia slide a leaf across the waves to the nose of a baby seal. Overflowing happiness, Bridie shouts back at the shouting waterfall, feels the freedom of shouting as though she is shouting them all down. Shouting down the bad Englishmen who put her and her mother on a ship out of Éire, shouting down the bad men at the orphanage.

Shouts so loud she shatters the mirror of herself, back in the Shipwright's Compass in Sydney. The mirror that beheld her painted face, that false face, full of pain.

Smashes that mirror to smithereens.

CHAPTER 24

On the beach two mornings later Bridie toys with a piece of charred wood. As she waits, hoping to see Manaia, she thinks of the copper-coloured children at the Parramatta orphanage who would have wasted no time in using this to mark drawings on scraps of peeled bark. She, Bridie, a pupil teacher, had taught them how to draw a circle, a head, scratching with their soft slate pencils on hard slate. Pointed to her face. Put in two dots. A line for her nose. Mouth one line. The children nodded, would draw in her way to please her.

When they scratched, their story appeared: men in coats with sticks protruding from their arms, sticks spurting at men whose faces, arms and legs were scratched to black. Not only men. Round circles and dots for breasts. Women. Tiny people, children. Drops of life water — blood — dropping from their sides, heads popping. A mother, a babe, mouths open, and inside the open mouths, scratch, scratch, a black cave of emptiness, life vanished.

Another picture, near-perfect depiction of men sawing at heads, two men and a woman. Heads lying beside headless bodies. She had gazed at the pupils she was supposed to be teaching, who were teaching her. Felt herself in their eyes, the girl who hit them for fidgeting.

When she showed Cuthbert the drawings, certain proof of a massacre, he stared, shook his head, pushed chin to chest, muttered that it was a sorry business. Innocent people killed to teach others a lesson — despicable thing, the killing of men who weren't culpable for any wrongdoing, the murder of women, children. He sympathised, of course he did, and so of course should she. But Samuel Marsden was not known as the flogging parson for nothing, and Marsden it was who founded the orphanage. The killings were a warning, ordered by the governor of New South Wales, governor of everything, Macquarie. The severed heads had been paid for — a barrel of rum and a shilling for each. So Cuthbert had heard, in the places where men talk, where the clergy listen.

Pulling herself back to the winter morning, to the cold beach of here and now, a little tired of waiting for Manaia, Bridie drops to a crouch. Curls one leg under the other, a comfortable way of seating herself on the sand, sure to hide her privates from the roving eyes of men.

What of the New Zealanders here in the Middle Island or the North or the other islands, she wonders — what stories will they draw, what stories will be erased? She tosses the charred lump of wood in her hand. Scrapes it against a rock. Draws her own map on this rock. Scratches to mark out the beaver of Robbie's hat, makes it a creature of the river. Scratches seals playing in a lake. Two large dots bring to life the whales, place them at play in the ocean. A large dot for the turtle, happy on its South Sea island, no longer a comb. In the scratches, the marks, the web of this life, Bridie suspends a dot for Manaia, another for herself.

She is coming now, Manaia, lengthening her stride, hair blown back by sand-salted wind. Accepts the gift of the rock. Holds it to her chest as tears well. Now she digs into the thick woven belt at her waist and passes to Bridie a long green stone. Familiar to Bridie, the look of it, but she can scarce recall that other time, that other place. Manaia points to a tear sliding down her own cheek, then to the specks on the green stone.

'Roimata,' she says.

'Roimata. Tears?'

Bridie understands that a stone could cry, for crying she is herself. Surprised at how hard it is to meet love.

The tiny biting flies are dense, the flax pods blacker, sky damp, swamp thick and dank: all the stinks are harsh. Clouds are poised for a fight. Sinister, Bridie would call it if she could make herself understood. She follows Manaia over the familiar route, but something has changed. Manaia notices, points at twigs broken, grasses parted, the tread of a large boot in the mud.

When they reach the fallen log a sense of doom pervades. Ahead of them, lying back with a satisfied smile on his bloated face, is Mallet. He of the Jonah conspiracy, one of the troublemakers who wanted to dump Cuthbert and Bridie at sea. Head in the shadows, Mallet is blocking the path. His shirt is open, coarse hairs fanning from his chest into a dark path to under his belly button; wending in a revolting line down to his trousers. Resting himself on a nest of ferns, legs crossed casual like, blocking the log, the bridge, at its far end.

Pipe smoke pours out of his mouth as he shifts his jaw to juggle the pipe. When he sees them his voice is inaudible, for the wide stream is trying to be a river, its song a sound he needs to rise against. Takes the pipe right out of his mouth.

'What do we have here, little Miss Madam?'

Fixed, he is, on Bridie.

'Running away with the seasonwife? I hear she's a better fuck than you. I've heard she—'

'Shut up. None of that is your business.'

Pretends, she does, that his words cannot rattle her, that she does not wonder whether there is truth to his words. Remembers the blubber finger, the curse on Robbie. Reminds herself of this.

'The two little wives sneaking off,' Mallet continues. 'I reckon he would be greatly interested.'

'You're skiving off yourself. What would the captain say to that?'

Has tried it on, her toff's tone.

'I won't be going no further. Not if you give me a little peck here.'

Plants a finger, taps the bulb of his left cheek.

'Or on second thoughts . . .' Cruel smile, crooked teeth, finger pointing to the black path curling towards his groin.

'You're mad!' she shouts.

He seems to assess, face shifting clouds.

'Joking, my lovely. Just Mallet playing his little game.'

Testing, more like, she thinks.

'What will you give to keep my gob shut?'

Bridie turns to Manaia, who says something she cannot understand. The New Zealand girl stomps once, twice. Strides across the log, leaps over this man's legs, whirls around, strong flash of her thighs. So fast she is, so strong. Bridie feels the pride of her like a great rushing wind that shakes them both.

Opens her mouth wide, does Manaia. Widens her eyes, eyes that pierce arrows into the man at her feet. Seems, as her eyes roll, her lids flutter, to see something that is unseen. Jerks her head as though she hears a scream, as though the sound comes from behind and around, not from her. Rolls her head back and around. Stomp of her feet. Hard thundering stomps. Maniacal, the scream, rising from within and around, seeming to bring a wind down from the trees.

Mallet raises his arms, tries to raise his voice. Fails. Seems, almost, to be blubbering. Casts his look on Bridie.

'Make this fucking witch stop, please!'

Not for the first time Bridie wonders whether a cruel streak is weakness in disguise. A strut, a sway, Manaia picks a clump of leaves, rattles them at him, leans down to him. Rattle, rattle, hiss; jumps back up. Regards Mallet as he heaves himself up, as he runs back across the log, brushing past Bridie, loping clumsily alongside the stream. Disappears into the darkness of the greenery.

For a moment the forest falls quiet, as though even the trees are making sure he doesn't return. Then the birds resume their drip-drop songs and chorus of gossip. Manaia lowers her head. Bridie marches across the log, reaches the New Zealand girl who is shaking, thinks at first that the shaking is part of the mad display, that Manaia is surely, fully and completely mad. Then changes her mind, for Manaia is shaking like a woman who finds a man running away from her a hilarious sight.

The feeling rises in Bridie, waves and ripples, great bubbles breaking inside her throat as the sound finds its freedom. Fear pushed away by laughter, like blue smoke pushed off by the wind. Squats, face to face with her friend. Hands pulling arms, legs twined, making of themselves a boat, a cradle. Rocking back and forth and back under green sunlit branches.

———

It is an afternoon like any other, and yet it is not. The trees swaying uneasily in the fresh wind are void of the chatter of birds. On her knees on the flat stones, Bridie crouches over the stream, scrubbing mud and oil from her only underskirt. She hears the bark of guns and stiffens. Resumes her task and sees the water turning pink. Looks upstream and sees blood bubbling under the rocks. Shrieking and trembling with terror, she rises. Runs so fast her body seems to have grown wings. The rain, the wind whip her, carry her, give her a freedom and a span of sight that could never be hers in human form. She stops when she comes upon clouds of gunpowder, where men disappear and reappear, hauling squirming bodies out of the water.

When the smoke clears, she finds that she has come upon killers. Landed, grounded, terror thudding her heart, she screams at them to stop. Has almost stepped upon one netted mother in the stream tearing against the rope cutting her skin. Another mother tries to cover her baby, half rolling, patting it with a flipper, turns her head to Bridie who feels her own self in the throes of death. Hoping against hope for escape, mouth gaping, trying to scream. In her eyes the agony and anguish of being both the betrayed and the betrayer.

She wishes the rocks could avenge the seals, that all the unearthed boulders and uprooted scrub on the hillside would crash down, a battering barrage crushing these men.

Gasps at the wounded, dying mothers, the raised axes of the men, and curses. Grasping the sense and senselessness of this new terror she prays to Brighid. All the way through the forest, all the way over the leaping boulders. Prays that the men have not found that secret pool where the baby seals swim.

On seeing the carnage she cries — cries for all the babies birthed not so long ago that have been clubbed, for the babies whose skin is being peeled from their backs as they lie dying. From deep within the earth comes a groan so agonising it meets the sadness of the sky.

CHAPTER 25

No amount of water falling over the cliff will cleanse the pool of this slaughter. Manaia sees the tauiwi stacking skins. She sees the mouths open in a howl, the rolling heads. Eyes locked in the confusion of dying.

The tapu of this place is broken: the mothers are dead, they will not have another season of breeding. The protection that would allow some babies to grow has been lost. She looks at Bridie. If she had never brought her to this place, the chain of birth and death and birth would not be broken.

Pukuriri. Anger is her fuel as she runs beside the stream, up the forest, into the clearing at the top of the first hill and back down into the forest. The anger she feels must come from Tāwhiri-mātea, the god of winds, because it stirs in her like the wind in a storm, and the wind is rising now. She can hear it in the waves that break in fury, in the trees that shake above her, in the long, thin cry of the kāhu that wheels above her.

Her feet stick and slide on the wet earth. She lifts her legs higher, pounds her feet harder, runs without stopping for food, water or breath, as though Ropi and the other men are chasing her. She must reach her village. When the clouds part and drench the leaves, her sweat mixes with the rain.

She slows in the night, feels her way through the forest, talks to the trees, takes her bearings from the roar of the moana and the voice of the awa. Finally, they come, the smells that tell her she is close. Her heart thumps at the thick earth smell of the dug and piled soil of the kūmara beds.

She screams as she runs towards the sentries. The screaming carries across the village like the song of birds that warn of a change in the weather. The scream is answered as women scream back at her and the screaming becomes a wind that summons the ranga-tira, the kaumātua, the kuia, the mātua, the tamariki. When she tells them the tauiwi are here to kill them, to take their heads and sell them, there is stomping and crying and tearing of hair and hands running like claws down faces, until Kāhu Kōrako tells them to be calm.

Sheltered by the arms of her whānau, Manaia walks in a daze, talks through the haze of light clearing the rain. She talks and talks, tells them about the killing of the seals, the scale of the slaughter, the unimaginable mass of bodies, all the dead tohorā. How these tauiwi want to take everything.

Their faces look baffled. Some moan, some shake their heads as though they are trying to clear the tears.

E kai, e kai, they order, but she does not have to be told. Her mouth waters with longing for food, for although she gathered and tenderised her own pāua, has steeped kina in wai from the stream, she missed the tang of pickled mussels, the pigeons preserved in their own fat and the sweet, tender kūmara. She missed the hand-woven bowls and mats. Her eyes fill with tears as she looks around. She has missed them all, her people.

One of the tamariki transfers water from a large bowl to a small bowl and Manaia sees them again in bubbles dancing light. Her eyes fill, remembering their eyes. Ngā kakerangi. The water falls.

———

Bridie's eyes are on the stars that pierce the cracks between the branches that form the roof. The stink is the stink of seals culled, skinned, piled up, their beautiful faces full of sadness. Every bone in her body, every muscle of her face is wakefully tense as she anticipates Robbie's return. She flies her gaze through the cracks in the branches. The comfort she seeks comes from stars.

Crunch of boots and Robbie seems to have fallen into the stack of damp driftwood, sliding into a tumble of laughter and rum. His curses become whimpers; she hears a thump as he lays the club under the awning. Watches as he ducks, hangs his lantern, slowly shuffles his clothing, his big hands slippery with oil. He tucks his right hand into his long coat and brings out a small bundle. Waves it in front of her, enticing her to stand. She reaches to stroke the fur of the dead baby seal. Orphaned and culled. A sob cracks her throat. He grabs her shoulders.

'What the Hell?'

Hearing the thunder in his tone she drops to the floor. As he raises his fist she stifles a cry of anguish.

'It'll make a fine muff,' says Robbie.

'It will,' she says. 'Thank you.'

'Thank you, *sir*,' he growls.

Out it comes, an Irish curse learned from her mother.

'Go ndeine an diabhal dréimire de cnámh do dhroma ag piocadh úll i ngairdín Ifrinn.'

'Don't be using your Irish gibberish on me.'

'Not even if it is a blessing of gratitude for the gift so kindly bestowed?'

The look in his dark eyes says he almost would . . . but does not believe her.

They slake the moonlight with shadows: four pick-axes, a sabre, a cutlass and a harpoon, tomorrow's grey dress, a shirt made solid with ox lard soap, a small skin — the memory of a seal. Robbie's hair and beard become scratching nests as his tongue and teeth scour her body.

But something deep within her remains untouchable and unreachable. Still joined to her bones, not quite free, not wind nor wings, her spirit takes flight and finds rest on a spear that hangs as a rafter. There it pauses while Robbie grinds her bones and flesh. She floats herself away, knows that the shift away from things too rotten to bear is a dangerous edge. Her mind follows the same track of thought over and over. If she fails to return, she will be estranged from herself forever.

When Robbie rolls away with a triumphant snort and humph she is landed back in Robbie's 'Fairhaven', his winter seat; his spring, autumn and summer seat. The base for his empire where he will be a merchant, trading land and everything else to the English. He is snoring now, the sound of him louder than the owl and its mournful call in the darkness. In the cramped, confined space her body is moulded by his bumps and hollows, while underneath, the damp seal fur stinks of the man and his stains.

———

Stirred into anger, they stamp as they fume, stamp and shout about the tauiwi who have proven themselves to be more ill-mannered, more ignorant and dangerous than they appeared during their first visit at the beginning of the season. This is the season of hunkering down, tending the fires, warming their knees, for enjoying the fruits that have been gathered and stored. It is a season for rest. These foreign men have shaken things up, stirred the forces of nature. Āe, their worst fears are confirmed.

Those who made her leave with Ropi tell her that she must stay home now, not return. Barely listening to the commotion, Manaia scours the crowd for Kauri. All the other rangatahi, his young friends, are jumping about, preparing to fight and he is — where? She asks Rima and Manutaki but they evade her questions.

Sickness rises in her puku when she closes her eyes, listens to all her senses except sight. Knows deep in herself that Kauri has been busy with another girl. She opens her eyes and sees him, pressing through the throng. His eyes are on her and at his side, yes, the kōhine. At least the girl has the sense to stand back. Assessing her, Manaia knows she could take her, this one, knock her to the ground, bash her head. Rima moves beside her.

'Kāo. Don't waste your time on them. She is not worthy of your fists. He is not worthy of your love.'

Manaia turns, shuns them and gives Rāwhiti the full force of her smile.

'Āe,' says Rima. 'At last you're awake, my girl. Rāwhiti is a more appealing man.'

———

Kāhu Kōrako has given her permission to state her own argument, voice her own plan. She has earned that right. She has barely slept for thinking it over, step by step, preparing what she will say. All the arguments about staying, all the arguments in favour of returning. If Ropi realises she has gone he will make his move.

She decides she must return and gather more knowledge for a surprise attack. Let Ropi and his men believe she knows nothing. The kaumātua listen, withdraw to consider. They discuss it among themselves and eventually concede that she is right. But it is danger-ous — if it goes badly it is possible they will never see her again. She sees their faces aching with sadness and feels torn. Feels shame and sadness for there is another reason for leaving them again, but she cannot share it with them.

She cannot abandon Bridie and Cuthbert, even if it puts her at risk.

She must find a way to save these tauiwi, for they have shown they care for her. Why? The voice is not her own — the question comes from outside her and it answers itself, the voice of this tīpuna. She must guide those who are willing to learn. She must save those who want to be saved.

CHAPTER 26

In the bright afternoon light inside the shelter that is part shack, part tent, Bridie listens to wind rustling shredded bark, crackling the canopy of dried skins. Listens to the din and caw of birds that swoop and flitter over the sand at the edge of the forest. The birds are tame, almost all of them. Big birds with splashes of colour under their wings laugh, mock and hop. Smaller dark birds rival one another with their mimicry of the drip drop plop pip trickle of water falling to a pool, songs of the sweep of valleys between forested cliffs, stretch of a branch, squelch in soft sopping cushions of moss, near-silent growth, notes running up and down threads as spiders weave doilies between fans of palms.

Company, these birds. They know her well, watch her as she washes, watch as she buttons her bootstraps, watch as she hauls water. Song after song, cloud after cloud, flap-whirring fall and rise of them. Reminding her they were here first.

Drifting her gaze now to the rafter of branches, hooked harpoons and spears. Crackle as the front flap gapes to shafts of shadow and light over the shell-crusted sand. The sea-tasting breeze fails to stir the taut ropes that link the canvas awning to the solid trunk of a tree. A tree whose branches hail the sky.

———

Dizzy and forgetful she is, under the weight of tiredness from the endless doing and undoing: the washing and hanging and drying and cooking and washing and log-carrying and fire-lighting and water-heaving and, again, washing. The slop clothes dried, turned about, worn once and splattered with mud and blood and sea salt, worn twice and drenched half clean by the rain, worn thrice and bloodied and muddied and set aside to be scrubbed clean and dried over again.

She tries to push it away, the fearful thought so large it is like a huge dog sinking its jaws into her skirt to reach the flesh beneath. She kicks at the dog but it will not release her. She needs to find out. Needs to open the trunks that have not been opened, that remain hidden from her eyes. She knows what she must do even if she finds what she longs to avoid.

She opens the small mouth of the chest that is filled with her gathered things. Takes out each shell, each pressed flower, each dried seed. Then she places her treasures back in the trunk, blesses each fine thing before it sleeps. She remains kneeling and prays to Brighid.

Now she looks across at the trunks — the large one filled with the gowns Robbie calls flumadiddle, and the other. The trunks strapped and buckled and chained. Brass padlocks hanging from rust-crusted chains. These are the two trunks that arrived with the pirate ship. The trunks Robbie has closely guarded ever since. She has often wondered at the contents, particularly because Robbie has taken such pains to warn her to stay clear of them.

She must know. She takes the flensing knife from the ridgepole where hangs her damp washing and his cleaned weapons. Kneels back and hacks around the hinges of the lid, making a wide hole.

The trunk is packed with guns. She counts a dozen muskets, eighteen pistols, several boxes of ammunition and powder.

Sweet smell of oil, fruit of a tree and another smell, slightly sulphuric. From a pocket in the side of the trunk she removes a crinkled pouch, pours into the pouch some powder. Opens one of the ammunition boxes, picks out two balls, drops them in the pouch. Takes a piece of oilskin from the trunk pocket and wraps the pouch over and under. Then she selects herself a pistol — to hold and keep and hide to shoot the living daylights out of Robbie if ever she can. Folds the gun into another oilskin cloth, gentle and firm. Folds it tight and sets these parcels aside.

Pulls down the lid of the trunk, shifts it back into place.

The smaller trunk is also locked but it takes her only a few minutes to scour out the key from the tin where Robbie believes it to be successfully hidden. Perhaps this trunk contains goblets, gold, pearls, rubies, emeralds? The lock is stiff and she is almost surprised when the lid opens. Staring at the contents she clutches her body, feeling the rapid beat of her heart.

Faces — human heads — stare back at her. Heads are in this trunk; heads severed from bodies and preserved. She looks at the one on top. Tufts of long hair, scalp shining where the hair is pulled back from his face as though he is balding. Perhaps he was an older man but it is hard to know. Any wrinkles are concealed under his tattoos. Dark whorls form ridges in his face. On his forehead the marks fan out like a fern. On his cheeks are lines that turn in on themselves like young fern fronds that have yet to unfurl. The dark inky substance is set into the skin and the skin in between forms paths all around his face. Her finger could walk his face through fronds and trees.

There is a circling path on his upper cheek that has not been filled in. She has heard the crew say that native tattooing is a fierce, slow business. Hours upon hours of sheer, steep pain. Those who cannot withstand the procedure succumb to fever and death or live with dishonour. She has heard Robbie's crew say they would never undergo the torture of the native tattoo, the tap-tap of the bone tool carving through skin.

She moves to her bed roll, feels underneath for the stone Manaia gave her. Sees the same black flecks in the green stone. Roimata, that man had said. Tears. The truth bites hard. The stone in her hand is the one he wore, the man she met in the street on that long-ago day. The memory a stabbing pain and each stab tells her that she knows now, she has proof. It was that man's head on the shelf in the cabinet in the back room of the Shipwright's Compass. That was the head of the man who smiled at her, who drew her hand to touch the stone in his ear. The stone she holds in her hand now has somehow journeyed from him to her, from Sydney to the Middle Island. How and why? She tries to understand what she is sure she is meant to know.

The eyes in the faces are closed and one has the look of a dried tear in the crease of his eye. Some have straight hair, some have thick curls; most of the men have topknots they must have tied on the day of their death. Hair worn coiled, hair locked with feathers. Hair young and black. Hair long and rolled short. Hair worn long on one side and bunched on the other. Hair with style and purpose for the day.

Her eyes are drawn to some faces in particular; then, feeling sorrow for those who hold her gaze less, she whispers apologies to them. Takes her gaze to theirs. One seems about to speak. Another to cry. One has something vital to convey. One is shouting, his shout silenced by this half death.

Her thoughts suddenly interrupt her — because what calloused heart could have taken this child from its mother? The tiny head, just a smudge of hair, a mouth that should be tugging a mother's teat. There, the babe who surely still wants to scream out against the wall of death. Next, she uncovers an older child's head, cradles it in her arms. The child wears a tiny feather. His little face should be crinkling in laughter. Silenced now by the wrongness of this too-early end.

A lament in her for all of them, welling high now. A lament joined by them, by the half-dead. They existed; their life persists — in the character of expression, in the manner of the style of them. In the high cheekbones and low.

She doesn't know how to say such things aloud but her jumbly thoughts deliver them and the voices around her, the voices of all the half-dead men and children, instruct her.

Cold corpse eyes, cold corpse lips. We do not want to sit on the shelves of curiosity cabinets in countries far away from our kin. This, they say, is not the release we deserve.

She can sum them up in simple arithmetic. Add four across and — she tucks her hands down — three layers of them. A round dozen. She can almost hear Robbie taking the order from the haberdasher. She remembers the merchant in Sydney — the judge — the lordy accent and high tone of the man who violated her. Recalls Robbie telling her that there were gentlemen and ladies in England who collected human heads as though they were china teacups.

Back and forth and back she rocks until the grey scraping sand hurts her knees. Words pour out of her mouth. She has no sense of her words or the places they might reach. Looking down at the mouths of men and the child and the baby barred from making their own sounds she finds something stirring in her. Even in this strange state of death some of them have something about them. She feels them around her as she still feels her ma. She longs to bring them from half death back to full life. If she cannot do this, she must do the next best thing. She knows Robbie only sees people preserved like apricots to be stored in trunks or shelves. A price on their heads like the price of seals or fish. But she sees people who deserve to be buried in the earth of the land where they walked, where they loved, and gazed at the stars.

She hears a voice that is not her own.

Closed now, the eyes that must have looked above the mountains and searched out the stars. The eyes that must have looked with love on parents and children. Who will search for them, seek them; where are they who cannot now be seen?

Another thought has risen from the ground to her heart and her tired thumping head. The people who loved these people must curse those who took them. Damn Robbie. But would they curse her too? Curse her children to come? She slams the trunk shut but there is no way of clamping down the presence. She turns away and hears the far-off sound of seals begging for life under the knives.

Some deep part of herself is trying to fly herself away but she can only make a half-turn and curtsey, the slow dance of disgust. She needs to sleep.

Sparks hurt her eyes. With the yellow and red of a hard-rock headache, she presses her face against the cold sand and listens to the waves, seeing the blue shield of each wave shadow. When there is only the hiss and splash of burnt light from the sea she opens the trunk again. Touches the cold dry skin; tells herself this is no worse than trying to revive with the bellows her near-dead mother.

The tent billows, cracks and flaps as she walks outside. Not a tremble from the trees — the only storm is at her feet and in the tent that is her house. She bows her head and the long sorrowing cry that comes to claim them reaches to the dead, bringing their spirits to within and she knows what must be done. She cannot save them now, but she knows about the circle of births and blessings and burials.

She walks three circles around the tent, praying with each stride:

Blessed Brighid, bless the dead and those who mourn the dead.
Do not bless the sinners, bless those who sin less. Bless those who bide and those who bind. Bless the wind and the sweeping tide.

Down at the shore she scrubs her hands with saltwater foam. Takes up an iron pail from the long hut, rinses away some nuggets of soil, dries the bucket with her skirt. Back at the tent she gently fills the pail with the heads, trying not to look upon them but finding the shape of each tattoo on a cheek or forehead or chin. Their lips appear to be sneering now, mocking her for believing that she can bury that which was once alive and full of talk.

She takes a blanket and Robbie's knife and, in several trips, carries the heads, the knife, the blanket and a spade. Tries not to look behind her at the trail of twelve ghosts.

Past the dunnekin, she walks up the sandy rise to the high part of the beach, past the washing line where the ground is mossy and soft. She digs each hole carefully, retaining a turf lid. Turfing is a skill she learned from Ma, who learned it from all the mothers and fathers back in Éire. Now there is a sob coming to her throat from the remembering. Her ma had even taught the supervisors at the prison how to preserve each precious piece of grass, dig it up and make it settle back down good and proper, like the pieces of the patchwork curtain around her bed.

Her thoughts chatter as she cuts squares with the blade of the spade and digs beneath. Digs a long trough. She takes the knife and cuts the blanket in half. Creates a bed for the heads with half the blanket.

Then she cradles each head in turn and she speaks to each face. She barely knows what she says — only that it is a greeting and a farewell, one and the same bound together. She places each in a hole in the ground looking upwards side by side, trying to imagine the body that would have accompanied each one. Places the baby and the little child side by side; knows they were loved and mourned as she is mourning now.

Her eyes turn to the sky — a sky like an oily rag stamped with pinchy-punchy finger marks of lamp black. It is raining now and in a moment it will all turn to mud, all of it. Anxious that Robbie and his crew will soon return, she hurriedly scoops up clods of black soil to pack the ground. She picks up the remaining piece of blanket and lays it over the upturned faces, closing the light on each one. The ground is muddying, muckying, and she thinks of the wet soil packing around the faces beneath her. Finally, she carefully lifts the turf into place. Rakes the ground with sticks, scatters handfuls of tiny grey and yellow leaves.

Back in the room that is part hut, part tent she takes the oilskin parcels containing the pistol and soft pouch of powder and balls and carries them up the bank to the cluster of cabbage trees. Overturns a dry boulder and digs with her hands. Places the pistol and pouch in the hole, rolls the boulder back in place and packs rocks into a small pile. Finding a piece of whale bone nearby, she stabs it into the ground as a marker.

In her muddy dress, face smeared with dirt, she stands still in the long fall of falling rain, breathing long and deep as she sings the keen of keening women. Keening is anger as well as sorrow. Anger that the window was never glazed, that bricks were never put to use, that the heavy door always held the snag of an autumn breeze. In her memory it was anger that keened so often, not love or remorse.

She shifts her song to these men and children and who they might have been had they not been felled and butchered. She tries her best to sing in Gaelic, for that is the only language she knows that wants to carry this song. She keens without a candle, without another woman to sing with her. The rain is in her mouth and the melody floats in green-grey melancholy, the words leaving her chest easily.

'It's hard to grieve for you, for you are strange to me, but I'm here wondering what you were doing when they snared you — hunting rats or raising spears, playing with children or cleaning eels?'

The wet missionary is crawling up the beach towards her. The slope must seem steeper to him in the rain.

Bridie continues her lament: 'Last night I dreamed I flew to a place where owls beg for pork. Now the autumn sea is ebbing but the leaves will stay awake. Have you cursed the ones who finished you? Have you cursed the one who plans to sell you? Have you cursed the man who promises me fishskin gloves and birdskin boots? He craves things that . . .'

Cuthbert is standing before her, solid in his fury and shouting frantically. She remembers how he came to her mother's house when Ma died.

His ranting words, proclaiming his disdain, scud in and out of the rain.

'Heathenish wakes express St Paul, immoderate will not rise shame deplorable, Christian vanity humiliation, Satan fed God, banish anti-Christian prayers, fasting alms, wholesome injunctions, woman's howl first crime not absolved, in case of detestable perseverance, practice excommunicated and denounced . . .'

She stamps her boots on the moss. A circle around him.

'Go now!' she screams. 'Go, go, go and leave me alone.' She looks back to her secret burial ground. 'The waves flow higher with their tears and the wind rises with their sighs . . .'

It is not a splattering but a sweet ash rain that is now drifting overhead with the gulls and the clouds. When she opens her eyes he is gone.

At first she believes the song she hears to be an echo. The cry is similar to her keening but the language is a stranger to her ears. Turning, she catches sight of a woman standing near the black eye of the forest. Rough hair, a straight gaze, square shoulders, muscular legs. Manaia. The wind cries and crests and the rain that falls now is like a veil over Bridie's hair. When she whirls around, the sea in front of her is calm. When she turns back, the forest is furiously quiet.

———

Drunk with ale the missionary had been when he left the singing and thumping of boots and tankards at the long hut. Drunk with fury when he saw Bridie keening up the beach. Now, coming away from her mad frenzy, he is rewarded by the soft whoosh of a shooting star. If he thinks rationally, he knows a star cannot make a sound, yet he's convinced he heard the wind of that star. A piece of sky coming so near — surely, what? A sign. A blessing? Looking up at the skyscape, the glitter and glimmer of every little planetary spot of life, he finds it hard to imagine that it is the work of one artist. How could all creation be the work of one creator? He calls out for an answer. In reply, instead of a single voice he expects a chorus.

Kicks at a shell in the silence.

His feet are bare for he is a wild man rather than a man on a mission. More alligator, less human. What is the difference between Robbie's mission and the Church's mission, which forced him, Cuthbert, to trade guns to the New Zealanders? There are no easy answers when life is not easy.

Boots lost, shirt open, he staggers as he wades the cold water, begging for sustenance from the sky. Singing about the stolen green of Éireann. Wading upstream from the sandy shore he feels something wiggle at his feet — the New Zealand dragon, the taniwha? Meanders with the meandering stream. Around him, in the pale path of the moon's light are mournful arms and feet of dead trees. He wades on until — miraculously — the trees are growing, tall and small, folding him inside their living arms. Stumbles, tumbles, falls flat on his nose on an island of stones. Running from his nose into his mouth is blood. The stream, this nice friendly path, is licking his mouth, a lovely dog come to lick, gulp, splutter.

Feels himself dragged up, hauled on a stretcher — no, cradled in arms. Perhaps his mother come to intercede on his behalf, ask Peter to let him in the gates, beg all the dead popes to forgive him for turning to the religion of the thieving English? But before this rescue something else happened. He is so tired he has trouble grasping what it was — has a dim recollection of a woman keening. Perhaps the keening remembers him.

CHAPTER 27

Bridie is well awake and rising to greet Robbie when she hears the stamp and drag of pebbles as he comes up from the beach.

He hangs the lantern and tips her chin and she smiles bleakly while his hands rob her pale skin of its coverings. As his cold fingers tug at her shawls she stays quite still, as she has before and before. Then his gaze is trailing the floor. She is sure he realises what she has done when he sees the broken lock but he opens the lid anyway.

The first blow fells her before she can even see his hand. Perhaps she could finish what he starts by forcing a cry from her mouth and crawling outside to rest on the bones of the fire but she does not wish to give up her cry to him. Huddled on the sand, she tastes the salt of shells and, as she is being pounded, tells herself that shells turn to sand turn to rocks. In rock she has seen the glitter of shells and solid lines harder than sand and — now, now, she tries not to cry. She winces and hears the hollering of him. She is what the sea takes in and what the sea throws out. Her womb is touching the sand floor and her spine is arching against the pole of the spear that stays straight with each strike. Hope is blue with whispers of lemon; waste is colour banished.

He's using his fists now, and all the curling blows are cartwheels spinning hatred.

Somewhere far behind her, using a tone free of challenge or rescue, Bill is pulling on him.

'C'mon, old man. There's a tasty stew waiting down there and the chums won't be starting without you.'

Robbie turns away, his laugh a scoff that comes with a spew of phlegm.

'Give the crew permission to eat without me.'

Falls into an exhausted, empty sleep, she does, until he returns with Tom, Bill and some of the other men.

'She's your sister so you'd better get some sense out of her,' Robbie tells Tom.

Robbie and the others take hurricane lamps and go back to the beach while Tom stays.

Bridie prays to the good Brighid, to Jesus the son of the father and Mary the mother of God and to the ghost — the holy; she prays that the men will not find the burial ground. She seeks sympathy in Tom's face and soothing from his small hands. Neither is forthcoming.

'Do you know what you've done?' he says.

He sounds like Robbie. Listening to this blustering boy, she wonders what happened to change him so. Where did he go, the brother who was briefly shaped by Ma's loving care? She pretends she cannot speak, thinks perhaps she cannot speak. But then she does — needs to hear an answer to her whisper.

'He made me play a pretty part, be a pretty face at the table but I am not what he calls me, a stupid dimber. I am my mother's daughter, a clever Irish woman. I played the part but all the while I listened to every word coming out of those drunken spewing mouths. I know the New Zealanders were tricked and murdered by Robbie's pirates. It's a bad, evil thing they are doing. Selling the heads is vile.'

'If it's so vile, why do the lords and ladies in England buy them?'

'Think, Tom. Those lords and ladies still behead the Irish. And the New Zealanders his men slaughtered have families who will seek revenge.'

'Their boats were burned and they don't have guns. We are a superior force.'

'Revenge, Tom. They will build boats, find boats. They will trade for guns.'

She is weary. He seems to have left himself behind. The sand whirs around the edges of the abode. The wind moans, turns to a high-pitched whine.

'Ding dong, Tom. Ring a bell in that great skull of yours. The English did it to us. In Éire. They stir up trouble, divide the people. Make the victims blame each other. Cause them to fight and then quietly seize control.'

'If Robbie seizes control, we're the winners.'

'Murder those smiling people who greeted us? You think that's all good and dandy, Tom? You think that will do our mother proud?'

She pauses. 'Anyway, they will wise to it.'

'You would warn them?' he asks.

The wind howls before she answers.

'It's wrong and she knows it,' she says, says it slow so he listens. 'All around us, raining down on us, don't you feel it? Her rage. When we create carnage we become the carnage. We can't wreak this havoc without her turning on us.'

'Don't start with Brighid and your stupid superstitious tripe.'

'Then think plain if you must. Think on the New Zealanders in the north who will come here and take us down if we do not take Robbie down. Think on that long and hard and do the right thing: help me take him down.'

He turns away from her, his feet trudging away in the rain that is pounding on the stones and shells.

'Tom!' she shouts. 'Don't think too long or you'll find your head lying beside your body.'

Loss is what Bridie feels as Tom leaves. She sees him in her mind, striding through the relentless rain and stinking fumes of rotting whale, towards the raucous calls of the long hut. She feels a huge sadness that Robbie and his crew have stolen his youthful idiocy, his softness. She wishes the missionary was around to defend her, to call his God to save her, but he creates his own absence, has perfected the art of disappearance.

For a long while the rain pounds, the shells clatter with a power that signals not the return of her brother or the violence of the wind. Each sound is a signal to ready herself for more pain. Fear trickles into her blood and bones, the ache of it dripping like cold water onto the dark, huddled creature of herself. She can turn to rock, for each drop of pain grows the heart of stone.

When Robbie is a shining wet shape, hooking his lamp to a stick stuck through the skin roof — bulky the silhouette of him in the wind-blown light — she bows her head, squeezes her face, presses her ears between the bones of her knees. Hears nothing, feels not one anticipated blow, looks up to see him grinning, teeth uneven, sweat greasing the hollows and mounds on his face. The look of him is the moon grown too full of itself, bitten by shadows on a stormy night. She reels as his large fist hovers above her. The fist wavers. Pulls herself hard into the floor of seals turned to skins turned to cover sand. Sags her body as he laughs and leaves. Relief does not last. It comes again. The crunch, the flap, the power that is darker than the raining wind.

At some point in the space between beatings and fear of them she drifts. A pale cloud begging the sky for release. Rouses as men rake their grumbles from the forest down to the long hut. Shapes are shadows, words are stones thrown hard. Woman is a bitch. A whore. A crack. Red blood that sheds monthly is a curse to be used against her, a stain of shame.

———

Still in a stupor of drunkenness, Cuthbert exits the long hut into the cold raining wind to clear his wandering mind. Drops his lantern as he tumbles, arms flailing, onto the wet sand. Recovering himself, he ponders how rudderless Robbie and his crew seem on land, finding contentment only when they can drown in flashes of lightning and thunder, blue liquor, brown ale. So easy it is to fall, become one of them.

The sky stretches around him like black skin; spears of rain are piercing his poor body, stabbing. Knows in his rational mind, to which he desperately clings, that the sky stretches beyond and around the earth. Perhaps the earth is an organ like the heart, under that vast skin. Goes a step further in his rational mind, for blood surely flows in the body in the way of water in rivers and oceans that cross the planet. Perhaps the New Zealanders are correct in their thinking that all life is descended from a great swirl of creativity — that every mountain, tree, rock, animal, fish, has a spirit.

Even on this moonless wet night he can see, all along the shore, the lumps of rotting flesh; breathes in nothing but the ever-present black burning stink of flesh melted in a cauldron. Perhaps this deadly environment has loosened his rational mind. That would not be surprising, he thinks, as he surveys the ghostly hulks of bones, the great rot, the lumps of disintegrating life, the everlasting stink, the rain piercing the black veil of boiling oil.

He is searching for comfort, for the warmth of the fire in the village where he had once lived in the north. Where he had found the thrill of love, the strength of belonging. He had listened to the kuia and koro telling stories to their mokopuna, and he had loved his wife who was young, but old enough. That wife had urged him to be strong, not weak; to be busy, not lazy. When she nimbly climbed a tree, she urged him to follow. He is sure that all life was like that once, surely in patches at least. Common land for common men and women, thatched roofs, flower paths.

The rain stops. He takes the patch box from the pocket of his wet coat, snaps it open, strikes the tinder, lights the flame, lights the lantern again. Walks towards a speck of light further along the cove, further from the long hut.

Drawing close, sees Bill the older under the iron roof of his shelter. The flames of his fire cower as he tries to shape arched planks. Would turn back to avoid the man's chatter but Bill is fastening him with a warm welcome. The heartiness drops like the wind to a breeze as the missionary nears. Bill's face now solemn.

'Is it conscience keeping you away from sleep, Mr Sky Pilot?'

'Cuthbert.'

'I can't shake from me the dread that we have all become weeds taking over a flower garden. Are we weeds, Mr Sky Pilot?'

Why is it, Cuthbert wonders, that night turns plain men into philosophers?

'We cannot possibly imagine, when we plant our seeds, what the Lord has in store for us,' he says, loathing the lofty sound of his own voice.

He remembers that the seeds and plants the missionary society sent to him in the north from Sydney had most often been mouldy and rotten on arrival.

'If your Jesus was here now, he being a carpenter, he might be some practical help to me. Wonder what he makes of all this hacking down trees for more and more puncheons to store all the oil?'

'Oil to light the world,' says Cuthbert grandly.

'Stretching the day to strike out the dark ain't natural. Man needs rest.'

The missionary feels pity for Bill, working all hours to meet demand.

'If you yourself could choose your future, would you stick with this life or venture to be something different?' Bill continues.

What is up with the man? Cuthbert wonders. Finds himself answering nevertheless.

'In the north when my New Zealand wife's niece sickened, I told her God was waiting for her. She took that to mean that God wanted her to die and so she did.'

Bill coughs, awkward.

'When I realised, I tried to undo it. Told her God meant her to recover, but she desired to see Heaven, she believed it had been ordained, weakened and died . . .'

Hears his voice fall away. Hopes Bill will say something profound to rescue him from this despair, but the man is quiet so Cuthbert continues.

'I tried to do a deal with Robbie Fitch, but when he came he spilled a bag of heads on the beach, the heads of their relatives . . .'

'Between you and me, sir, Robert Fitch has a knack of creating havoc and stepping neatly aside.'

'I am not a sir, I am a simple man, Bill, who has made a great many mistakes.'

'That being the case, might I suggest that you be yourself, talk straight when you talk with me in the dead of night. No offence but I don't need no pretensions.'

Cuthbert hesitates, for he has come to believe the meadows, rambling roses and clipped hedges in his voice.

'Irish, ain't you?' Bill's tone is kind.

Cuthbert considers that he had not fooled Bridie's mother, Róisín, either. She had asked his mother's name and nodded when he replied Eileen — Eileen Murphy. Name like ours is the peat that fuels the hearth, Róisín had said. What would Róisín say now? Protect my children, be a good, gentle guardian. He has failed terribly in that so far. So many failings.

'Forgive me my rudeness,' Bill says now. Serious, the tone on him.

'We turned from the old religion, converted to Protestant so my father could keep hold of his land,' Cuthbert confides. 'Broke my mother, it did.'

'Now we are talking honest like, what do you make of the native girl you've been shacking up with — is she a fly-by-nighter?'

'She is not a fly-by-nighter or a witch, not anything of the sort. Wherever do you get this ridiculous notion?'

'You've been seen coming from her bed.'

'From her whare, her house. From talk and healing. She makes poultices to heal my wounds.'

'Working, are they?'

'Like a miracle.'

'There you are, see?'

Eyes meet, the light of the fire inside their eyes.

Cuthbert tries to tell Bill what he felt in the north, and what he has learned now from this young New Zealander. The night after night storying, the sharing of kindred thoughts and ideas. The messages she receives by listening and watching the stars, the moon, the plants, and hearing the ancestors. Not to mention — but he is mentioning it — the knowledge passed down from her mother and her grandmother before her, back to all the women she can name, all the men she can name. The memory arcs back to where they came from, what deeds they committed, where they came from before this place, the web of lines back and back to, well, the other world.

He wonders if it is the liquor, this rambling in him. Vomits. But he cannot stop, not even with Bill suggesting that he do so now — turn in, succumb to sleep. Remembers how his mother spoke of the binding, how people are bound one to another, in marriage, in families. He has been part of that undoing, breaking the bonds.

'I've been used by the Church, Bill,' he says. 'Turning people into ranks and files and divisions — an army, a navy and rulers. Do people revere the rod rather than the hearth?'

Answers himself before Bill can dredge up a response.

'They are our hosts. If we come in friendship we are greeted with hospitality. If we attack, they will seek revenge just as we would. Robbie — so many men — fail to understand. The New Zealanders see women as the heart, the womb, the eternal force. They sent this young woman because she is special. The heart should not be harmed.'

Bill coughs, phlegmy. He is unconvinced.

'I reckon she's a witch on account of Robbie's finger. He hadn't touched a seal at that stage, had he? Yet the thing swelled up after he was with her. I reckoned then she must be some kind of witch.'

Cuthbert sighs. Here we go again, he thinks.

'Let me assure you — so you can assure the men — she is not a witch. She can hear those who have gone before, that is all, and she listens to nature.'

'My grandsire was like that.'

'And my mother.'

Bill stops scraping his piece of wood. Stares into the fire.

'Forgive me if this seems like blasphemy, Mr Sky Pilot, but it seems to me that we're on the verge of losing something with all this over-doing. The gutsing, boozing, fornicating and killing. Chopping all the trees, taking all the seals.'

He passes Cuthbert a rutted earthen bottle. Presses his arm.

'There's something you need to know, sir — Robbie is after killing you. He is after killing the New Zealanders too, on account of needing heads for his wrongful trade.'

Shakes his head, Cuthbert; finds his whole body shakes with it.

'I was afraid so.'

Their conversation pauses as the rumbling sound comes to them — of men, out of the long house and up the beach, jeering, yelling, the sounds thin with the wind.

Another fit of coughing. Cuthbert wonders if the man is long for this world.

'Those heads the girl buried, he preserved them his self. Him and Jake. Wanted me to help but I says, "Sir," I says, "I am too busy with my coopering, better you use the men who are skilled with butchering and fishing."

'Do you understand? Robbie's pirate coves brought them heads all freshly gutted so Robbie could practise his processes of preserving.'

Wonders, Cuthbert does, how he could not have realised, but then it was all part of the bloody horrible work they do — the work he tries not to observe closely.

'He needs confining, does Robbie, but I don't rightly know how to confine him and the others.'

Bill looks at Cuthbert. Is the man inviting a mutiny? Cuthbert finds himself sick with fear. With so many bad men all around, how could the good possibly win?

'I fear we shall all be for the pot if he keeps going,' says Bill. 'They eat people, don't they? When I saw you coming I thought, "Here's my Irish friend with his conscience. He'll know what's to be done."'

'Guilt guides me.'

'God, you say?'

'Guilt!' Realises he's snapping.

Bill pats Cuthbert's back, the way of it, one mate to another.

'Might I suggest you act quick now, Mr Cuthbert, and let guilt guide you in the right direction.'

CHAPTER 28

The ruckus ceases momentarily as Robbie shoves the bench. Tankards slopping as elbows lose their propping place. Assures them he does, assures the men who stole the vessel and turned it pirate — bravo to them, one and all — assures the whalers and sailors and coves — bravo to them as well — that he will return swift and sure to rumble the rest of this wild night.

Outside the long hut, fumbling for his cock in the darkness, he throws his gaze into the black sea and sky. No man has ever managed to convince him of the existence of a divine presence. Murky it sounds to his mind — he has more faith in the weather than God.

Inside him forever, the stinking black river, the memory of old moping ships on the Thames. Demeaned, humiliated, stripped, outcast from war those prison ships. Rotting hulks, their gallantry forgotten. Double-ironed he was, on cause of shouting obscenities when the guards stripped him of his silver pocket watch. Burned on him the irons — a flinch becomes a burn mark, a seeping wound, a scar. He learned hardness the hard way. Fight and you die. Think, plan, act the battle in your mind's eye until each possibility is tested and you might just beat the buggers who run the game.

He scratched Latin on the ship walls, spoke in the flash lingo the guards could not comprehend, invented new words beyond their ken.

His first sight of Sydney was sails, ships, rocks, the wide cove, the bay, the glistening sea, the sky folding white on blue, the breath of the land, the whole country stretching into the back of beyond, yielding herself to him. Cock-a-hoop, he was, transported with joy. Hope floated like a buoy bobbing bright on the water, and his anchor was solid rock.

In the long hut behind him his men are laughing at some fine joke. Looking down at his cock now he tells it that it is letting him down. He had tucked it away but it wants out again. It isn't flowing right — painful squirts. Is it another curse that makes him piss pins?

He has sailed, and served, and stolen — learned from men who behaved worse than he himself behaves. If he bides his time and works hard he could own one ship, and another. His ships could breed, become a fleet.

Sighs as his cock releases a satisfying squirt. Looks up to the stars. If there is a God up there it is a man like himself, strong and quick to fury, who has no mind for forgiveness of sinners because He understands that men must sin; that is why He sent Jesus to forgive them. That man, if he exists, deserves a good strong name.

A name like . . . Goliath.

'Goliath!' he yells. 'Prove yourself! Rouse a storm! Rake lightning!'

Far off down the beach he sees a little fire. There he could burn Bridie for spurning him. For making a fool of him. Two dozen muskets he'd paid for those heads. It makes him want to wrench her neck as though she were a chicken.

Tucks his cock away and walks a circle as his fury mounts.

Whenever he takes her, he feels she's not there, feels the shudder in her when he puts her hand on his cock. Why, she only displays the art of fakery when she's afeared of him, but she will curse him to hell and back if she thinks herself safe from a beating, and when she believes he's out of earshot. Her mother's daughter all right. She should be grateful.

'Hear me, Goliath,' Robbie yells. 'Pour your wrath on that bloody girl!'

Back in Sydney so many dimbers follow him, beg him, want him. Even the true dames, the sterling ladies look at him and blush. But the Murphy women — mother, daughter — are ravens on the rocks, sirens taunting men, calling them to their deaths.

Clear-sighted his rage, like a spyglass that finds a face in focus. The face of Róisín. Even in death she has such power over him. He tries to shove off the thought that she haunts him for stealing her hair, hair threaded with such bright light. He cannot forget the fresh plums in her cheeks, the greenery of her eyes misting with love. Love for that weak fawning bugger who, like herself, was from that planet of the urinals. Ireland.

Jimmy. Bloody Jimmy. Robbie had stood it for nigh on nine months till he could not stand more and then — only a word or two in the right ear, while handing over the right amount of coin, to have the mighty Irishman sent back to the bush felling trees, to be buried under a felled tree.

How she keened, lament coursing out of her, frightening mad, saying Jim's death were no accident. Robbie longed to tell her that it was for her he had the man killed, for kindness, for all that he could earn whaling, sealing, heading — being a headsman — and return to provide.

The sickness that took her after the Irishman's death repelled him. Beauty diminished. Feverish accusation in the green of her eyes like she'd received some kind of message from that bugger on the other side.

'I hope you are happy wedded up there!' he yells at the black sea and sky, at his cove, good old Goliath.

Scuffs his feet in the sand. The sky is void. No moon to mock him, to glide along womanly, to remind him of all that is lost and will never come again. He turns back to the long hut, to find the men, to bring them out to have some fun. To drag the wastrel out of the abode, make her earn her keep.

The long, hollering cry shivers along the beach, coming all the way to Cuthbert and Bill from somewhere near the long hut. The cry brings down all the night, shredding darkness, spitting blood. Cuthbert gropes for the tinder, strikes it, lights his lantern. Runs after and overtakes Bill, who is already clumsily running towards the sound, boots unbuttoned, causing him to stumble.

Feet bare, sand damp, his breath cold and loud, it is Cuthbert who reaches the sound first. The light of the lantern stabs randomly at black sand, black waves, snarling lip of the sea, and then at a huddle of grim-faced men. Pushing through, he sees the broken look of her. Bridie.

Her legs are at odd angles, blood on her thighs. Swollen blue eyelids. He bends, picks up a hand that flops lifeless in his own.

He looks up and around at the men. His voice comes from a savage place deep inside, down, down, dragging up from the deep, dark well where rage waits. From the murk of every bad memory he brings forth his venom. Anger and hatred spear each of them — each pirate, each sealer and whaler and sailor. He faces Robbie, Jake, Mallet, Ivory. Faces Tom.

'You disgust me, you vile, depraved monsters.'

When he tries to pick up Bridie's battered body, pain rouses a whimper. She cries and the cry terrifies him. Gently he tries again to take her from this evil company.

A moan freezes him. Long and shuddering, like the wind in agony. The sound takes them all inside a terror, sucks them inside to drown. Mallet starts to speak but Robbie hisses.

The moan is carrying a flaming torch and the flames spit and brush at men who clutch their wrinkled, unbuttoned pants, their pale thighs and limp cocks.

It is Tom who raises an arm, seems ready to strike at the shadow behind the light. But the shadow reaches out and seizes the boy's hand.

Tom screams. Raises the back of his hand in the light to show bite marks. The sand is whirling, the wind shrieks. Unafflicted, Cuthbert and Bill watch Robbie bow low, suck-sucking dry sea dust. Watch in unison as the dust storms into eyes and onto the tongues of the men, who choke as they struggle for breath, heads pushed down by an unseen hand.

The shadow crouches beside Bridie, cradles her. Rises.

Astounded, Cuthbert watches as the men try — and fail — to lift their heads, Tom and the men in a semi-circle: Mallet, Ivory, Jake, Robbie and the pirate men who sound like bleating goats.

In the swirling haze of the sand, tending Bridie in her torment, is a figure. Female, he thinks. Manaia? All around the wind is an unseen force, whipping up sand, circling, creating sand-devil whirlwinds. The tone of the storm has shifted to a soft, high wail. The men who have done this thing crouch, a circle of shame.

The figure rises and Cuthbert glimpses strong female arms holding Bridie as she flops over a shoulder. Together they make a shape that shifts into the centre of the storm and away.

CHAPTER 29

Robbie pushes last night down. Makes it sink like the moon that is sunk by the sun. Puts last night's happening, the sudden storm and the strange business of Bridie's rescue down to the fugue of liquor. This is a new day, with whales and seals to cull, flax and trees to chop.

Musters the men. Strides down the beach marking the boundary of the sea with his cutlass, as he did the day after their arrival.

'We won't have a seasonwife running this station, will we, lads?'

'No fear.'

Who spoke up? Of course it was Mallet. Most of the men are as sullen as the swollen sky. The only one to be trusted is Bill, who won't look him in the eye today. The rest are moody and moody isn't good. Could turn against him if a stronger man stepped forward. A man like Mallet. He must show his own strength.

'Only thing good for the New Zealanders is a bullet in every mother's son.'

'Aye, every mother's son of 'em.'

Mallet dutifully mimics the words, but he is undutifully dangerous. Robbie looks for Cuthbert. Time to divert the men and drive away any thoughts of mutiny. He'll hang the bugger up and give him another lashing. Claws for breakfast, entertainment for the men. But half an hour later, Mallet and Jake and Bill and Tom and every other bugger who searched report that Cuthbert is nowhere to be seen.

———

Cuthbert feels the terror of being caught in a trap as surely as any fox or hare rasping for breath as hounds and bugles bay for his death. He is not one of these hunters, men who lust for the thrill of a kill, whose bloodthirst will never be satiated.

Regrets — so many of them. If only he had stayed in the north rather than fleeing down that beach to Robbie and his men, rather than returning to Sydney to be another whipping missionary. Bitter regrets that cannot be shed.

If the way back is lost to him now, the way forward seems equally out of reach, but he must try. Stumbling in the dark, holding his lantern high then low, boots sinking and sliding, arms flailing against flax, ears straining for the whooshing, whishing sound of Manaia carrying Bridie, in the sinkhole of darkness he sobs. Beckoning like a friendly host laying a grassy bed is the invitation to curl up and fall into a forever sleep. He does curl up, lies on the damp moss, but he cannot rest. When dawn comes he is awake and ready.

As the forest unfolds into fern trees and the log bridge across the beds of kūmara, he feels such relief. When he sees the double fences and gates of the kāinga he is overwhelmed. Tears drawn from a well of happiness rather than sorrow, for surely he has been guided to this miracle.

Hastily he removes his garments outside the gates. They have been contaminated by the bad actions of bad men, and removing them shows that he does not stand with them. The sentries regard him, order him to wait. He waits for a scowling sentry to return with a scowling response. Worse even than the frown of the sentry who remains is the piercing wind.

He stares up at the frozen shoulders of the hostile mountains. Not close, the mountains, but not far off either. Down the groin of the hill, across the forested valley and up another forested hill. Mountains worshipped as ancestors by the people of this place. Cold trickles painfully into his bones. Blighted, he is, by the misery of miserable weather, by the raining forest and now this frightful wind. Wonders whether he has ventured foolishly into another mistake.

He would love to pick up the garments at his feet but dares not. This cold nudity is his asset. He has no weapons hidden, is ready to be washed clean in whatever ritual their tohunga desires as long as he can keep his head, hold onto dear life.

With his manhood shrivelled to almost invisible, they must surely see that he is humbled, if not humiliated. Not a warrior or a warmonger, not an attacker or a defender. He is become nought, nil, a lion who has lost his mane, a bird in want of feathers.

The sentry returns. The other sentry raises his taiaha, says something that Cuthbert doesn't catch. The men laugh.

He is dragged into the river, the water colder than the wind off the mountain. Regrets his willingness to suffer. Under pain of cold his stomach tightens, is a fist, pounding him for release. He wishes the karakia would be over, and then it is over and he feels exalted as he leaves the water — a surge, a thrill, ecstatic, like the thrill of draining himself into a woman.

Halfway under the low gates he pauses, reminds himself there is no going back. He forces his mind towards an image of light at the other side of this darkness. Hears a woman calling the karanga, welcoming him forward, paying heed to those who have gone before, and he feels the shiver of entry to another world. He comes out into the light, blinking, goosebumps on the sad folds of his skin, looking around trying to recall the geography of the place.

A criss-cross of paths to the sleeping houses to the left, the meeting house of the rangatira further along in front of the large, shell-paved courtyard. The domed guest sleeping house must be somewhere behind that — possibly further over to the right, the entertainment house somewhere further over to the left, and the kitchen and dining houses over on the right.

This is the map he drew in his mind back when he came with

Robbie, and when he snuck out and listened to the men debating at night. If Bridie has been brought to this village, he needs to find her. Please God let her be alive.

His head thrums as he stands before the rangatira, recognises one of them. Plucks his courage to perform a humble oratory about himself — where he comes from, his mother, his father, their land stolen, their language taken. He himself stolen. That he does not stand with Robbie and the others who have wronged Bridie and Manaia.

He speaks plainly about Robbie's vile nature. About his weapons — the pistols that could kill many men in one killing spree. Finds himself describing Robbie's plan to kill all the rangatira and enslave the survivors. He tells them about the heads — heads that have been taken from people in the north and the survivors who must now be lamenting their loss. Trades heads, does this bad man, Robbie. And not in the way tangata whenua trade heads — as tools of peace, to return and treasure.

Cuthbert explains that Robbie kills only people with the finest tattoos. He has been known to offer to spare captives only if they select lower people to be similarly tattooed so he, Robbie can behead them too. After the heads are preserved, he sends them far from their land and people to lands of strangers where the heads are not revered but mocked, sullied.

'Robbie — Ropi — is a bad leader working for bad leaders,' Cuthbert ventures to add. 'He lacks all the qualities that make men listen and women sing.'

He hopes the rangatira will like the poetry of this last sentence, for he stands before people whose waiata and whaikōrero and karanga would move the greatest bard to weep, borrow and steal. In the soft grey mist of his tears, he adds that he is sorry for all the grief, for the betrayals.

Sees himself being appraised, finally, by Kāhu Kōrako. A majestic bird of a man, with white-feathered hair, long brown-feathered cloak, who talks animatedly with the others. In the pause, the wind ruffling the feathers, he waits, Cuthbert. Wonders whether, all in all, he went too far. Like a prophet who believes he stands firm on rock but is in fact on a crate in a town square, rambling ruin, raving damnation.

Kāhu Kōrako is raising a hand, has a question.

'Why did you not share this knowledge with us before? Why did you let him marry one of our women, the girl Manaia?'

He thinks swiftly, does not want to lie, can see no other way forward. Had he known? Tells himself he did not realise it would all go as badly wrong as this. Knows that he did, but how to tell them that he was different then? That his friendship with Manaia, the way she healed some wounds and opened others, awoke something in him. He could lie but then they would know that he was no different to Robbie. In truth, he should have acted sooner; he should have had the courage to stand up and warn them before Manaia joined Robbie.

He is crying because this matters so much. Somewhere Bridie is dying or dead. He surveys the faces before him, these fine tattooed faces enshrining the wisdom of generations. Feels in the wind, in the crying wind, his mother crying, her crying face. Before he left her, his dear Irish mother, Eileen Murphy, she had handed him a warm pebble.

'From my heart, and before that from Orcan's Well,' she said. 'Swallow it and Éire, your country, will be inside you always.'

Through the sea of his tears Cuthbert finds Kāhu Kōrako nodding, as though thoughts have wings, as though messages have flown between them. Tears from deep inside well up and out, flow a trail down his cheeks as the old man moves forward and holds Cuthbert's shoulders.

'Mō tāku hē,' says Cuthbert. The words leap from his tongue. 'Mō tāku hē.'

Because he is so deeply sorry.

Beyond the grasp of his understanding, the karakia uttered by the tohunga is a prayer that seems to come from behind and yet beyond.

Above and yet below. Stirred from the old world to the new, intoning depths to reach heights. Cuthbert finds himself fascinated by the layering of the song, the strange words that his soul seems to understand. Fear abated, he is soothed, restored.

Several hours later, bathed clean, hunger sated by steamed fish and sweet potatoes, thirst quenched by fresh cold water, he gratefully accepts the gift the tohunga hands him. A feathered cloak. Runs his fingers along threads that perform a geometric dance at the border. Triangles and squares, each thread weaving a way back to its beginning.

Somewhere behind the carved logs that form the gates to this safe place his old clothes lie, to be burned or buried or both.

Relief floods him, for he has shed his old skin.

CHAPTER 30

The crush, the folding down of herself, the weight. These Bridie struggles against as she strains to wake. As though she is a house and men are jumping on the roof, pounding rocks on the shell that would protect her.

The room is like a steaming bowl. Canoes are filled with rocks that puff steam. Glowing from shells of abalone are tiny flames, flax wicks in puddles of fish oil. Rainbow light. Someone scoops water on rocks, steam hisses. A woman fans a fern frond, fans the steam that rises from rocks in the carved hull of an old canoe. Cradled, Bridie is, in one of these, in a canoe floating in an ocean of leaves. Leaves on her hair, on her face, her hands, her breasts, her wounds.

Whales keen, their lament long and high and strange. Verses composed in a place beyond words. She reaches for the whales, which turn into the faces of women. Mothers. Not the women of The Rocks or the women of Éireann but it matters not; these women sing for her, nevertheless. She wants to thank them but she cannot find the strength. There she is, Brighid, dear Brighid.

Manaia puts a hand in hers. Her tears gentle rain on Bridie's chest.

'Roimata,' says Bridie, and sees Manaia smile like a mother hearing her child's first word.

———

What he sees when he looks at her hurts Cuthbert. The women have ushered him inside the healing house. They continue singing softly as he braces himself, sickened by her injuries. The cut on the bridge of her nose, the swollen brokenness, the sweat glistening in the pores of her skin. Her lids made heavier by swelling, her lips cut, her cheeks bulging and pebbled with bruises. Some cuts are deeper than others, some bruises are black. One eye is closed, the other squeezing open.

'The bean sídhe wanted my comb, but the turtle buried itself in my skull,' Bridie tells him.

Her words are strange, her voice surprisingly strong. He strokes her forehead, wondering if the insides of her head are damaged forever. His hand finds warmth but not fever. Reaching across him, a woman with a face disappearing into lines, and fingers that dance playfully like those of a child, squeezes a fistful of kūmara flesh, dribbling the juice into Bridie's wound.

'Kūmara is the native potato. It assists with healing, stimulates the body to repair itself,' Cuthbert tells her.

He is about to detail the other plants that have been applied to her wounds, to stem the blood, to ignite healing, when Bridie cries, 'Do you see it? Half the comb is buried in my head!'

When she turns her head to the side to show him the great trough, he feels astonishment stretch his features. Too far inside to ever safely dig out is the ridge of the brown mottled shell.

'Robbie raised against my head the very same axe they use to chop trees. But that turtle split itself in half. One part dug into my skull. The other half flew out and clawed him in the face. Manaia will show—'

'Settle down, do not upset yourself,' he says.

'Settle *yourself*.' Her tone is a slap, cold and hard. 'It's the deeds of men that upset me. Manaia has the other piece of the comb. She took it from the sand when she rescued me.'

He looks at the comb in Manaia's hands. One part of the turtle in her head, the other in the hands of her rescuer, a woman. She is right about the deeds of men. How could she not be upset by their actions?

In this healing house, songs thread one woman to another, incantations invoke the atua of peace.

'You are safe now,' he assures her. 'These people care for you.'

But she is listless, not hearing.

'After the comb broke, after the turtle rose up, I screamed, and that scream came from my roots as though I were a tree whose roots reached down under the ocean, trailing all the way back to Éire.'

Blethering she is, her chest rising, tangled hair wet, skin dripping sweat.

'But they knocked me down, those bastards. Mallet, Jake, Ivory, Robbie and the others — and Tom! Tom, my bloody runt of a brother, stood there doing nothing.'

Manaia steps forward, speaks firmly, and Bridie demands that he translate.

'In the traditions of the people of this place the turtle is a guardian. It guides people to a safe shore. It guided their ancestors,' Cuthbert says. 'They say this turtle protected you. This makes you special. They are gifting you with a cloak to honour you. These are her words, mind, not mine.'

'Yours would be different then?'

Cuthbert puzzles, treads carefully.

'I am appalled at the attack on you, but this turtle comb business is — seems fanciful. A story is a dent in reality. You and Manaia are young women who met in the land of dreams and superstitions.'

She laughs. Miserable, the laugh.

'So I'm rendered forever fantastical with this comb in my head.'

'I'm simply suggesting you might recover more rapidly and fully if you push away your imaginings.'

'Yet you cannot deny we are stuck to each other now, me and this turtle guardian, for it has buried itself in me.'

He is about to speak again but something stops him — a voice coming from inside and outside of his self. Has he not shed the skin that carried this tired old Church voice? He reaches back, remembering the life he had in the kāinga up north before Robbie with his guns and head-hunting. Without the local people, who nourished them with fresh food and water, so many Englishmen would have starved — and yet how were those people repaid? Calculated betrayals led to calculated conflict that resulted in total chaos.

Manaia's mother, Rima, distracts him from his musing. Bridie begs him to translate again. Really, he would rather not.

'Her assessment of me is that I speak with my eyes but I do not see. I listen with my ears but I do not hear.'

He moves aside as Manaia lifts Bridie's head to drink water brought to her in a bowl. The water smells like the heart of a mountain. He feels himself pushed away by the women.

Bridie sips, raises her hand, signals for him to wait, that she must speak before he can venture another word.

'When I worked with you at the orphanage we both knew, did we not, that the name of that establishment was a lie? Those children were wrenched from their mothers as I was from mine. You tell me why the Church wants to shut out women — we are the threads between this world and the world beyond, but we are not supposed to rage or mourn. We are not even supposed to keen.'

She is correct in this, as she is in so many things. He silences women just as his father tried to silence his mother.

'It's not my fault, Bridie. The Church's position on this is clear. Those who keen are hearing the voice of Satan. To keen is forbidden.'

Where did he come from, this self who sounds so tediously pompous? Just when he thought he had shrugged him off.

'You might as well try to cut the winds that cross the ocean,' says Bridie.

If he stabbed his finger in the Bible would it give him a way to answer her? But the Bible is left behind on his bed roll. He put it aside and it did not follow him to this village of feathered cloaks, flax candles.

'Doleful sermons weaken the body and the soul,' she continues.

Her voice is softer, and he knows it is only right she admonishes him so, for he is ashamed that he failed to rescue her from Robbie and his men, failed to rescue her and Tom and Manaia. He needs to feel ashamed. Puts his head in his hands.

'You want to be English but you are not. Murphy you are, not Cuthbert. You're only fooling people who want you to be fooled.'

In the darkness rendered by his hands he remembers how he tried to stop the singing hands and mouths when Róisín mourned the only protector who was good to her. How he tried to stop Bridie and the other women keening when Róisín died. Should he tell her that it is fear not anger that makes him act so? That he was fearful when she keened all those poor dead? Frightened of the sound that seemed to come from under the land and reach out through the women to the heavens?

He removes his hands.

'I've been used like a spade shovelling dirt over the truth. The Church — the establishment — needs to suppress rebellion, not only in Ireland but in England.'

'Are we children of Satan?' asks Bridie. 'Or are we men and women and children who want our own stretch of land to work with the sun and sleep with the moon?'

This brings from him a smile. She has been through so much and here she is, the poet in her, causing him to walk in fresh fields of reason. In this place of healing it is women who are forcing him to reach inside and outside of himself. Shedding his garments for his skin to be washed and prayed over, that was one thing, but this is another. It feels as though he must descend to ascend.

Manaia taps him on the shoulder.

'Kei te māuiui ia, me moe ia.'

Yes, Bridie needs to sleep so she can heal. He wonders whether they will ever trust him.

'Kei te māuiui ahau, kei te māuiui tōku wairua. Kei te pōuri ahau. Kei te mataku ahau i a Robbie rātou ko Mallet, ko Jake mā.'

Has no idea if he has used the correct kupu to convey to her that he feels sick in his soul, and that he is sad and fearful of the others, Robbie, Mallet and Jake in particular.

'Kei te marama ahau.'

She nods. Manaia does understand, but something is troubling her.

'Whakarongo mai, e hoa.'

He is listening; he is all attention, and anxious.

'Ka haere mātou ki te pā tūwatawata.'

She tells him they are all leaving for their fortified village. Will they allow him to accompany them? Surely they will not abandon him after he has shed his clothes and bared his soul?

'Ka haere tātou ki te pā?' He hears the shake in his voice.

'Ka hoki mai koe ki te kāinga o Ropi.'

His heart sinks at hearing they would have him return to Robbie after all this, after healing his soul and shedding his old rotten garments. It seems they want him to be part of some trickery against Robbie.

Do the New Zealanders trust him enough to reveal the whole plan or does Manaia even know? He wrestles with asking her and decides it might be better not to know. At least that way Robbie cannot torture the truth from him. If he refused to go, would they take him with them? He shudders.

'Ka pai?' Manaia asks.

'Ka pai.'

Not at all ka pai, but what choice does he have? He has passed through a gateway and there is no going back now. He is among them, and they are placing trust in him. If he refuses, well . . . he has no idea what would happen.

Perhaps this is his chance to finally draw a line between himself and Robbie, show courage. Return, but with his new skin.

CHAPTER 31

Restless in a dome-shaped guest-house, smaller than the one he shared with Robbie and the other men at the beginning of the season, Cuthbert wrestles with his predicament. Fear is a knot in his stomach, but if he could fight its cause he could surely relax and sleep. What is the worst that could happen? Head on a pike. He wishes he had not asked himself; better still, not answered.

What does he want? He remembers Bill asking him that. He knows what he does not want — to return to Sydney, to travel upriver to Parramatta, to shove God into the shocked minds of infants who have been torn from their parents.

He wants — he wants — to go back to the New Zealand village he first lived in, up in the Northern Island. Perhaps it is possible. He could take someone from here; surely someone would agree to venture up north with him, help him to put his case, test the waters. He could vouch for them and they for him. Surely New Zealanders from here could assure those good people up there that he, Cuthbert, never wished to bring death to these shores?

He will humble himself, because it worked here in this place, appearing naked and on his knees. He will apologise to them too, that community he abandoned, explain that he did not mean to be an agent of harm. Resurrect relations with his Māori wife and her family, live among them as one of them.

Surely it is possible to go back?

———

In her pain Bridie reaches back to the past, to the New Zealand man she met in Sydney, gives herself the gift of imagining him. Imagines herself reaching up to touch the long stone of green. Her finger traces a trail from the soft lobe of his ear to the dark specks in the stone.

'Roimata', he says.

'Tears', she says.

'Tears,' he says.

'Roimata,' she says.

Wet, her face, her hands. She flaps her wet hands. He takes her face in his hands and she opens her eyes . . .

When she sees it is not him but Manaia holding her face, the fantasy shrinks. The present hits her with a force she cannot push away.

She closes her eyes and sees the truth. For the whole season she has nursed fantasies of returning to Sydney and seeking him out, imagined him as a sailor fresh off a ship, imagined him as a farm worker on Marsden's estate, imagined him returning from the bush. Imagined she could escape Robbie's clutches and find her true protector; they could protect each other.

Sure, she was, that she would find him if she searched every fusty smoky corner of every rumbling ken, scouring streets and lanes, seeking him out amongst all the sailors and adventurers. She even thought that if she learned enough words of his tongue she could describe him, enquire his whereabouts by visiting his people.

Imagined even, begged of Brighid, that she could go back to that afternoon with her ma, give Ma the coin for the bonnet so she can buy it, own it, wear it, so she could look like a settler instead of an Irish convict. But she cannot go back. Ma is dead, her hair stolen — her body too, most like — and that New Zealand man is not in her future. She pushes the question from her mind but it keeps coming back.

To face the truth, she must face the past. Place herself back in that room at the back of the Shipwright's Compass, with the lordly judge.

If she looks closely at the cabinet in that room she will see what she wants to push away, but she wants to keep him living, cannot bear to see his head on that shelf. In a cabinet like an ornament. She screams, screams and screams. Hears singing and wonders if she is dead at last, whether women are keening her as they keened her mother. Opens her eyes and sees that the women are singing for her to heal.

So easy it would be to stay in this place. Under this spell of singing, she feels not just a strengthening of her body but something new inside and outside of her, like a light; her own flame strengthens in their company. She wants to rouse herself, raise herself up, warn them that New Zealanders who live in Sydney to work, to ply trades, to sail the world are considered prey by the English. English head-hunters. English body-snatchers. That the body-snatchers have crossed the ocean, that whalers are headers.

The hands of those killers have mishandled her, harmed her, harmed Manaia, will harm more men and women. She needs to warn these people, urge them to flee as far away as possible from Ropi — she has started calling him this herself now — from Robbie and his men. And yet, and yet, there is Tom.

Like the wind snatching a flame, Robbie has been. He tried to snuff out her light, but she is alive, and he must pay for this season of killing.

———

Men and women smile at Cuthbert as he wends his way back to the healing house. He wonders what they make of him. Perhaps they smile because they believe he was party to Manaia's return. Tamariki skip along beside him. Scream in horror, giggle in delight. Inside the whare he finds that Bridie has drifted into sleep. He needs to wake her, show that he is not his old self, he has changed.

He touches the tattoo on her arm, smiles tenderly as she slowly draws open the curtains of her eyes.

'It's not only men who carry the pitchforks and spades in a rebellion, it is women,' he starts in straight away. 'Strong and brave women. The bean sídhe was attracted to your comb but it met a spirit that would not let go.'

'This doesn't sound like you.' Bridie looks at him. 'Sure, tomorrow you will be back to quoting the Bible.'

Silence lies in the shared tears. Hers and his. He squeezes her hand. Her eyes, clear now, smile at him, the green of them like Éireann fields, like the eyes of her mother, approving him for seeing beyond all those fences that keep people confined.

He feels unburdened, as though he has indeed pulled up all the palings that contained the field of his mind.

Manaia has placed her hand in Bridie's.

'Me moe koe.'

'Yes, sleep,' he says.

'Thank you, Murphy the sky pilot.'

He turns to thank Manaia.

'Āe, me moe ia. Tēnā rawa atu koe. E noho rā.'

Bridie's eyes shut, but as he makes a motion to leave she shifts her weight onto an elbow, raises herself up.

'We need to go back. Save Tom.'

It is not a question but a command.

CHAPTER 32

Sombre the atmosphere in the long hut like heavy cloud after a summer's day. Jaunty, wild, fantastical festivities had raged the night. The weather had raged too. The sand, the grit of it in Robbie's eyes, on his lashes, in his beard and hair; it even coats the sea biscuit and grates in the bottom of his dish of tea.

Through the square of the window the morning sun is hidden behind a grimace. The sky full of boxers punching fists. Only a handful of men have turned up to break fast at the bench where Nob is dishing out the tea and plates of fried cod. To his irritation Robbie sees that something is bothering Bill. The big man won't meet his eyes.

When he rises from the bench, Robbie rises too, follows him as he returns to his coopering station. Feels fed up to his eyeballs — and other balls for that matter — with the man for always being on the edge of fun, for shouldering a certain burden of morality. For offloading onto others his smouldering judgments.

Wrong, Bill is, for the wrongs done are caused to him not by him, Robbie. There's an action and a reaction, and that is a fact. Bill should instead be directing his anger towards the stupid ungrateful dimber who buried the heads, and the seasonwife who spent the season laying a curse on them all.

Bill's head is down, hat pulling a low shadow over his eyes, as he strides back and forth pulling out the warped planks from his cooper's hut.

'I want a word, Bill.'

'Can't stop, sir. Work to do.'

Robbie regards the piles of wood, the half-finished and quarter-finished puncheons. Solid worker, Bill, he won't deny that. The four men who work with him are back in the long hut, the sluggards. But Robbie can feel a cloud of judgment coming from the man. Feels a desire to pull out his knife and drive it straight into his throat. But he needs the vessels Bill makes, and he wants to win the approval of the old man, who has served alongside him and who now serves under him. He needs to explain Bridie's disappearance.

'She's been kidnapped,' says Robbie.

'Who's that?'

'The dimber. Bridie.'

'Right you are.'

'Stolen by the New Zealanders. Missionary's gone too.'

'I see.'

The tone of the man, like a father talking to a child who claims to have seen fairies supping a dish of lap for their afternoon tea.

'I've a plan. We'll attack, shoot the tattooed buggers. The men might even skin a few, while I grab the dimber.'

'May I venture to say—'

'You may.'

'—that I see a small tear in the canvas of your plan, sir.'

'Being a cooper you would be a master strategist.'

'Thank ye, sir.'

Is the man mocking him?

'Might it be better if you—'

'Shut your gob. Shut your fucking idiot gob.'

'Sorry, sir.'

Robbie sees his head cooper anew, not as the wise old confidant, but as the village idiot.

'Look at me.'

'All right but I won't talk, sir.'

The halfwit clearly does not understand the whole plan, or surely he would see the sparkling brilliance of it.

'If she is killed,' Robbie, continues, 'it'll be their fault, not mine. And then . . .' He wants to say he would rejoice.

'You would rightly mourn, sir.'

Idiocy confirmed. The whole marvellousness of the plan must be confided, must be approved. Bill's refusal to give him the nod is driving him to madness.

'The story we would take back to Sydney is that they are killers — slaughtering, eating a woman who is little more than a child. That would bring the weight of the New South Wales government down on the New Zealanders, might even bring a man o' war to wipe them out. And who would profit from such an attack? Who has already staked his claim to the land, the whole fucking bay?'

'I see, sir.'

'Good. Marvellous. Fucking brilliant, is it not? And we must waste no time. You stay here, keep the fires burning and get the puncheons ready. We will put off soon.'

He marches off, for it's all settled now, and Bill can lump it.

'Bastardly gullion.'

The words stab his back like a knife plunged and twisted.

'All the fucks in fucking Hell, what did you call me? I see you judging me, you and the sky pilot all cosy, but you try managing a station!'

'Beg pardon, but all you heard was my phlegmy cough and the roar of the sea on stones.'

The man makes a show of coughing, spits phlegm. Smart enough, Bill, to play the halfwit, it seems. Call his bluff, he will.

'Aye, well, you stay put and keep up your coopering, but Bill the younger—'

'What about my boy?'

All attention Bill is now, rising from his little stump of a stool. Smug satisfaction melts in Robbie like rum seeping through the aches and knots in his spine.

'Your lad will get his first taste of bloodshed. An advance, an attack, a victory.'

Such merriment he finds in watching the cooper muse on the fact that his boy's life might be cut short.

'Please sir, no sir. Don't take him, for it will put me behind. He helps me out when he can and he's a good watch, as you know, sir.'

'Pity, isn't it, that your coughing and the voice of the sea were so rude to me? The boy comes with me.'

Times it perfectly, the stride in the striding away, leaving the clod of fear to bang and break on the simpleton's head. Hears a sound, and ducks. Is Bill throwing something at him? Surely not. A whoosh, a feathered thing — a spear with a clutch of white feathers. A New Zealand spear? He looks up from the bank of cockles onto which he has stumbled. Sees a flash of blue-black. A parson bird. Sees Bill nodding, cupping his hands to his mouth, calling out.

'A sign, that is. An omen.'

Robbie turns his back, resumes his stride. Even if the bird did seem to aim directly at him, seem intent on stabbing him with its vicious little beak, it was not — nor will he ever deem that it was — a fucking sign. Even it were, a sign of what precisely? Sign of nothing, that's what it was. Nothing.

———

Every part of Manutaki is awake. This sentry knows that being important to the people does not mean being arrogant, proud. He is guided by love and a desire to protect. His eyes protect his people. His feet have carried him far, so far. He knows now he is walking towards the scent of danger. The tohu are clear. The mist, the sound of the trees, the strange light coming over the water that seems not to come from the rising sun but some other place beyond. Now his eyes are on mist gathering and spreading over the waves in the cove. This is the place where the tauiwi captain and his men endlessly hunt. The stench of death is all around. So much death.

His eyes catch something moving through the mist as it peels back from the land. Two ghost waka, red-brown the colour, like the feathers of the weka. Two vessels sliding through mist, slipping over the quiet morning waves. He wonders if it is a tohu, atua, wairua that he sees, but as the mist shreds he catches a glimpse of the wide pāua eyes, the threatening lolling tongues on the carvings of these war waka that are drawing into the shallows.

Out they leap, bold warriors splashing through the water, weapons raised as they thunder up the beach. He must alert the other sentries and the rangatira. A ripple of fear but a thrill too, for he has walked further, spotted what others have not, proof that young eyes are useful but old legs can walk far, old eyes can see far.

He, Manutaki, strides quietly. He is intent on returning swiftly to the village when he sees a boy sitting on a platform like a fat little pigeon. He cannot risk calling to the child and being spotted, so he crawls under the canopy of fern to the cleared land on top of the hill. From his vantage point he hears the boy — who must be a sentry like himself — call down to the beach, a sharp warning cry.

A warrior running up the shore glances in the boy's direction. Manutaki ducks. Slides over to the boy, who is now climbing down the ladder from the platform. Pulls the boy and tumbles him over and over. Tucks him under an arm and runs. But his breath becomes heavy and his feet slow. He realises he has to leave the boy or he will not make enough speed to reach the kāinga, to warn his people.

At the first hollow under the roots of a large kahikatea he puts the boy, covers him with fern, motioning at him to be still. The young sentry's tears move him, remind him of his own sons when they were young. They are grown now and living with their wives in their own whare with their own children. His heart swells with aroha. He tries to reassure the boy but the child is terrified.

As he runs he prays, prays to Ranginui and Papatūānuku, the gods of sky and land and all that dwell within.

All around him he hears the whisper and roar — the tīpuna are here to remind him he is not alone. Above the heaving ocean he runs into the dark forest. Long flying strides of his old, strong legs, breathing through his body all the way from below his feet to above his head. Up the hill, above the valley of harakeke, through the forest of tall trees he flies. Plunges under the wet fans of fern trees and up again and down. Pounds over the platforms that bridge the kūmara plantations. Signals at the sentries not to blow the pūtātara so as not to alert the attackers or those who are being attacked.

Two women stand in front of the strong, carved posts of the gate where ancestors carry ancestors. Restless women pacing in front of the ancestral beings. No need for him to ask how they know. The knowledge of danger must have been conveyed to Rima and Manaia by sentries in that other realm, the dwelling place of departed souls.

CHAPTER 33

After yet another rowdy night, the floor of the long hut where Robbie lies is sodden with rum. He wakes to a grating sound coming to him over the slink and slip of waves. Eases his pocket watch out of his damp coat.

Ten minutes to the hour of six. Not yet dawn. Keenly he listens until he can be sure — yes, it is the sinister scrape of a wooden belly sliding on shells, deadly sound of canoes slipping into the crusted sand. Moves fast — fast as a boy. Pushes Mallet, who lies belly-up beside him on the floor. Huskily he whispers. Move, fucking move, move, move.

Five men rush to the unfinished end of the hut. Robbie pushes the first two into the hesitant light. Hears the shocked gasp, the stagger and fall. Darts out and under the commotion, arms pummelling, thinking only about himself, the need to fight low, aim for the groin, an old trick he learned in Black Lion Yard. Only two warriors at this end, and the mist, the dear mist is rolling so he can hide behind its curtain. Hears the blunt thwack of a stone axe cracking a skull, another whack against the throat, the gasp and rattle of death. From the warriors come laughter and jeers.

In blind muddlement, in rolling roils of mist, he can hear the rhythm of men clubbed before they have a chance to wake — all his pirate coves, all his crew. He makes a dash up the bank and into the forest. Mallet, whose breathing seems laboured by shock, runs with him. They are joined by Jake and Ivory. So far uphill it is, the forest.

He curses the clearing of it, but fortune comes with the mist that tumbles over them, becoming a blessed shroud.

Panting hard, they stop somewhere near the top of the hill, well off any hint of a path, deep in the forest. Silence but for their panting and the burble of water. They move slowly and quietly until they are sure there is no one hunting them down. Crouch themselves on a log, arses cushioned by moist moss.

'Anyone got a gun, pistol, musket, anything other than fucking nothing?' asks Robbie.

Vigorous shaking of heads.

'This whole mess is the fault of those crank cuffin pirates. One fucking rule, I says, is don't leave no one alive. Take the lot, I says. They can keep each other company grinning in a glass case.'

'There's always someone left to come after us,' says Mallet.

'Not if we put a bullet through every mother's son of them.'

'Favourite phrase that, ain't it? Favourite fucking phrase and look where it's got us.' This from Ivory.

'Would you like me,' asks Robbie, 'to shatter your stinking teeth and force them down your throat? Because I have a mind to turn a witless fucker into a toothless, witless fucker.'

'We'll wait it out. Hide and wait,' Mallet suggests.

Robbie nods, eases himself up off the log. Walks a few paces, picks a handful of leaves, shits, wipes his arse with the leaves.

'Sitting and waiting is for cowards,' says Ivory.

The man has much to learn.

'You wouldn't be so brave if your eyeballs were swallowed for break of fast. Listen all, are we men who want to live?'

Aye and aye.

'To life, to us all fucking keeping on fucking living,' says Jake, as though he has a tankard in hand.

To Mallet, Robbie confides the plan after taking him aside.

'That bastard Ivory is—' Mallet starts.

'A liability. Here's the plan. First, we stay and hide. Even if it takes a day or three. We have water and we can kill a rat or two. We don't go back till the canoes have gone. Aye?'

'Aye, Captain.'

———

Only when the New Zealand warriors from the north have retreated does Robbie order his remaining men to make their way back down to the beach. The slaughter has been swift, the warriors successful in avenging the murder of their people by Robbie's pirate associates. Surveying the damage, Robbie feels frustration mounting. A mockery has been made of his work, his careful planning. In one morning the northern warriors have rendered it all undone. On the beach, he regards the motley collection of survivors. Musters the miserable bastards.

'They hacked off the heads of your sea beggar friends — and our good mates,' says Nob.

Someone — Ivory, most likely — whimpers. Infuriates Robbie, this sign of weakness.

'They should have taken your heads too, it seems, for you lost them, and your guts too, for fucking garters,' Robbie snarls.

His plan — the whole of it — was contrived in haste, but when he hears himself laying it out now to the handful of men, the beauty of it astonishes him. So masterful. Strategical.

Mallet and the others will depart for the ship and stay anchored in the cove. When the local natives come for himself, the captain, as they surely will, he will employ his powers of persuasion. Chuffed, he is, puffed full of joy, for he's mulled it over and, even though so much is lost, it need not be — surely it need not be — all lost.

'They've played into our hands, see? We'll tell the toffs in Sydney that we were brutally brutalised, savagely attacked by savage New Zealanders, that they took my wife, slaughtered our men. That they cooked our men. Ate them.'

'Did they?'

'Most certainly.'

'Meanwhile, Mr Sky Pilot will persuade the natives who live near here of our good and great intentions. We will plant the seed in them that they themselves could be attacked from the north at any time.'

Nods at Mallet. Mallet nods back.

'Through the sky pilot, Cuthy, I will vow to the New Zealanders that if they let us leave for Sydney . . .'

He pauses, for the men cheer at the name of their beloved township.

'. . . we will come back with guns and axes, harpoons and blankets and more guns. Yes, we will honour our deed with them.'

'Our deed?'

'To buy all the land. Don't play the fool, Ivory. It's not the time.'

'Why will they believe the promise that we will return?'

'We will leave them the dimber, and one or two of our most useless men.'

A gleam in Mallet's eye, Robbie sees. He knows Ivory will be one of those useless men.

'Pretend they attacked us and stole the Irish girl,' says Mallet. 'My oath, Captain Fitch, that's fucking brilliance.'

'Aye, we will push for the New South Wales government to grant us a force, the navy, a man o' war. When we return we will clean the buggers out. A bullet for every mother's—'

'—son,' says Mallet.

The men, his coves, clap and cheer. Stop when he reminds them that there is much to do before they celebrate. As they row out to the ship, Mallet's voice sluices through the wake.

'Brilliant, fucking brilliant.'

Robbie slips his pocket watch from his waistcoat, squints his eyes, for the light on the rim is bright.

Ten minutes, the long hand says, to the hour of noon.

CHAPTER 34

Bridie chides herself for thinking the sweet potato from yesterday tasted dry, for she is sick of dry food. Misses butter, longs for a dob of cream as she did on the whaling station, struggling to eat yet another dry sea biscuit. She longs for butter here when the people so proudly present her with more potato. Stupid, selfish thoughts such as might be entertained by the sterling, the rich, conceited settlers of New South Wales. Childish moaning. Not that she had spoken aloud, but no doubt Brighid heard and thought to teach her a lesson. It all starts to unravel right after her selfish thinking.

When Cuthbert tells her the rangatira of the village have decided to hold back, she asks what he is talking about.

'They have determined not to interfere. They do not want to become embroiled in a bloody war. They say they must have reason for seeking utu on the tauiwi. And they shall have it.'

'What on this earth are you are talking about?'

'You haven't heard? It's been spreading like a merry little dance of a fire, heading down one path then another till it has gobbled the whole kāinga.'

'Talk straight!'

'Sorry, I forget sometimes that you do not comprehend their language. Manutaki saw war canoes landing in the cove.'

'In our — Robbie's cove?'

'Warriors from the Northern Island come to avenge Robbie's pirates,' he says.

'But Tom, my Tom . . . I have to go, and you — you know him, you must please come.'

'I am stricken with fear for him but I can pray, we must pray. I am sure they will not touch a child, and to run towards this would be foolish. I cannot stand by and watch you get yourself killed in a massacre. And besides, you have not yet recovered.'

She will not heed him, barely hears him. She needs to escape all the gentle kindness, the healing hands, the loving songs, the love of these New Zealanders towards herself, a selfish butter-loving stranger.

All she can think on as she rises is her brother. His sandy hair, baby cheeks, sun-stained spots of Sydney's summer on his face, colour of tea, those spots. She dons the finely woven cloak Manaia has gifted her.

She had hoped that Manaia might come with her, but she will not. Afraid for her own people, or tired of playing guardian to a stupid Irish girl. Cuthbert will surely follow, she thinks, but he does not. After all his beguiling talk, that man has not changed. As she crosses the bridge over the kūmara plantations she hesitates, looks back at the elaborately carved ancestral gates. No one has come with her. She is alone.

Alone when she enters the forest, alone when she skirts the hill and walks alongside the stream near the seal pool. She cannot turn back, she must keep walking forward. She prays to Brighid, to Jesus, to Mary, to anyone she can think of, even to her mother.

'Please let Tom be alive. Please do not let me be killed by vengeful warriors.'

———

Beside the skeletal hulls of whales and the shrugged-off skins of seals are other forms, oddly mangled, strangely familiar. Gulls plummet for pickings along the shore. The smell is burnt flesh, but not like the back yard stink of Caddock's butchery or the pungent sickly stink of whale. This is the singed smell of burnt hair. Unbidden, the words singing around and around. Fee-fi-fo-fum, I smell the blood of an Englishman.

Wanders, she does, in a haze of smoke. If any of their own were wounded or killed the New Zealanders have taken them away over the sea, for there are no warriors on the beach. Some men she recognises only from their material remains. A corpse burnt black, charred fingers hold a bone fragment of scrimshaw. Sadness and fear curdle in her belly. She hears the words of the song round and rounding in her head. Be he alive or be he dead.

Outside the long hut she finds the body of Bill the older, whose ring shines from the middle finger of his disembodied hand, his charred torso hung over two hoops he had been rendering for puncheons. She imagines him raising one in defence. Bill did not deserve this.

A shrill voice behind her — Bill the younger, sliding, running towards her. There is no time to hide this from him. When he sees his father's hand, he writhes in distress.

'I called a warning and then I hid. Had not the courage to come down,' he says. 'I'm sorry, Pa. Sorry, sorry.'

She strokes the boy's shaking shoulders.

'Tom?' he asks, eyes bloodshot from lack of sleep.

'Let's look together.'

She senses it, even before she sees him. The world is already different, emptied of him. The small body lies still, the mouth open, as though he awaits a piece of sugared candy, the spirit of him flown before it had time to grow.

She would scream but the silence forbids it. Silent, the birds, even the waves are whispering her to hush. The words come again. Fee-fi-fo. Be he alive or be he dead. I'll grind his bones to make my bread. Fum. Fuck. Fuck.

Bill is on his knees, blood on his hands as he touches his friend. Blood. She feels the great rack inside her give way but she holds on, she must wait.

'We must go now. I doubt any good men survived this.'

'The captain, Robbie — I seen him and Mallet and some others head into the forest,' says Bill. 'Didn't see no sign of them again.'

She hopes the warriors found them and gutted them. Fee-fi-fo. Clasps Bill's hand. Leads him around the remains of men, the huge hulls of whales torn apart, the bones scattered, many taken as treasures no doubt.

Inside the tent she finds the empty chests, her garments strewn, some gone. She picks up her emerald gown, slips it over her head, draws the cloak back over her shoulders. Pulls the plum red over young Bill's head, the boy struggling until she admonishes him.

'It's not for you. Take it off when you see Manaia — red is her colour.'

That the guns have gone makes her fearful. She bends a little, speaks urgently to Bill the younger, reminds herself there is no need to call him that now. So sad and small he seems, a child swamped in a gown. Shoves him in the direction of the cabbage trees and the hill straight up from the beach.

'Run back up to the watch hut and hide somewhere at the top. I think some good people will come soon. Manaia and the others. They will look after you.'

'One already did care for me — saved me.'

He tells her and she realises he has encountered the strong and gentle sentry, Manaia's uncle Manutaki.

'Robbie says they deserve a bullet, every mother's son,' he says. 'It is terrible wrong to say that, isn't it?'

A sound — part anger, part sob — is forcing itself out of her. She holds the boy in the dress close, closes her eyes and feels the moan of the keen rising. Shuts it down.

'It's on account of Robbie that your father and my brother are dead. Bill, your father, was a decent man.'

Shaking, she looks to the dismembered limbs outside the long hut, at the abandoned whales, mounds of seals, the strewn bones, dead trees, charred remains of men who sailed and sang and hunted. Unrecognisable in death. What's it all been for?

'It was harmony so fine here when we arrived, and now it is Hell. So go, get out of here.'

He seems to sleepwalk.

She yells after him.

'And stay well clear of Robbie.'

CHAPTER 35

Devious dark eyes on her she senses; knows he knows how to keep himself alive. Her feet carry her but she is elsewhere, thinking ahead. Back when she buried the heads she also buried a pistol, a purse of powder.

Bridie stumbles towards the clutch of cabbage trees. Under trees she kneels. Wades her hands through the grass to a pile of stones, to the whale bone marker. Removes the boulder, takes out the oilskin parcels, the gun, the pouch.

She unwraps the parcels and props the gun between her knees. Shakes the pouch of powder. Barrel up, she pours the powder inside the gun. Takes a ball from the pouch and presses it hard into the muzzle. She is about to take the ram and force the ball down when she hears a shift in the shells. A scrape. Like a foot pressed down.

It is in a fresh roll of sea mist that he appears — his naked feet, the slight protrusion of his belly, dry gristle stink of him, and beneath the tangle of his beard that mouth, that ever-open, mocking, swearing, jeering trap.

Cocks her gun. Fires a cloud. Hears the bark of the gun, sees him fall. At his agonised shriek she could dance for joy. Moves slowly forward, each step the edge of a precipice. Sees him crawling, flapping an arm. Shudder, shudder, twitch. Moving towards him, she raises the pistol as a club.

So fast, the movement of him rolling to his knees in front of her.

He jumps, seems to angle away but her wrist jerks as he pushes the gun out of her hand.

'Surprise!' he laughs. 'Thought you could fell me with the barking iron, eh?' Cough-laughs at his own comedy. Shoves his fuming chops in her face.

'Alive I am, and oh, so well, you stupid bog-trotter, despite your best efforts. You really cannot do anything right.'

Keep trying, she thinks. Don't give up. When he pulls her hair she bites hard the stump of his finger. Rejoices as he howls, sobers when he draws his knife, shivers as he holds the cold steel against her neck. Out of the corner of her eye she sees him roll the handle of the knife, feels the blade turn, the point pricking her skin. Stepping back, he mock-nurses the wound. Takes a finger, wipes her blood. Sucks.

'I will hack off your head and have it for supper. Come to think of it, I'm awful hungry. Who do you think they would blame, the cannibal natives or Captain Me?'

'You buckeen, you bastardly gullion, Robbie Fitch!' She is not done yet.

Satisfaction as his jaw tightens, a nerve twitching.

'So you're fly to the cant — you can thank me for that, you fly-by-nighter,' he says.

'I'll be thanking you surely when your hooves are dancing a jig upon nothing.'

'But it is a beautiful thing, my plan. See, I go back to Sydney, tell the toffs — including your man the judge — that these New Zealanders, these savages, killed the men and your brother Tom. It's not a bounce, it's only putting the slide on the truth.'

'It's a complete lie. The people here have been kind to us. Those who killed my brother and the others came in mourning and anger after your coves went after them, besieging and beheading.'

'The press will love the notion that the savages attacked us for no good reason, stripped you down to a perfect state of nudity, ill-used you. Play the spoiled lily and you could be the Queen of Sydney.'

'A rigmarole you've conjured, so roundabout nonsensical they'll never swallow it.'

'As usual, my dimber, you underestimate the sophistry of this deception. My plan is perfect. Toffs crave deceit. As they say, 'Mingere cum bumbis, res saluberrima est lumbis'.

He crouches, squeezes his buttocks.

'Piss and fart, sound at heart.'

Again, she sees, he's entertainment to himself. She tries another tack.

'You think the New Zealanders you've harmed will wave from the shore, bid you a peaceful farewell?'

'Cuthbert will do my bidding. On my behalf he will assure them that I will return from Sydney with guns, blankets and more than enough flumadiddle to make up for their losses and their travail.'

'Never believe it, they won't.'

'You will also assure them it's the truth. See, young Bill bolted straight for the forest and into me. I will chop his fucking head off if you don't inform that grumbletonian sky pilot and your native mates that I must be set free so I can return and pay them handsomely.'

'Except you won't.'

'Surely, I will pay them with something better than coriander. One cannon ball, maybe two would finish off the buggers. We'll burn out the survivors.'

She can see his mind working, a knot on the side of his jaw twitching, eyes shifting, can see he is planning aloud as he goes along.

'Here's my considered answer.' She spits at him, makes herself grin as he wipes the glob from his cheek.

———

The night seems to be at its darkest pitch as he drags her to the longboat and puts out from shore, turning the oars and singing — singing about a dusky maiden and a king taunting her. Pauses in his singing once they are far out from the shore. She, shivering in the cold wind, he merry merry. Fee-fi-fo, she thinks. If only.

'You know the New Zealand girl, my seasonwife, she wasn't like you. Very engaging, that girl. Relished every moment of my bedding her.'

The words seem to spill out of their own accord. 'Touch of you is so loathsome she turned it on you. Have you forgotten how you lost your finger? See the stump of it? That's your reminder. Not much bigger than the size of your cock, as I remember.'

Bitter the stink of his laughing breath.

'I could toss you.'

Wishes she wouldn't shiver but she does; shivers so violently she is almost sick.

'But I won't. Why? Because I am your one and only protector. The only man who has ever tried to offer you a proper future, and I can still save us both if you will try to be as clever as myself. Because all this' — he waves an arm — 'all this is a great big mighty bloody fucking loss, has set us back, I'll admit that. So we need to recuperate our finances somehow. So let me think. Yes, yes. When I rescue you from the natives you can come back to Sydney. We will make a report in the paper about how sad it's all been, a fragile flower abducted by savages. We'll raise funds by rousing pity.'

'May all the good gods damn you, Robbie Fitch. Brighid, Jesus, Mary and—'

'It will matter not,' he says. 'My god is Goliath the giant.'

'Who was felled by a boy.'

'No he wasn't.'

'I tell you truly, Goliath was felled by a boy with a slingshot.'

As she says it, Tom comes to mind. Tom swinging up in the rigging, holding a hand to the wide sky.

'I'd forgotten,' says Robbie.

'Forgotten Tom?'

'No, you stupid dimber. About the slingshot. What was the boy's name?'

'David.'

'I'll switch my allegiance. Davey, that's my God. Clever lad who felled a giant.'

————

He orders her up the net of ropes while he ties the boat to the ship, holds the boat steady as she climbs. In darkness she stretches her arms and legs, grabs at the web of ropes, feels the weight of hurt in her arms. Remembers Tom as she climbs, weeps as she climbs, looks down below, to Robbie tying the boat to the ship. Fee-fi-fo. She looks down to the black water. Could she float herself back in the black waves? He grabs her ankle, reading her thoughts.

'Drowning ain't a pretty death. And remember, I will cut young Bill's throat.'

She feels him climbing up behind her; soon his breath will be on hers, his body will crush her.

For one glittering moment before she throws herself over the taffrail she raises her eyes to the wide field of stars. Somewhere in that constellation are Ma and Tom, their names forever on her tongue and in her tears.

Something draws her down, over the taffrail into softness, a hand on her mouth. Cradled in arms, she looks up to see Robbie climb onto the rail, raise the lantern, steady himself. He gives one shocked yelp as a strong arm pulls him back to the deck. Manaia holds a lantern to Robbie's scowl and a young New Zealand man stands behind him, pinning the big man's arms.

Bridie looks about her. Among the figures huddled on the deck, she sees Cuthbert and Bill. Young Bill still wearing the red gown, now shredded, which makes sense because Manaia is wearing a red ribbon around her forehead.

'Tihei mauri ora!' yells Cuthbert. 'Huzzah! Huzzah!'

'But how?' Bridie asks him.

'If you spoke their language you would understand. She was never going to leave you, and neither, it turns out, was I.'

'May the ruffin cly thee, you fucking rantallion!' cries Robbie.

'And fuck you,' says Cuthbert, rising and stepping over Mallet, Jake and Ivory, bound and lifeless. 'I believe I should have said that a long time ago.'

He gives a hand to young Bill.

'Would you do the honours and shut this man up?'

Young Bill saunters towards Robbie, a swagger to him.

Bridie watches as the young New Zealand man hands Manaia a large stone patu.

''Twas those savages killed your father, Billy,' says Robbie.

'It was on account of *you* they came for us!'

'Me?' says Robbie. 'I'm only one link in a long chain—'

He seems about to say more but young Bill smashes his small fist on Robbie's jaw.

Robbie shakes his head, annoyed and baffled. Manaia steps forward, eyes rolling, jeering. Leaps high and down to strike the patu against Robbie's head.

Bridie dances. Dances for the living and for the sake of a sweet moment in time worth saving, and for all the good people who deserve Brighid's protection. Links arms with Manaia and dances, around and around and back and forth. Manaia laughs too, laughs and laughs. Then the young New Zealand man puts his arm around Manaia and pulls her to him. She leaps onto his back like a child, clinging to his shoulders, whispers in his ear.

'Who's this then?' Bridie asks Cuthbert.

'Rāwhiti.'

'I have a plan,' mumbles Robbie.

Bridie marches over to him. Takes the cravat he so fondly wears. Binds his struggling mouth with the cravat. Spitalfields, the cravat, finest silk, as he likes to tell them at every opportunity. With all the fury she has stored up over the winter, like sticks she has stored to burn, she faces him.

'I have a better plan,' she says.

CHAPTER 36

All the possibilities swell inside him. It won't be easy to face his New Zealand wife, Cuthbert knows this. By now she might well have taken up with someone else. Regardless, he must explain to her and her whānau that he was not in league with Robbie, that he did not know there were heads in that sack, he did not.

He must convey to them his regrets at the bungling stupidity of the mission in trading guns and failing to stand up against the whalers who were head-hunters. Humble himself, tell them he regrets his cowardly decision to abandon his wife and her people rather than stay and explain. Regrets above everything the rash decision he made on that golden sand to pledge himself to Robbie and sail to Sydney. It was a selfish decision made in a fleeting moment, which put him back to being a servant, bound to powerful men — traders, churchmen, whalers, headers.

He puts it to young Bill that he could take him under his wing, become a father of sorts. It matters, this, for he feels his skin changing colour as he puts the idea, feels the pleasure when Bill the younger, and fatherless now, agrees.

After two meetings Kāhu Kōrako informs Cuthbert that a group of young men will leave with him for the north. These men will assist him in sailing the ship, to gain knowledge, to return and share knowledge with the people who remain.

Manaia drapes a kahu kererū over him. This cloak is finer than any coat he has ever owned, any cloak from London or Sydney. As she takes hold of his shoulders, tears slip from his eyes to his cheeks, to his chin, to his chest.

During the hongi he feels his breath being drawn from the light under the black water of a deep well. Hā ki roto. He releases his breath in love and relief, to the wind, the sky, and all the trees shaking above the beach. Hā ki waho.

She steps back, her eyes smiling kindness. Tells him that his wairua, his spirit, is almost healed, but if he falters he should return and she will heal him again.

They all farewell him then, each taking his shoulders in the hongi. Rima, Kāhu Kōrako, Kauri, Rāwhiti, Manutaki.

Burgeoning freedom is what he feels when the sails crack, when the scudding wind fills them out so that they float above the water, taking the force of the wind inside, unfurling the light.

He sees them grow smaller, the people, all the whale bones, the makeshift houses, the long hut. The place Robbie called Fairhaven has the chance now to return to itself. He can barely see them, Bridie, Manaia and the others, as they wend their way back up the valley, the hill, the next valley, the next hill to the kāinga.

Above them a harrier hawk flies, returning, no doubt, to its peaceful nest.

―――――

Outside the ring of warmth, on his knees, mouth stuffed with raupo, hands bound with flax, is Robbie — struggling, shivering, falling.

The rangatira have deemed that the other prisoners will not be despatched, for death is an escape they ill deserve. Rather, they will lighten the load of those who serve. Ferrying rocks, digging traps and laying logs over deep ravines. Manaia and Bridie have been accorded the honour of deciding Robbie's fate.

In a circle around the outside fire Manaia's mothers warm their knees. A log cracks and interrupts the discussion. An older woman pokes Robbie with her foot.

Manaia rises to speak and the other women bow their heads to listen. Likes this, Bridie. Imagines how it would be for the Irish women to stand and list the crimes of the English — unwelcome landlords stealing land and food and homes, banning the language and stamping out the customs.

No translator is needed for the anger that flies from Manaia.

'We could carve him up and eat him,' says Bridie, whirling on her feet when it is her turn. She demonstrates, dancing out the mime. Gobbling him up with her hands. The women shriek with laughter.

Back and forth, in her language and theirs, her gestures and theirs. She pretends to crush him like a louse. Manaia pretends to slit his throat. The women slap their legs and point at Robbie's terrified expression.

Then it all seems to stop. The laughter dies, the wind that has been stirring the fire and brushing their hair sinks to a whisper. Words will be Bridie's weapon.

'Kei te mōhio ahau,' Manaia says, gesturing to Bridie, who also understands.

Over him Bridie stands now, for she will curse him in English.

'I want you to understand,' she says, 'every damning word.'

———

The weather obliges. Clouds are swollen black clods, the trees curl and shake their fists. She untangles it all, takes herself back to The Rocks of Sydney, to the Abbess and the judge and the trapdoor.

As she screams it out, her curse, the clouds let fall the dirty black rain, the wind screams up from the earth and down from the sky. All the anger and the agony for Ma and herself and Tom. The anger at what he did to Manaia. Claws at the soil, she does, digs and tugs until she clenches in her hands clumps of moss and bark and sand and soil, throws these at him with her words.

Casts her spell back, unwinds the binding of him to her, the damage of all he has done. Casts it back on him.

'Hark back, ruffin, to the time before you set sail, before you stole our ma's hair. May the wind on the cliff from that night find you here, cause you to fall on this wild shore. May gulls feast on your eyes and your ears. May a shark gobble your hairy balls.'

She stops, mock-considers. Takes on a toff's voice to query the price of heads. What is the market price? What coin would his head fetch? He leans forward on his knees, hands straining against the flax rope. Manaia and all the others, all the mothers, the daughters, the sisters, stand and hiss.

It will be a long while before their anger burrows into a hollow in the sand, ready to rise if these crimes are committed again.

'You turned on your hosts, stole from them. What kind of marriage did you make with this girl Manaia? A marriage of trickery, a short season where you would take, she would give? The season of stealing. The season of raping. The season of killing.'

Manaia presses into Bridie's hand a stone. She turns it over, sees the stone she touched that day all the way back in the store-room in Sydney. Sees the tears in the stone. Rubs the stone until she feels the rhythm thrum in her palm. All that is frozen melts, water-turned-stone-turns-water.

'Do you know who you stole this from?'

Robbie shakes his head.

Manaia kicks him.

'Do you remember what you did to him?'

Shakes his head. Another kick.

'This man walked, he talked, he loved, he laughed — and you stole from him that most precious thing: life. His spirit does not belong in an Englishman's cabinet. He will haunt you every day until he is returned to his people. Hear me? This curse is on you and your children and your children's children.'

The wind stirs the fire and the women begin moaning. The moan becomes a song. If the dead felled for the London markets could speak, what would they say? If the silenced Irish could speak, what would they say? The answer is a song rising up from the earth and down from the sky. Turf the soil to see the darkness beneath, turn it to green so it may sprout again.

Bridie needs the season of suffering to end, but it cannot, not quite. She unbinds his mouth.

'You will become our — what is the word? Mōkai?'

The women nod.

'Our servant. Our slave. You can serve us.'

'I'd rather you slit my fucking throat.'

'You will work from the crack of dawn to the last fall of light through every season. Fine weather and foul.'

Still clasping the stone, she reaches for Manaia's hand. The song passes between them and rises to her lips.

'Such a fine game comes to mind. The huntsman can become the hunted. You will run, but you can never run far enough.'

———

A sorry-for-himself tear slides from the crack of Robbie's left eye when Manaia holds the looking glass to the ugly tattoos on his face. His beard gone, shaved by a shell, the tattoos so horrible, so roughly made, a stick figure hanging from a gibbet, the broad arrow, and a thing that looks like a worm crawling under his nose. Disfigured he is, forever.

'E oma!' Manaia orders, prods him with a spear.

He scrambles to his knees and tries to run, stumbles, picks

himself up, runs proper now. Hears children, turns and yells for them to leave him bloody alone but they follow, taunting, waving spears, laughing. Into the darkness he runs, tumbles over a rock, rolls.

As he gets up, an image comes to him unbidden of the man he chased on the outskirts of Sydney. Is this what the New Zealanders mean by utu? He pushes the thought away. Terror courses through him, causes pain so sharp he feels it slicing through his breastbone. Brave, that New Zealand man had been, turning, facing his hunters, taking them on. A good man, cast down by him.

———

Crunch of leaves, crack of a bough. A shout — Bridie calling to Manaia in the New Zealand language. He knows she is carrying something, but what — a spear, a gun?

He sees it for a moment — the forest, the sun squeezing through branches, leaves littering the carpet of moss at his feet. Would consider it spectacular if he had time to pause. His breath is ragged, the forest is dense, and all the trees bend away from him. Sydney is so far off. So much sailing and running, and he must run now. Find a cave, hide.

He has made it down to the beach, is dragging his body for breath. Hears the hunting party crashing through the trees towards him. Nearly upon him, and where can he go to escape them?

Women, bloody women.

———

As they skip back, leaving the game of seek-and-chase for another day, Bridie smiles at Manaia, tickles her armpit. Manaia puts an arm around her, encircling her shoulders, then drops the arm and runs off. Following her, Bridie weaves along the path above the valley of flax, around the stream near the expanse of light. Bereft now, without the sparkle of seals. Feels a darkness stir her soul — a shadow, a warning. Shakes her head.

Just ahead, where the speargrass meets the trees, Manaia is waiting. With one leg on a rock, seeming to hear something, she shakes her head and leaps along the path. Bridie continues along the path towards the people who have claimed her as their own.

Their pace quickens, so hungry are they for the companionship of the people of the kāinga. Striding faster, ignoring that ripple, that whisper. Will not stop again to close their eyes and listen to all the senses.

Must not turn to see the blot of ink that dribbles down to spoil the page.

A ship drawing from the horizon into the cove.

Author's notes

This novel started life as a short fiction, 'A Perfect State of Nudity', written in 1995 and published by Penguin. The novel was written on various shores: in Aotearoa New Zealand, in Sāmoa, Tokelau and the Middle East (Saudi Arabia, Bahrain and Qatar). It was written during a time of personal and professional upheaval, in breezy fale, wafting seawater and frangipani; in souks smelling of coffee, oranges and hummus. Sometimes it was written in places where women must hide behind curtains and in places where the story becomes a veil.

It seems fitting that after so many landing places this novel landed in Te Kōrero Karoro, the haven of chattering seagulls, my home, New Brighton, between the estuary and the sea.

Although the story is purely fictional it is based on a perspective that has been hidden from the colonial narrative. Indigenous histories in colonial countries tend to be crushed, sometimes confined to graveyards. The voices of the poor, of the illiterate, are also crushed, their voices are denied and redirected, their languages stamped out.

And yet the truth has a way of rising up and out.

As a young newspaper journalist in the 1980s I covered the Ngāi Tahu land and fisheries claims before the Waitangi Tribunal. I experienced the hospitality of Ngāi Tahu, staying on marae throughout Te Waipounamu. I was nurtured by whāea and kaumātua; I was respected and treated with the utmost kindness.

While I was working for *The Press* in Christchurch a preserved Māori head came up for sale at an auction house in London and my newspaper editors tasked me to write about how such heads were stuffed. I told them they could get stuffed and get another journalist to do that job.

I was gratified later to read a fine piece by Bernard Levin about that head. Levin admonished the auction house, and anyone who would trade in human heads. What stuck with me was that Levin lamented the lack of imagination that sparks empathy. He said that these were the heads of people who had thought and lived and loved, who had looked at the stars.

His article made me think deeply about writers, about the surface level and the deeper level of stories — about the stories we tell ourselves.

This fictional work binds many threads woven from non-fiction. During the course of this research I was shocked to find a letter in which a man blithely referred to murdering a Māori man in the environs of Sydney in the 1830s. The unknown victim had been killed for his head and his skin. The head of a Māori woman was also offered to the buyer.

The letter was reproduced in a pamphlet as part of the Otago Provincial Histories Collection. It had been discovered and published in *The Countryman* in 1939, a hundred years after it was sent to Henry Aglionby, MP for Cockermouth in Cumberland.

Sydney, New South Wales,
20th May, 1839.
My dear Aglionby, — I have great pleasure in informing you that after considerable trouble and difficulty I have at last succeeded in procuring you a capital specimen of a New Zealander's head, and as soon as it is well cured and properly dried I shall send it to you by the first ship that leaves this colony, and I think that you will agree with me in considering it as a beautiful and curious ornament for the handsomest room in your house.

I fell in with the possessor of the head by the merest chance while proceeding from Sydney to South Cove, going through the plains with a party of Natives, and after a long chase we succeeded in bringing him down by a rifle shot, which fortunately did not injure any of the ornamental tattoos on his face, which I doubt not you will admire as much as I do.

If you would like his skin, I have it drying, and will send it to you the first opportunity. Some of the tattoos on it are exceedingly beautiful, particularly on certain parts, but one figure has suffered a little by the ball having passed through it.

Let me know as soon you can the receipt of the head, and tell me at the same time if you would like the head of a female, as I shall have great pleasure in supplying you.

Believe me, My dear Aglionby,

Ever yours sincerely,

I. W. WILLIS.

Reading about this murder led me to wonder more generally about the presence of Māori in Sydney during the early nineteenth century. I am enormously grateful to Rohan Howitt, who shared his honours thesis, 'Poihākena: Māori travellers and workers in New South Wales, 1793–1840'. His research into the establishment of an early Māori community in Sydney has proved invaluable to me in writing this novel.

Early on I was assisted by Grace Karskens, who generously supplied a huge array of information on early convict settlement in The Rocks, even before some of her own work had been published.

Bridie is named after Brighid, the Celtic Goddess, and the Saint of the same name. Serendipitously, in the year of the novel's publication, Brighid has for the first time been honoured by Ireland's Government with a public holiday on February 1st. It is the first Irish public holiday named after a woman, coinciding with Imbolc, the traditional Gaelic festival for new life and fertility.

Bridie's voice came to me in dreams, an insistence that women married whalers, walked these shores, and that their stories were not kept or conveyed. Author Joan Druett has written extensively on whaling wives at sea, but there was little written at that stage about shore station wives. Bridie's Irish character is inspired no doubt from my own Irish ancestor, Mary Jane Laverty, among others.

A base of fact in the novel stems from my own research for an MA in Creative Writing at the International Institute of Modern Letters at Victoria University in 2003, during which I found that some European women preferred to remain in Māori communities after their supposed 'capture'; given the chance, they chose not to return to European life.

The cant, the flash language Robbie uses, was drawn from sources including *Musa Pedestris: Three centuries of cant songs and slang rhymes (1536–1896)* by John S. Farmer, and *A Classical Dictionary of the Vulgar Tongue* by Francis Grose (first published in 1785) and *Memoirs of James Hardy Vaux, vols 1–2* (1819).

The verse on pp. 20–21 has been quoted from *The English Gipsies and their Language* (1874) by G. Charles Leland, Trübner & Co, UK. Please note that the term 'Gipsies' or 'Gypsies' is regarded these days as derogatory, the preferred term now being 'Romany'. Robbie, though not Romany, would have heard the language during his London days where language rich and ripe flowed around him. Bridie would have learned the verse from him. My interest stems from the fact that I am descended from Romany myself.

Readers wishing to know more are encouraged to read works by scholars Anne Salmond, Harry Evison, Atholl Anderson, Te Maire Tau, Vincent O'Malley, Ranginui Walker and Buddy Mikaere, among others.

Glossaries

Te reo Māori

Te reo Māori is one of three official languages in Aotearoa New Zealand, yet arguments persist about this language's right to live alongside English. Colonisation separates people not just from their land but from their language.

During my MA studies I was fortunate to have as a supervisor, Jane Stafford, who has written extensively about the way Māori have been rendered in fiction by Pākehā authors. Early Pākehā created Maōri who were noble savages or savage warriors; they bore little resemblance to real people. Some contemporary Pākehā authors, aware of that trap, felt uncomfortable about portraying Māori for fear of misrepresenting or being judged as appropriating their culture. Well-meaning writers not wishing to cause hurt or harm opted instead to avoid writing Māori characters altogether. Consequently, Pākehā authors have sometimes inadvertently wiped Māori from the cultural New Zealand landscape, rendering them invisible.

While Māori should not be confined to the margins of historical fiction in Aotearoa, it is equally important that authors research and learn language, rather than simply putting a Māori cloak on a Pākehā character. The question will long be debated as to whether Pākehā authors in this colonised country have the right to write about Māori characters at all. I still struggle with this question. Fortunately, Māori authors have written — and will continue to write — outstanding novels. I encourage readers who wish to immerse themselves in the Māori world to read books by those authors, including (but not limited to) Patricia Grace, Witi Ihimaera, Keri Hulme, Paula Morris, Whiti Hereaka, Kelly Ana Morey, Monty Soutar and Becky Manawatu.

This te reo Māori glossary is provided in the hope that one day it will be superfluous in this country. The future I look forward to is a future in which both Māori and English will be used fluently, and the boundary between them will be fluid.

Te reo Māori words and expressions

The translations on the following pages capture the context of the words and phrases as they appear in this novel. Literal translations of words are available from Te Aka The Māori Dictionary — maoridictionary.co.nz and other published dictionaries.

āe	yes
āniwaniwa	rainbow
ao	world
aroha	love
aruhe	fernroot
atua	god
awa	river
E haere ana koe.	Go away.
e hoa	friend (a term of endearment)
E iti noa ana nā te aroha.	A small thing given with love. (a whakatauki — proverb)
E mōhio ana ahau.	I understand.
E noho rā	Goodbye (to someone who is remaining)
E oma!	Run!
E pukuriri ana koe?	Are you angry?
E tatari!	Wait!
hā ki roto	breathe in
hā ki waho	breathe out
Haere atu!	You go!
Haere mai!	Come here! Welcome!
hau	wind
He aha te kōrero tōku whaea?	What did my mother say?
hīkoi	walk or march
I nei	No way!
hinau	a tall tree that produces edible berries
hongi	touching noses in greeting to share breath
iho	downward flow or essence, inner core
Ka haere mātou ki te pā tūwatawata.	We will go to the stockade.
Ka haere tātou ki te pā?	Will we all go to the pā?
Ka hemo anake te tou o te tōtara.	Only the tōtara makes that farting sound.
Ka hoki mai koe ki te kāinga o Ropi.	You will return to Robbie's place.
ka pai	fine, ok
kāhu	Australasian harrier hawk
kahu kererū	native pigeon feather cloak

kai	food
kaimoana	seafood
kāinga	home, unfortified village
kakerangi	seal
kāo	no
kāore	no
Kakare kau nei te tau o taku ate.	You've stirred my emotions.
karanga	call or summon
karewao	supplejack, a climbing vine
karoro	southern black-backed gull
kaumātua	elder(s)
Kei te kōrero mō te houhou rongo.	He wants to make peace.
Kei te marama ahau.	I understand.
Kei te māuiui ahau, kei te māuiui tōku wairua. Kei te pōuri ahau. Kei te mataku ahau i a Robbie rātou ko Mallet, ko Jake mā.	I am sick, my soul is sick. I am sad. I am afraid of Robbie, Mallet, Jake and others.
Kei te māuiui ia.	She is sick.
Kei te mōhio ahau.	I know.
Kei te ngenge ahau.	I'm tired.
Kei te pēhea koe?	How are you?
Kei te pīrangi ahau ki te houhou rongo.	I want to make peace.
Kei te pōuri ahau.	I'm sad.
Kei whea te tau ō tāku ate?	Where is my beloved?
kererū	native wood pigeon
kete	basket (old word of Indo-Oceanic origin)
kina pākira	sea urchin
kiore	Polynesian rat
kōhine	girl
kopakopa	kidney fern
kōrero	talk (n), speak (v)
Kore rawa ahau, e wareware ki tēnei manaakitanga ā mate noa ahau.	I will never forget your kindness and hospitality until I die.
koro	old man, grandfather
korowai	cloak

kuia	old woman, grandmother
kūmara	sweet potato
kupu	word(s)
kurī	dog
mahi	work
mākutu	witchcraft
manaakitanga	hospitality, kindness
manuhiri	guests, visitors
marae ātea	open area in front of the meeting house
maro	loincloth, kilt
matakite	seer (n), foresight (v)
mata pūkana	stare dramatically and fiercely for effect
matua	uncle/parent
mātua	uncles/parents
māuiui	sick
mauri	life force
māwake pā roa	persistent rainstorm
Me moe ia.	She needs to sleep.
Me moe koe.	You should sleep.
mere	flat stone club (weapon)
moana	ocean
moko	tattoo (also tā moko)
mokopuna	grandchildren
Mō tāku hē.	I'm sorry.
mutu-whenua	waning moon on thirtieth night of the lunar month
naenae	mosquito
namu	sandfly (small biting insect)
Nā te aha koe i te tōmuri ai?	Why are you late?
ngaio	a New Zealand native tree — *Myoporum laetum*
ngākau	heart
nīkau	a native palm tree — *Rhopalostylis sapida*
oriori	lullaby
pā	stockade, fortified village
pākoro	storehouse
papa kāinga	communal land

Papatūānuku	the earth mother (goddess of the earth)
pārahirahi harakeke	sandal made from flax plant
pātaka	raised storehouse, usually elaborately carved
pātengi	kūmara storage pit
patero	fart
pātiki	flounder
patu	club (weapon)
pāua	abalone (shellfish)
pipi	a species of small edible shellfish
pītau	edible young fern shoot
pīwakawaka	fantail, a native bird
ponga	a native tree fern (silver fern)
pōuritanga	despair
puhi	adorn with feathers (v), virgin (n)
pūkana	dramatic eye-rolling gesture
puku	stomach
pukuriri	anger, angry
pūmoana, pūtātara	conch shell trumpet
rangatahi	young people
rangatira	leader
Ranginui	sky father (god of the sky)
rātā	tree with red flowers
reperepe	dowry
roimata	tears
ruru	owl (morepork)
tahi, rua, toru	one, two, three
taiaha	long wooden weapon
tamaiti	child
Tama-nui-te-rā	personification of the sun
tamariki	children
tā moko	facial tattoo (also moko)
Tāne-mahuta	god of the forest
Tangaroa	god of the sea
tangata whenua	people born of, and who belong to the land
tangi	weep, mourn (v), funeral (n)
tangihanga	funeral

taniwha	water spirit or monster
taonga	treasure
tapu	sacred
tara	female genitals
tarata	lemonwood tree
taua	war party
tauiwi	foreigners, strangers
Tāwhiri-mātea	god of wind
Te Kore	realm of creation from which all things are stirred
Tēnā rawa atu koe.	Thank you very much.
Tēnei te ao o ngā tauiwi	This is the world of the Europeans.
tī	New Zealand cabbage tree, *Cordyline Australis*
Tihei mauri ora!	triumphant exclamation meaning first breath of life
tīpuna	ancestors
tī rākau	stick game
tohorā	baleen whale, specifically southern right whale
tohu	sign or omen
tohunga	esteemed specialist in specific high level knowledge
toroa	albatross
tōtara	a New Zealand native tree
tuangi	New Zealand cockle
tukutuku	woven panels in a meeting house
uhi	tattooing chisel
utu	retribution/restoration of balance, includes peace offering
wahine/wāhine	woman/women
wai	water
waiata	song
wairua	spiritual essence, soul
waka	canoe
weka	woodhen, a brown flightless bird
wētā	a large native insect
whaea	mother/aunt
whāea	mothers/aunts

whaikōrero	formal speech
whakapapa	genealogy
Whakarongo mai.	Listen to me.
whakatauki	proverb
whānau	family, extended family group
whare	house
wharenui	meeting house, similar to a community hall
whare harakoa	place of entertainment
whare kura	secondary school, house of learning
whare moenga	sleeping house
whare takiura	place of higher learning
whekī	variety of tree fern — *Dicksonia squarrosa*

Cant, slang and flash (whaler slang)

Language represents race and class. Even today people are judged on accent, spelling, the use of certain words. In the era in which this novel is set, the most colourful array of words in the English language belonged to the poor.

There is no such thing as pure English. The working class has fed the upper class in every way, including language. For decades I have researched the ballads that poured from fields and inns out to the streets, in songs of the sea and songs of the land. All were alive with cant, the language of the secret alleys and underground stairs. The knowledge it yielded was not accessible to all.

Archaic, invented, creative, clever, this cant was drawn from Shakespearian theatre and old dialects, from French, Romany and Latin. It rolled off the tongues of men like Robbie and women like Bridie. The working poor used oratory as a tool of survival in the tragedy and comedy that formed the theatre of their lives. As that language has largely disappeared (bring it back, I say!), I have included a glossary to aid readers.

Cant, slang and flash (whaler slang) words and expressions

abbess	mistress of a brothel or pub
adzooks	an exclamation
barking iron	pistol
baubles	testicles
beau nasty	a man whose fancy clothes do not disguise his ugly nature

bint	a derogatory term for a girl
bog-trotter	a derogatory term for a member of the Irish diaspora
bounce	tell a lie
broganeer	a derogatory term for someone with a strong Irish accent
buckeen	a shabby dandy, aspiring to the upper echelons
caulk	skin (of a merrow)
chaffe	eat or drink
chav, chavi	Romany terms for boy and girl, respectively
chiv lis adré	Romany expression — 'put it in'
chuckle-headed	stupid person
cock-a-hoop	exulted
cordwainer	shoemaker
coriander	money, coin
cornstalk	child of a convict, usually Sydney born
cove	crewman, henchman
crab-sneak	someone who thwarts a plan, an untrustworthy person
crack	a derogatory term for a girl
crank cuffin	sworn brother or ally
crimpers	criminal class of trader
cunny	female genitals
dimber	a term for a woman, either affectionate or mocking
dunnekin	outside toilet
fartleberry	excrement released with explosive force from the posterior
flaybottomist	someone who whips people as punishment
flumadiddle/flumdiddlery	fancy clothes
flunkey	manservant or liveried footman
fly-by-nighter	witch
fustilugs	glutton
gingabobs	testicles
grumbletonian	someone who complains in a lofty manner

gullion	a worthless person, or someone who is easily deceived
Henshall's coin	first coins minted in Australia using old Spanish coins
lap (supping a dish of lap)	drink (having a drink)
long white ash	whalers' term for longboat oars
lushed	drunk
merrow	mermaid
moll, mot	derogatory terms for a girl
ninnyhammer	silly or stupid person
rantallion	a man not well endowed
ruffin	devil
rumbler	hackney coach
rumbling ken	disreputable drinking house or brothel
rundlets	small barrels
sea beggar	privateer, pirate
sky pilot	missionary
spoil-pudding	moaning or mean-spirited person, a party-pooper
stiff-rump	arrogant person
sterling	British settler in Australia (not a convict)
thornback	old maid, spinster
toff	member of the upper class
topper	top hat, but can be a generic hat

Gaelic

Minimal Gaelic is used in this novel for the sad reason that it died out in the colonies after the transportations and diaspora. Bridie's mother had the tongue; her daughter did not. My Irish ancestors were among those who lost their language and their ability to live in their own land.

Thanks to an Irish renaissance, the language is being reclaimed around the world. Irish glossary translates the terms used in this book.

Gaelic words and expressions

bean sídhe	banshee, a spirit who foretells a death

caoineadh	keening: Irish singing for the departed soul
Éire	Ireland
Éireann	of Ireland, e.g. people of Ireland
Go ndeine an diabhal dréimire de cnámh do dhroma ag piocadh úll i ngairdín Ifrinn.	May the devil make a ladder of your backbone and pluck apples in the garden of Hell.
mnàthan-tuirim	keening women
murúch	an Irish mermaid
Ná bí róbheag is ná bí rómhór leis an gcléir.	Don't be too small and don't be too big with the clergy.

Acknowledgements

I am indebted to my mentor, Geoff Walker, who patiently midwifed this novel. In 2019 I received a mentorship from the New Zealand Society of Authors, which enabled me to work with Geoff and receive his glorious insights and magnificent wisdom. He has continued to assist as a mentor, guiding this novel to publication. Through every labour pain Geoff has been there, all the way to the final delivery.

I am grateful to Buddy Mikaere, who checked the Māori language and who insisted that the koha for his service be a donation to a refuge to keep women safe from violence. As this novel is about a man's violence against women, this koha was gratefully made and is especially fitting. Thanks also to Layton Lowe for his language expertise. Any mistakes in te reo, the poetic language of this land, are inadvertently my own. As Cuthbert would say, 'Mō tāku hē.'

I am indebted also to Bill Manhire for his encouragement and for seeing in me so many years ago the writer I have now become. His vision helped me progress to this point. I am equally grateful that he set up the International Institute of Modern Letters at Victoria University, which has produced so many good writers in the islands of my country.

My supervisor during my MA in Creative Writing at the IIML, Jane Stafford, gave strong, helpful, kind advice. I remember my toddler picking the spines off her first-edition books and her kindness when she saw my horrified face. Thank you, Jane.

Rohan Howitt is deservedly mentioned in my author's note. Thank you also to Thomas J. Oertling, at Texas A&M University. As the author of *Ships' Bilge Pumps: A history of their development, 1500–1900*, he generously corresponded directly with me regarding leaks — and life in general — on ships. Any mistakes are mine, not his. Thanks to

Joan Druett for her communication and comprehensive publications, fiction and non-fiction, on whaling wives.

I am grateful for the hugely supportive learning environment of Te Wānanga o Aotearoa, and in particular the gentle guidance of my kaiako, Beulah Parris and Sipola Parris. Thank you to Tā Tipene O'Regan, whose mind is a universe, and who opened so many doors in my own mind during the Waitangi Tribunal hearings into the Ngāi Tahu land and fisheries claims. I am thankful for Huirangi Waikerepuru, who opened the first door. He kōtuku rerengatahi ia: The white heron flies only once.

My dear friend Henare Rikiihia (Rick) Tau kept the door open, and I am grateful for the love, humour and manaakitanga I received from him and Ngāi Tahu kuia Kera Brown, Rima Bell and Anne Thompson, who took me under their strong, beautiful wings.

Thank you to the Samasoni and related families, Samoan and Tokelau'an, for all the Pasifika love. Thank you, too, to that fine support crew, the Edmundson clan. Thank you to Trudy Fersterer and my extended Fersterer whānau.

I could not have written this novel without my dear friends. Karo Bythell fed me wonderful meals, proofed my work and rekindled me whenever my spirits flagged. Lavinia Kingi-Kaui gifted Māori names. She and her wife Mahina Kingi-Kaui kept me nourished in heart and song. The following people have helped me save my life and fulfill my authorly dreams: Diana England, Vicki Thompson, Vanora Bennett, Zahra Romana Barber, Zena Smirani, Evelyn Mary, Elizabeth Braggins, Andrea Hannah-King, Rosemary Thompson, Roger Boyce, David Garb, Paul Hopkinson, Carol Penaia and Chrissie Martin. In France, Jan Barwick-Claudy, Judy Blair and Glenda Arnold. Te Owaina Gerrard helped me grow up and I still feel her gentle strength. Her children and mokopuna are part of my family.

Thank you to Louise Russell at Bateman Books, sensitive, insightful and caring beyond measure, and to the rest of the super-talented team at Bateman for seeing the merit in this book and sending it into the world. To my trusted editor Rachel Scott, thank you for your skill in fine-tuning the manuscript. To Keely O'Shannessy, thank you for your vision and talented execution of the cover.

Thank you to Irish speakers Michelle Carroll and Martin Connell for their keen Irish eyes in checking the Gaelic text.

Thank you to the Lime Square Poets and all poets in and outside Ireland. If I had a muse, it was the English author Mary Anne Evans (George Eliot), a cousin on my paternal side. Any donations to the George Eliot Foundation in England will help maintain her legacy.

My brother Philip England read several drafts of this novel. He has been my greatest cheerleader, encouraging me when I was down. Thanks to him, his lovely wife, Gina, and their family for being there in every sense.

Thanks also to my gorgeous sister, Karen, her good man, Andrew Wilson, and all my nieces and nephews for their never-ending support and kindness.

I am grateful beyond measure to my husband, John, my New Zealand Irishman, my lover, my devoted reader, for binding his life to mine and generously overlooking how difficult it can be to live with a writer. I am indebted to my sons — Kelynge, ever and always my teacher and my spiritual guide; Ben, the wise peacemaker for his kind counsel and *The Seasonwife* musical playlist; and Marco, my last-born, a poet and saviour. My sons and husband are good men. Without them, this book would have remained dormant.

Thank you to my mother, Elaine, remembered for her sparkling love of life, who taught me to read, who instilled in me an appreciation for all things Māori — the language, culture and people.

Thank you to all the good people who build the platform that lifts the soul.